SUNSHINE THROUGH THE RAIN

Ellen is settled in Edinburgh when one day her sister begs a favour: can she come and look after her farm and three children while she has a much-deserved holiday. Ellen loves her nieces and nephews, but the animals are a bit of a worry... After a manic yet fun weekend, her world is shattered when a freak accident kills her sister and leaves her as the children's legal guardian. Desperately juggling her responsibilities, Ellen is driven to find a compromise between her old life and her new: one the children will accept, and that will allow her to keep something of herself as well.

SUNSHINE THROUGH THE RAIN

SUNSHINE THROUGH THE RAIN

by

Gilly Stewart

Magna Large Print Books
Long Preston, North Yorkshire,
BD23 4ND, England.

British Library Cataloguing in Publication Data.

Stewart, Gilly
    Sunshine through the rain.

    A catalogue record of this book is
    available from the British Library

    ISBN   978-0-7505-4241-8

First published in Great Britain in 2015 by Accent Press Ltd.

Cover illustration © Jacinta Bernard by arrangement with
Arcangel Images

Published in Large Print 2016 by arrangement with
Accent Press Ltd.

Magna Large Print is an imprint of Library Magna Books Ltd.

Printed and bound in Great Britain by
T.J. (International) Ltd., Cornwall, PL28 8RW

For David

Chapter One

'So, how would you feel about coming down and house-sitting for the weekend?'

'What? Me?' Ellen had been eyeing her reflection in the hall mirror and letting her thoughts wander. Jessie had sighed over their father's slow decline, asked after Ellen's work and her on/off relationship with Richard, confirmed that the children were all in good health. Discussions of possible surprises for her brother-in-law's fortieth birthday had continued for months. Ellen had failed to realise that all this talk of cheap flights to Prague heralded a *decision*. 'Sorry. What did you say?'

'I said, would you mind house-sitting while we're away? Please.'

'You mean you've booked?'

'Yes! I can hardly believe it. I wanted to do something special for Sam, he always works so hard. And turning forty is an event, isn't it? Gosh, aren't we getting old?' Jess laughed.

'When did you say you were going?' asked Ellen cautiously. House-sitting a small farm wasn't exactly her cup of tea.

'On Sam's birthday, of course. The first weekend in February. So in two weeks' time. I hope he likes the idea. You know how he hates leaving the farm for more than a few hours, or leaving the kids, for that matter.'

11

'You're leaving the kids?' Ellen wished she'd been paying attention sooner. 'All three?' She had never looked after her nephews and niece for more than a few hours. Now Jess thought she could manage a whole weekend?

'Of course. I feel bad, but we could hardly afford to take them, could we? And this is a special occasion, it'll be the first time we've been away on our own since – well, since Angus was born. Sam used to dream of going to Prague when we were younger, but it wasn't possible in those days.'

'It sounds great. I'm really glad you've finally done something.'

'So you'll help out?'

'Erm... Well, tell me what this house-sitting would involve.' Even as she spoke, Ellen knew it wouldn't just be the three children. There was the little terrier, Monty, and then all the farm animals...

'There are the hens, of course, but they're Callum's responsibility so you won't need to worry about them, and Angus'll do the horses and dog. I know Angus is only twelve but he's really good with the animals. There are the cows and the sheep, but there really won't be much to do for them, it's not as though it's lambing time yet.'

Ellen thought of her own well-ordered life. Monday to Friday she lectured at the North Edinburgh College. Weekends she pottered around her flat or went walking or climbing with like-minded, child-free friends. She knew absolutely nothing about kids and animals. And how old were the younger two? She was pretty sure Callum was ten, and Lucy couldn't be more than seven. Oh goodness, that sounded so young. She crossed her fingers. 'Nothing to it, then.'

'Exactly. So will you come?'

'Well.' Ellen took the phone into her tiny kitchen and checked the calendar. 'I'm supposed to be going away that weekend with Richard and our usual group. You're not exactly giving me much notice.'

'I know, I'm sorry.' Jessie paused. 'Couldn't you do it, just this once? You go away with Richard pretty often, don't you?' Jessie didn't usually ask for things. Ellen tried to imagine what it was like not to have had a proper adult holiday for twelve years, and failed.

'Seeing as you've already booked. I do think it's a great idea for you both to get away. And I haven't seen the kids for a while.' She took a deep breath. 'OK, I'll do it. Friday to Monday, you said?'

'Yes. Thanks, Ellen. You're absolutely brilliant. I promise never to ask for anything again.'

'Not this year, at least.'

'Not this year *or* next. You don't know what a relief it'll be to know that you'll be in charge.'

Ellen didn't have nearly so much confidence in her ability. 'Hmmph. Just make sure you come back on the Monday, I think four days will be my limit. The college owe me some time back, but I can't push it too far.'

'Of course. I'll be desperate to get back after four whole days. And if there are any problems with the house or animals you can ask our new neighbour Kit to help out. He won't mind.'

'New neighbour?' As far as Ellen could remember, the nearest house to Craigallan was at least

13

half a mile away, which didn't constitute neigh-bourliness in her opinion, and was inhabited by Jess's best friend. 'Has Clare moved?'

'No, of course not. Don't you remember me telling you? We sold off a bit of our land to raise money. The man who bought it is building a house entirely himself, he's got amazing plans, and meantime he's living there in a caravan. I really admire him.'

'Oh,' said Ellen. Somehow she just knew what was coming next.

'He's a fascinating guy, I'd like you to meet him.'

Ellen was all too used to Jess introducing her to suitable men. Jess didn't appreciate Richard's aloof good looks. 'Hmm.'

'His name's Kit Ballantyne. He's a vet, early-thirties. He's really lovely. I'll ask him to call down while you're here.'

'There's really no need.'

'I'll mention it to him.' Jess didn't give up easily.

Ellen rang off as soon as she could. She enjoyed chatting to Jess, but just now she needed to get over the shock of what she had agreed to.

A whole weekend of children and animals. She looked around her calm, white little flat and shook her head. It would certainly be a contrast.

She loved it here, living on her own. That's what people didn't realise. Her mother had taken to making hints about her and Richard tying the knot, but it wasn't what either of them wanted. Richard had one expensive failed marriage behind him and Ellen – well, she was perfectly happy with the way things were.

She sighed as she took a pencil from the drawer

and crossed out the climbing weekend on the calendar. She wrote in 'Craigallan' and shook her head in disbelief.

Richard was unexpectedly annoyed when Ellen told him she couldn't make the weekend in Perthshire. She broke the news to him casually when they were having an after-work drink in one of his favourite bars, a discreet little place in Edinburgh's New Town. 'So, I'll have to give my apologies, which is a nuisance, but can't be helped.'

'Why can't it be helped?' He frowned, his handsome face sulky. 'Why can't someone else babysit? Does it have to be you?'

'There doesn't seem to be anyone else.'

'But Ellen, you agreed to come with us.'

She reached over and touched his hand. 'I know I did, and I'm sorry to let you down. But it's no big deal, is it? It's not as if I'm essential to everyone's enjoyment of the weekend.' Or even anyone's, she thought, as he withdrew his hand from beneath hers.

'Everyone else will be in a couple.'

'You could come to Craigallan with me,' she suggested, but without much hope. It wasn't likely that Richard would be prepared to fritter away valuable leisure time on other people's children.

'No thanks.'

'Look, it isn't that I *want* to spend a weekend looking after three children. I'm the one who will really suffer.'

'So why go?'

'Richard, Jess asked me to do her a favour. She doesn't ask often.'

'And when did she last do something for you?'

Ellen pulled a face. He was missing the point here. This was family, it wasn't a case of tit for tat. 'What would I want her to do?'

'You're right. You don't need favours, do you?'

For some reason, that thought seemed to please him. Ellen didn't bother to explain that she didn't need favours because she was careful never to get into situations she couldn't manage. Life was better that way.

When they had finished their second drink, she said, 'Shall we get something to eat in town, or do you want to come back to my place?' Richard never had more than two drinks on a work night. 'I haven't got much in but I think I could just about stretch to a stir fry, would that do?'

'Thanks, but I'd better get home. My day's work's not finished yet.' He patted his briefcase affectionately. She wondered if this was his way of punishing her for not fitting in with his plans. If it was, she didn't mind. An evening alone in her little Dean Village flat was never a chore.

She made herself a salad and ate it curled up on her sofa, reading the latest murder mystery that she had picked up on her weekly trip to the book shop. Richard couldn't understand why she hadn't moved on to reading novels digitally, but she liked the feel of the book in her hands. Later she would mark assignments on *The Impact of The Euro on European Economic Stability* and then perhaps have an early night. Or a long, lazy bath in her recently refurbished bathroom? She felt the tranquillity of her flat settling around her, and relaxed.

The Friday at Craigallan was easy. Jess and Sam had done all the morning chores and packed the children off to school before they left. All Ellen had to do was arrive before the younger ones came home and she managed that fine.

Craigallan was a long, low, white-washed building, more a cottage than a house. The older part had two storeys, the rooms on the upper floor low-ceilinged with tiny dormer windows. A nice enough place, if not exactly Ellen's taste. Jess had left the back door unlocked. There were apparently no worries about break-ins here.

The first hour went well. Lucy in particular was delighted to see her Aunt Ellen, showing her around the house and the animals. It had been a good idea to bring presents – sweets and comics, which even Angus seemed to find acceptable when he arrived home. They weren't bad kids, as far as kids went; she felt her fondness for them returning and wondered why she had left it so long since her last visit.

In the early evening seven-year-old Lucy had been invited to a birthday party in Dumfries. Ellen solved the problem of what to do with the boys by bribing them: if they came to the supermarket with her, she would feed them at McDonalds afterwards. Their parents disapproved of McDonalds, so this was a treat indeed! Lucy was almost willing to forego the birthday party for it. So far so good. Ellen couldn't remember when she had last had a Big Mac herself, so the experience was almost exotic. Really, she didn't know what she had worried about, it wasn't that difficult to keep children happy.

'Auntie Ellen, did Mum remind you about the Rayburn?' asked Angus after demolishing his burger swiftly and in silence.

'The Rayburn?' Ellen wracked her brain. 'What about it? Did she put it on the list?'

'Don't know. She said to be careful we didn't let it go out. It's a bugger to light again if you do.'

Ellen frowned at the language but suspected he was repeating a phrase from his father. 'It's solid fuel, isn't it? I'd forgotten.' Damn. What a time to remind her, when they were thirty minutes' drive from the house and Lucy's party didn't finish for another three quarters of an hour.

'I put some anthracite on when I got in from school,' said Angus. 'It might be OK.'

'Good. Well done.' Ellen hadn't noticed him doing it, but that wasn't very surprising in between visits to the horses and the hens, walking the dog and making a half-hearted attempt to unpack her suitcase in the tiny spare room.

'Can I have a McFlurry?' asked Callum, who clearly couldn't have cared less about the Rayburn. Ellen cared; without it, there would be no heating and no hot water.

'Yes, why not?' she said. They still had some time before collecting Lucy and she didn't personally think the occasional ice cream did much harm, no matter how many additives it might contain.

Callum jumped to his feet and shot across to the serving bar. Angus rose more slowly. At twelve, he was only two years older than his brother, but tall and lanky, with a pale face that often wore a worried expression. Ellen handed him the money and he muttered something that

18

might have been thanks.

The Rayburn was almost out when they arrived home. This meant that instead of taking Monty straight out to empty his bladder and then getting Lucy and Callum off to bed, the four of them spent the next half-hour coaxing it back to life with strips of newspaper and kindling.

'Don't your parents have any fire lighters?'

'No, fire lighters are unnecessary,' said Lucy. 'Dad never ever uses them.'

'They might not be necessary, but they'd certainly be useful.' Ellen added them to her mental shopping list. 'Angus, isn't there any way of getting a better through-draught in this thing? I'm going to start hyperventilating if I have to blow on it much more.'

'Not sure,' he said, pushing back his long fringe in a nervous gesture. 'Dad and Mum do the Rayburn mostly. Maybe this thing?' He pulled out a vent near the chimney and sent a cloud of smoke into the room. 'Oh, sorry.'

'Push it back in! Ah, leave it there, that seems to be better. Yes, Lucy, what is it?'

'Auntie Ellen, I think that Monty's done a piddle.'

'Oh no.'

'Callum, you should've let the dog out as soon as we got home. It's your job.'

'No it's not. I feed him, Mum does everything else.'

'But Mum said we had to help Auntie Ellen.'

'Never mind,' said Ellen, standing upright with a sigh. 'Let him out now, will you, and I'll use some newspaper to clean up the mess. Where does Mum keep the old newspapers?'

'I think we've just used them all on the fire,' said Angus.

Ellen swore silently and tried to smile. 'Not to worry, at least the fire is well and truly lit. I'll find something else I can use.' Possibly, she added to herself. That was the problem with people who were so keen on recycling. She had forgotten how seriously Jess and Sam took that kind of thing. They didn't leave piles of old newspapers around because they reused them.

Ellen thought of her Edinburgh flat, and told herself there were only three more days to go. Three more days of sharing family bathrooms, sleeping on that less than comfortable spare bed, of being responsible for everything but never quite in control of anything. Already, she felt hemmed in.

On Saturday afternoon, the roof fell in – sort of. Jess had phoned in the morning to check that everything was all right, and Ellen had assured her, fingers crossed, that it was. The house was baking hot from an overheated Rayburn and Angus and Callum had been bickering since they got up, but nothing serious had gone wrong.

The rest of the morning was spent doing chores according to the lists left by Jess and Sam. Ellen was surprised at how amenable the children were. She didn't remember that she and her sister had been this good about doing jobs, but perhaps her promise of an afternoon trip to the swimming pool had acted as an incentive. She wondered what a normal weekend was like at Craigallan, and smiled at the thought. Jess would no doubt be baking, Sam out in the fields with the boys, friends dropping in for coffee and a chat. No one could accuse Jess of being lazy, but she had that way with her of seeming to exist in happy chaos, while always making sure the essentials were done.

Ellen had to do things her own way, and was quietly satisfied as she ticked the last item on the list.

It was when they came out of the pool that her doubts returned. The children were tired and grumpy, and it was pouring down. The rain fell so hard that the ten minutes Ellen had spent re-styling her short hair were entirely wasted.

'I want to sit in the front,' wailed Lucy when Callum got there before her. 'It's my turn to sit in the front, it's...'

'Just get in,' shouted Ellen. She had no intention of refereeing an argument in the rain. 'For goodness sake, what does it matter?'

Lucy looked at her from wide, blue eyes, now tearful, and put her swimming bag down with a bang.

Ellen felt the children's resentment deepening as they drove back to Craigallan. She had forgotten that Jess and Sam didn't believe in shouting. Jess had explained that, in the long run, it was always better to give a quiet explanation. Sam's patience occasionally snapped, but she had never seen her sister waiver.

'And what shall we have for tea?' she said brightly as they drove up to the front of the long, low, white-painted house. 'I don't think I can justify chips two days in a row, but how about pizza?'

'I never had any chips yesterday,' began Lucy, and was brought up short by a resounding crash. Ellen had parked at the kitchen end of the building. A couple of inches in front of the car a massive slate had come down and shattered on the paving stones.

'That was close,' said Ellen, taking a breath.

A second slate fell and hit her offside head light. This time slate and head lamp shattered. 'Oh sh – sugar.'

'This doesn't look good,' said Angus, craning his neck to look up through the rain. 'We've never had two down at once before.'

'Damn right it doesn't look good. What about my car?' Ellen reversed and parked at a safer distance from the house. From here, between the waves of rain, you could see where the slates had come from. There was an ominous hole just above the gutters.

'Dad said those slates'd had it,' said Angus. 'He said he'd better replace them before something like this happened, but Mum said there were more important things to do.'

'Looks like this time Dad was right,' said Ellen. 'Let's get inside, shall we? Don't go anywhere near that corner, I don't want one of us being hit.'

'Old buildings,' said Callum, knowingly, when they had reached the warmth of the kitchen. He was a solidly built boy, with his father's wavy brown hair. Now he sounded just like him, too. 'There's always something.'

'At least the rain's not coming in,' said Ellen, examining the ceiling.

'Not yet,' agreed Angus.

'Can I go and watch television?' said Lucy.

'Yes, off you go, all of you. I'm going to get myself a glass of wine and have a think about this.'

'We'll need a fire. It's really cold in there. Will you light a fire, Auntie Ellen?'

Ellen could feel her patience wearing thin. Why did everything have to be so difficult? What wouldn't she give for lovely gas heating that sprang into life at the touch of a switch? With an effort, she swallowed down a retort. She might be exhausted but it wasn't the children's fault. She shouldn't take it out on them.

'I'll do it,' said Angus.

'Angus, you're a star. I bought fire lighters, use one if you like.'

It was bliss to have half an hour on her own, sitting at the long wooden table with a magazine and a glass of wine. This room was cosy and she rather enjoyed the snuffles of the little border terrier curled up before the Rayburn. She seemed to remember that Jess and Sam spent a lot of time in the kitchen, and she could see why. It could do with a lick of paint, and Ellen wouldn't be seen dead with cupboards like those in her house, but there was something very comfortable about the place. Her sister and brother-in-law had made a good life for themselves down here. Busy and impoverished, but not bad for all that.

She took the dog out for a stroll before bedtime and examined the kitchen roof as best she could in the moonlight. The slates shone wetly, showing a gap where the two had fallen. Eventually she decided that, as the rain was dying down, she would keep her fingers crossed and hope for the best. It had lasted decades, surely the rest of the slates would stay put until Monday?

To Ellen's relief, Sunday did not go too badly.

The roof stayed on, the children were bearable. When the phone rang at teatime, she wondered whether to answer. It was probably her mother or Jess, checking up on her yet again, and she really didn't have time to chat. It was ages since she had cooked a proper Sunday dinner, and it was harder work than she remembered.

But there was the off-chance that it was Richard, so she picked up the receiver, hoping for rather than expecting his voice.

There was a long, crackling pause, the normal precursor to Jess's calls, but this time the voice on the other end was unfamiliar.

'I speak to the household of Mr Moffat?'

'Yes,' said Ellen, with a jolt of fear. A foreign accent. 'Yes, can I help you?'

'To whom do I have the pleasure of speaking?'

'Ellen. Ellen Taylor.'

'Ah.' The speaker coughed nervously. 'I have the household of Mr Samuel Moffat?'

'Yes, yes. I'm his sister-in-law. I'm Mrs Moffat's sister. How can I help you?'

'I speak from the hotel in Prague, in the Czech Republic.'

'Yes?'

'I have to tell you there has been the accident.'

Ellen could feel her legs quiver beneath her. 'Yes?' This couldn't be happening.

'Mr and Mrs Moffat, they are on holiday in Prague?'

'Yes?'

'I fear to tell you, madam, that they have been hurt. I fear to tell you that Mr and Mrs Moffat are unfortunately dead.'

Chapter Two

Kit Ballantyne sat at the dry end of his caravan and stared out of the window. It was too dark to see anything, but he could hear the falling rain clearly enough, and he didn't have much faith that the patch-up job he had done the previous night would hold out if the downpour worsened. Hell and buggeration. There was no time to waste on caravan repairs just now. Once the house was ready he would take it to the scrap yard, which was the best place for it.

The rain made him think of Australia. He hadn't seen much rain when he'd been over there, and that very fact brought those dry, sunny days to mind. He wondered what Sally was doing and told himself it wasn't very surprising she hadn't made it to the UK yet. All Australians knew that Scottish winters were the pits. Perhaps once spring was here she would get herself organised. And maybe by then he would have worked out a way to keep the whole of the double bed dry.

It was almost a relief when his mobile rang. He didn't want to sit here thinking. Being on call, he couldn't even have a beer. Work was the best thing for him. The call was about a calving somewhere

25

up the Dalveen Pass. He checked the calf jack and other equipment in the back of his beaten up estate car, and headed off down the track.

The calving was difficult and depressing. The calf had come too early and the farmer had called Kit too late. He managed to save the heifer, and the farmer expressed surly gratitude for this, but the process of extracting a dead calf was one Kit particularly hated. Hard work, and only a carcass to show at the end of it. He sluiced himself off at the outside tap when they finished, declined the unenthusiastic offer of tea, and climbed back into the car.

He was shivering now, the sweat dried by the bitter wind and the water icy on his hands. He turned the car's heater on full and cursed as his mobile rang again. What was going on? The beginning of February was supposed to be a quiet time, which was the only reason he had agreed to do three nights on-call in a row.

The number flashing on the phone was his mother's. Which was possibly worse than work. He stopped the car, sent up a silent prayer for patience, and answered it.

'Kit, darling, it took you ever such a long time to answer. I was worried you might not be there.'

'I'm here. I've just finished a calving the other side of the Dalveen.'

'Jolly good. Kit, darling, I'm phoning about next Saturday. I've got Alistair and Debbie coming for lunch as well as yourself and, do you know, I couldn't for the life of me remember what time I had said for you all to arrive.'

'Mum, I don't think its next Saturday, I think

it's Sunday. Didn't you say Sunday lunch to Debbie?'

He held his breath. There was no knowing, these days, how his mother would respond.

'Sunday?' Her voice was plaintive. 'Have I got it wrong again?'

'We all get confused, Mum, but I'm pretty sure it's Sunday, 'cos neither Al nor I are on call then. I'll tell you what, why don't I check with Al in the morning and ring you back then?'

'Thank you dear. That would do nicely.'

Kit sighed. He loved his mum, she had always been his main supporter in life, but there was no denying her memory wasn't what it used to be. He was starting to think it had been selfish, opting for the caravan instead of his old bedroom at home. But he'd wanted to be on-site for the house, and, he had thought that being back in the area, dropping in at home a few times a week, would be more than adequate. Now he wasn't so sure.

He drove slowly past the Moffats' place, not wanting to disturb them, and was surprised to see lights on in almost every downstairs window. Perhaps Jess and Sam had just arrived home, or maybe that townie sister didn't have quite their attitude to conserving the world's resources. The thought of Sam and Jess made him smile. He hoped they had had a really great time, away on their own. Jess would never have got around to booking the trip without his encouragement, so that was at least one good thing he had done. He retired to his slightly damp bed feeling happier about life.

It can't be true, Ellen was thinking. It can't *possibly* be true. Things like this don't happen in real life.

After the phone call she had returned to the kitchen and sat in petrified silence for five minutes or more. She could hear the crackle of the chicken in the oven, the dog snuffling, the rain on the window. All exactly as it had been moments before but now totally different. And she, Ellen, the decisive one, had had absolutely no idea what to do next.

It might be a mistake, she told herself. She tried Jess's mobile but it was switched off. Jess never switched off her mobile when she was away from the children.

What on earth had happened? Why hadn't she asked? She'd been so stunned she hadn't managed to question the stranger, and when she tried to phone the hotel back there seemed to be no one at this time of night who spoke English.

Ellen somehow got through the evening without saying anything to the children, although Angus certainly suspected something was amiss. She couldn't tell them until she knew for sure.

Once she had ushered them off to bed she tried the Embassy in Prague and then the Home Office in London. But all she got was answer phones. Maybe that was a good sign? Maybe, if something really had gone wrong, someone official would have contacted her by now?

But eventually, the waiting and wondering was too much for her, and she phoned her parents. She needed to talk to someone. And they needed to know, didn't they?

Afterwards she sat shivering beside the Rayburn, waiting for her mother to arrive and make everything all right. The drive from Stirling would take a couple of hours, plus arrangements would have to be made with Moira-next-door. Her father's illness had progressed to such a point that he couldn't be left alone for long. Poor Dad, he would hate being beholden to a stranger. Feeling sorry for her father was something real amidst this sudden horror.

When she heard tyres on the track she ran to the window, but the car drove on past. It must be the caravan man. Chris? Kit? Wonder what he was doing up at this time of night. Think of something else, think of anything, don't think of Jess.

She sat back down and pressed her fingers to her dry eyes.

When her mother arrived they hugged each other tightly, neither speaking. What was there to say? Ellen put on the kettle and went to check that her mother's arrival hadn't disturbed the children.

'The poor babies,' said her mother, her voice almost a whisper. She must have been crying as she drove, her eyes were red and puffy, but now she was trying to be strong. 'What will we say to them?'

'I don't know. Nothing, yet.' Ellen gripped her mug in her hands. 'We need to know something definite. I can't just say – your parents *might* be dead – can I? We need to be sure.'

'You don't think we should wake them to-night?'

'I don't know, Mum. I don't know.'

'I suppose there couldn't have been any mistake?'

'I don't think so, but...' Ellen knew she was procrastinating, but even the decision to delay speaking to the children was still a decision taken, and it made her feel very, very slightly better.

They knew finally, irrevocably, that it was true, when a policeman and policewoman arrived at the rarely used front door soon after seven the next morning. Neither Ellen nor her mother had gone to bed. They had called Jess's mobile again and again, with no success.

'No,' said Vivien Taylor, when she saw the police car. Her face was grey, almost the same colour as her hair.

'You look after the children,' said Ellen quietly. 'I'll deal with this.' And somehow she did. After a strangely elongated interview, which according to the clock had lasted less than ten minutes, she let the two police officers out of the front door once again. Now she was going to have to tell the children. Ellen felt ice-cold, no blood flowing in her veins.

'What's happening?' said Angus. 'Why is Grandma here? Who were you talking to?'

'That was the police.' Ellen nodded stiffly to her mother. She had been chivvying the children to eat, but now she turned away to hide the tears that were welling up.

Ellen took a deep breath, trying to speak past the lump in her throat. 'My dears, there's no easy way to say this. I have some very bad news. Your parents ... your mum and dad ... they've been involved in an accident in Prague.' She paused. It was hard to make her lips move properly. 'The ... the police came here to tell us ... to tell us that they have both been killed.'

She tried to keep her eyes on all three faces at once, but it was Angus's expression that held her. His thin face was usually pale. Now it was white, the eyes staring, bloodless lips ajar.

'No!' he said.

'I'm so sorry.' Ellen moved to pull him close but he resisted her. She put her arms around Callum and Lucy instead. 'My darlings, I'm so, so sorry. I don't know much about what has happened yet. I just know they were in a taxi and there was an accident. I'll try to find out more, and we'll look after you, don't worry. But just we now need to be brave and try and comfort each other.'

'I don't believe it,' said Angus. 'I don't believe you! How did you know?'

'There was a phone call last night. And then the police came around this morning and – and confirmed it.'

'The police? How would the police here know?' His voice was beginning to rise. 'It doesn't make sense. Where are my mum and dad?'

His grandmother had turned back now, wiping her tears with a white cotton handkerchief. She looked stronger once the words had been said. 'I'm afraid it's true, Angus. I'm so very, very sorry, darling.'

'That's why you're here, isn't it? You knew already. You've both known since last night.'

Lucy had started crying and clung to Ellen, Callum was slumped like a deadweight in his chair, both of them mutely accepting. Only Angus was refusing to take it in. It made no sense to Ellen so why should it to him?

31

She said quietly, 'The phone call last night was so strange, the man didn't say much, I didn't know what had happened ... I hoped...'

His face went from white to red in an instant and tears sprang to his eyes. 'You knew and you didn't tell us. Anyway, I don't believe you. I don't.' He jumped up, knocking his chair over, and ran from the room.

Kit was asleep when someone hammered on the caravan door in the late afternoon. He could tell it was late afternoon because it was already going dark, and he cursed himself for not having set the alarm clock. He'd had a second call-out at 4 a.m. and then spent the early part of the morning in the vet practice, filling in the partners on his night's work and confirming social arrangements for his mother. It had been nearly lunchtime when he finally got back to bed, by which time he had been too exhausted to notice its cold discomfort.

He pulled on a pair of tracksuit bottoms and gave the door the sharp tug it needed to make it open.

Clare, Jess Moffat's best friend, was standing at the bottom of the steps. She was a potter who lived at the edge of the village. Kit didn't know her well, but thought of her as something of a free spirit, always cheerful, bright in her hippy clothes. Today there was something strange about her. She stood holding her small daughter by the hand, staring up at him with a fixed, anxious expression. 'So you are there. I'm so glad.'

'Hi. Can I help?'

She chewed her lip and glanced back down the

track. She looked as though she might be about to cry, which made Kit uneasy.

'Look, can I come in?'

'Yes, of course. Sorry it's...' He pulled open some of the flimsy curtains and cleared a bench so she had somewhere to sit.

'Something bad has happened,' said Clare in a whisper. 'Something really bad. I only heard when I picked Grace up from school just now. I asked why the Moffat kids weren't there and... Look, the head teacher told me that Sam and Jess have been – have been killed. Both of them. Something must have happened, while they were away.'

'Dead?' said Kit faintly, putting out a hand to steady himself.

'Yes. So we've got to go down to the house now. Are you coming?'

'Go down? Why?' Kit felt panic. 'Won't we be intruding?'

'We're their nearest neighbours. We must go and offer help. I've bought them a candle.' She gestured with the brown paper bag she was carrying. 'I thought you should come too.'

'Oh. I see.' Kit's head was spinning. It wasn't possible. He couldn't take it in. Jess and Sam had gone away on their first holiday in a decade, one he had encouraged them to take. And now they were – dead?

'We won't stay long. We'll just offer to help, so they know they're not alone. I'll have the kids if need be and you can do things around the house. And help with the animals. There's a lot to do, as you know, and Jess's sister Ellen won't have a clue.'

Kit managed to get his visitors out of the

33

caravan while he changed into something slightly more presentable. He still felt stunned, but he allowed himself to be towed down the track by the child Grace, a diminutive of her mother in long skirt, long jersey, and long, loose hair. He couldn't seem to take in that Sam and Jess might not be coming back. *Were* not coming back. His steps dragged as they approached the kitchen door. What on earth would he say? Sam and Jess were his friends, he had had supper with them only a few days ago... He really couldn't bear to face the children.

The kitchen was just as Kit remembered it; a square room warmed by the solid fuel Rayburn, the too-big table piled haphazardly with the debris of family life. Now, however, it was not Jess's plump, cheery face that turned to greet him but that of her mother Vivien and a tall, stylish woman who must be the sister.

Clare went forward and kissed both women solemnly on the cheek. 'We heard the news in the village.'

'Ah,' said Jess's mum. 'It's good of you to come.'

'We won't stay. We just wanted you to know how sorry we are. And that we're here and willing to help. We're thinking of you all the time.' She took out her gift with a flourish, a squat white candle on a pale blue pottery stand. 'I thought you might like to light this tonight, to remember them.'

Vivien's eyes filled with tears. It looked like she had been crying a lot. The other woman just closed her eyes tightly for a moment and when she opened them they were the same dull hazel colour, no tears, no expression at all.

'Thank you.'

'I know the shock must be awful,' said Clare gently. 'Have you thought of what to do next? Will one of you need to go over, to wherever it is?'

'Probably. We've just been talking about that. It was a car accident. I suppose there'll be police enquiries – and things.' It was the younger woman who answered, her voice as blank as her expression. 'We want the funeral to be here, for the children. Otherwise we haven't decided anything.'

'I can have the kids for a night or two, if that would help,' said Clare. 'And...' She looked pointedly at Kit.

'Yes, and, er, I'll help around the house, farm, I mean, whatever. I'm Kit Ballantyne, by the way. Jess and Sam's nearest neighbour. That is, I was...'

'Pleased to meet you,' said Ellen, glancing at him and then away.

'Is there anything we can do just now?' asked Clare. 'I could have Lucy for a sleepover...?'

'No. Thanks. The children are watching television at the moment, but they won't stay there long, none of us can settle. I think we'd rather all stay together, for now. Thanks.'

'Of course. I'll pop up and see you again tomorrow.'

Kit edged towards the door. The reality of what had happened was starting to sink in, and he felt sick with the horror of it. 'And I'll have a quick look over the beasts now, shall I? I'm more than happy to do anything you want. I could do the evening feed for you?'

'Thanks, but no. I think Angus wants to do it.'

Clare went and embraced both women again. This time Ellen's eyes started to fill with tears and the pale face that had been so frozen quivered. Kit's impulse was to turn back and hug her himself, to make things better, as though she were a child or one of his injured animals. He paused for a moment, drawn by the stricken face, and then Vivien moved to put her arms around her daughter. Kit turned and hurried out.

Chapter Three

Ellen sank down onto one of the hard kitchen chairs. She wanted to rest her head on her arms and weep, but she was determined that today was the day she wasn't going to cry. Since the offer of help from Jess and Sam's nearest neighbours, a fortnight ago, she hadn't seemed able to stop the tears from falling.

But the funeral was over now and the children were back at school and she *had* to get her head in order. It would be easier if there wasn't always so much to do. It was already ten o'clock. She had been up since six and this was the first chance she'd had had to sit down. She had tried to take over more of the morning chores today, to ease the children's return to school. Poor children, poor orphaned children.

She wondered how they were getting on and then decided not to think about that. It would only start her off again.

She ran her fingers through her drooping hair. It really needed a cut, and new highlights were definitely overdue. She hadn't a clue when she would have the time, but it cheered her up a little just to think about it. Something normal, that was what she needed. She also needed to get more of her clothes down from Edinburgh. She was sick to death of these once-white jeans. Perhaps she *was* getting a little better, if she could think of things like that.

'Coffee,' she said aloud. She heaved herself to her feet and tripped over Monty, the ageing border terrier who had taken to following her about all day long. 'Oops, sorry, sunshine. Coffee, and then I'll make a list of all the things I should do.' Yes, that was better, far more like the old Ellen.

Just as the kettle came to the boil, the phone rang. She cursed. It had been like this since the news got out. Phone calls and visits, offers of help, nosiness. She wasn't used to this. In a city you had privacy, anonymity.

'Ellen?' For once, it wasn't one of the neighbours, but a person from another life.

'Richard! Hi.' She was surprised and pleased. He rarely made personal calls during office hours.

'How're you doing?'

'OK, I suppose.'

'That's good. Must be a relief to have the funeral out of the way.'

'Ye-es. Thanks for coming down.'

'I felt I should. It was good to see you, even with so many other people around. A shame we hardly had a chance to talk.'

'I'm sorry. It was a bit – chaotic. I did

37

appreciate you coming, though.'

'No problem. Glad to be of use. How else would you have got that black suit?'

'Yes, thanks for that.' Even if it was the wrong suit, one she'd meant to throw away years ago. But it had been black, which was the main thing.

'I was wondering, now that you've got that out of the way, if you've decided when you're coming home?'

'Oh, Richard, I don't know.'

'Haven't things been sorted out yet?'

'No, not really, we're all a bit...'

'You need to make a start, Ellen. The longer you leave it the more difficult it will get.'

'Yes, maybe.' Ellen resented his tone. In another life, she would have agreed with him, but now the world seemed a different place. She ached with the loss of Jess and it was impossibly difficult to focus on even the smallest thing. 'Things are still a bit strange here, with the children, and people dropping in all the time, and trying to sort out the animals...' Her voice trailed off as it threatened to overwhelm her again.

'The neighbours still dropping in, are they? Really, I don't know how they have the time.'

'Yes. Well. They're just trying to help. Or maybe it's always like that round here, I don't know.' Ellen was realising how little she had known of her sister's life from those brief, rushed visits.

Richard returned quickly to the important issues. 'What has your boss at the college said, about you taking so much time off?'

'They've been pretty good, so far. Annie McFadden is covering my lectures. I'm on compassionate leave, at least that's what I think it's called.'

'But of course that can't go on indefinitely.'

'I know.' Ellen felt a wave of panic. It was all very well telling yourself you had to take one day at a time, but how could you, when there were so many things to worry about? 'But I can't come back to Edinburgh just now. Who will look after the kids? I can't just leave them.'

'I thought you said your parents would take over?'

'Did I? Yes, of course, but it won't be for a while. My dad is really not well, and Mum's not as young as she used to be...' The panic went up another notch as the meaning of the words sank in. She took the phone over to a chair, stumbling over Monty, and sank into it.

'Have you seen the solicitor yet?'

'Yes, sort of. I mean, he came to the funeral, and we had a brief chat. I'm going to see him again sometime this week.'

'The sooner the better,' said Richard. He sounded impatient. She supposed he wasn't used to her being so indecisive – she wasn't used to it herself. 'After that you will know how things stand.'

'Yes, maybe. I'm going to have to come up to Edinburgh one day soon to pick up some clothes. Perhaps we could meet for lunch?'

'Lunch is never easy. An evening would be better.'

'I have to be back for the kids in the evening. Look, I've got an idea, why don't you come down here next weekend?' Her spirits rose very slightly at the thought of familiar adult company, someone to lean on.

'Sorry, no can do. Had you forgotten this is when we were going to do the Laraig Dhu? I gave your apologies to Hal, you don't need to worry about that, I realised you wouldn't be able to make it. We'll split the cost of the cabin between the rest of us. But there's no way I could let them down as well.'

'Oh.' The idea of climbing the Laraig Dhu with five or six carefree friends was so far beyond Ellen's ability to picture that she didn't even feel jealous. 'I hope you have a good time.'

'I'm sure we will. There's a call for me on the other line, must go. Keep in touch.'

'Bye,' said Ellen, but the line was already dead. She could picture Richard in his immaculate office, his attention already on the next problem, Ellen forgotten.

She sat staring into space for a while. Then, just as she was collecting the energy to move, there was a tentative knock on the door. She groaned. She hadn't even made that coffee yet.

Her visitor was Kit, the large, scruffy man who lived in the even scruffier caravan up beyond the copse. 'Morning,' she said, making an effort. He had been very kind, helping with the animals, and had come to the funeral, too. And at least it wasn't Mrs Jack, from the bungalow opposite Clare's cottage. She had also attended the funeral and popped in more than once with offers of help but there was something about her perfect hair and complacent expression, the way she looked around, as though making unfavourable mental notes, that made Ellen wary.

40

Kit smiled gently. 'Hi there. Sorry to disturb you. Just thought I should mention a couple of the ewes look like they might be starting to lamb.'

'Oh, no.' Ellen hadn't yet got her head around coping with the animals already at Craigallan. The thought of more frail new ones was terrifying! 'Isn't that a bit early?' It wasn't yet the end of February and still felt like deepest winter.

'I suppose Sam planned it that way. You can make more money from the first lambs of the year, but it's harder work.'

This was not the sort of news that Ellen needed. 'God, this is never ending. What do I have to do?'

'Nothing, just now. I'll keep an eye on them for you if you want. If nothing's happened by tonight you should get Angus to bring them into the byre.'

'OK,' said Ellen with a sigh. 'OK, I'll do that.' She knew nothing about animals. The block of flats where she lived didn't even permit cats.

The man had a thatch of messy hair and a broad face with sleepy brown eyes. Just now, they were watching her with concern. 'Look, why don't you sit down for a minute and I'll make you a coffee? You look all in.'

'I...' Ellen tried to stand up taller. She clearly looked a wreck. But the effort was beyond her and she sat down again, suddenly. Her legs didn't seem to want to hold her today. 'That would be great.'

That brief moment of optimism seemed a long time ago. Now she wanted nothing more than to throw back her head and wail. Where was Jessie? It would have been better if Ellen had died and

41

Jessie was still here, it really would. No one needed her as the children needed Jess and Sam. Why was life so cruel?

She let out a shaky sigh and watched as the stranger quickly and competently made them both a drink. He was familiar with this kitchen, and even that fact made her chest ache. He had known Jess and Sam better than she had.

'Children off to school?'

'Yes. I think they wanted to go. They didn't say so, but they needed to get back to normality. Whatever that is now.'

'They're lucky to have you.'

'Hmm. They'd rather have their gran, I think. I mean, if they can't have their parents. But they can't have Gran either, just now, 'cos Grandad needs her.'

'How is your Dad doing? Is there anything they can do for Parkinson's these days?'

She looked up in surprise, and then realised that he would know about her father's illness from Jess and Sam. He seemed genuinely interested, watching her with quiet concern.

'Not a lot, with the stage the disease is at. He probably shouldn't have come down for the funeral, but he wanted to. It was important to him and to Mum, so I suppose it was worth it. But now they're both worn out. It's put him back.'

'It's not surprising.'

'No.' Ellen cradled the mug in her hands. It might not be surprising but it was upsetting. She was used to her parents being there to help out when she or Jess needed them, but it wasn't like that any more. 'How's your house coming on?'

she asked, brightly. She had to remember other people had lives, too.

He smiled ruefully. 'Not as quickly as I'd like.' He began to tell her about his problems with the planning department, but she found it hard to concentrate on anything just now. Richard's phone call pointing out all the things she really should be sorting out hadn't helped.

He paused, expecting some kind of response from her. 'Sorry, I sort of lost track...'

She felt embarrassed, but Kit's expression was sympathetic. 'No worries. Time I was off. I'll have a look at those ewes for you.'

'Thanks.'

'You're welcome.'

She went to the door to say goodbye, and he paused and looked down on her, his eyes kind and concerned. He pulled her into a warm, friendly hug. 'You'll be fine. You're doing fine.'

She was surprised at the gesture, brief as it was. Her circle of friends weren't the touchy feely type. 'Well,' she said, moving quickly back. 'Well, thanks for coming down.'

'You're welcome.' He considered her with a slight frown, as though she was a puzzle, and then he let himself out of the door.

As Kit walked back up the track he decided that now was the time to throw himself into the building work. He had procrastinated long enough. It had taken forever to get planning permission and he still didn't have a Building Warrant, but was that reason enough to delay? Sal had always accused him of being a ditherer. Well, he would prove her wrong. He had done his duty by calling in on his neighbour, and checking on the ewes, now he should get to work.

Keeping busy had the additional benefit of stopping him thinking about Jess and Sam – Jess and Sam and his role in sending them away. He still couldn't get used to the idea that he would never see them again, that they had set off on a carefree holiday – and not come back. How could taking one little trip in a taxi go so wrong?

He couldn't begin to imagine how it felt for Ellen and the children. Why oh why had he so blithely encouraged Jess in her plans? But don't think about that now. A bit of practical work was what he needed.

He spent the rest of the morning striding his plot of land, marking out the foundations with metal poles and string. He had always been quite interested in that techy kind of stuff at school and now it was coming in useful. He had his spirit levels and theodolite and with the aid of the plans (which he had drawn up himself) it wasn't too difficult to mark things out. A digger driver called Robbie was coming to look over the job some time that afternoon. Now there was something definite for him to see.

When his stomach reminded him that it might be lunchtime, Kit stood back and examined what he had achieved. He could picture the house without any effort at all. Wood and glass, south facing, lots of light and solar panels. He hoped it was as easy to create in real life as it was in his head.

He felt better for the physical effort. There was nothing like getting your hands dirty.

He fired up his computer and automatically checked for any e-mails from Sal. It had been a relief to get the phone line put in last week, but so far it hadn't made communications from Australia any the more frequent.

This time a message did flash up, and even before he had read it he felt the foreboding.

I don't know how to say this so I'd better do it straight out. I'm not coming over to join you. I'm sorry, but it's not going to work out. To be honest with you, I've met someone else here. He's English too but he wants to stay in Oz and I've realised so do I. I'm really sorry.

I hope things work out for you.

Take care,
Sal

It was so brief that Kit read it right through without taking a breath. Then he read it again. He sat there for a while, letting it sink in. Pretty, bouncy, carefree Sally would not be joining him. Had found someone else. Was no longer his.

The good humour created by the morning's work evaporated. He felt winded by the suddenness of it. Even though he had begun to have his doubts, because she had delayed her departure for so long, he had never thought she would do something like this. He had *trusted* her. He buried his face in his hands, rubbing them over the unshaven chin as though he could rub out his thoughts.

He tried to focus on anger rather than the hurt. How long had she known this other man? How could she keep Kit stringing along? How could she end it all by email? If that was the kind of person she was, he was well rid of her. He didn't need anyone, especially not someone who thought he was English!

And yet his thoughts kept drifting back to Sal's bubbly laugh, her zest for life. He gazed around the messy caravan with distaste. No wonder she hadn't wanted to come over to this. He didn't like it much himself. It was a disaster. Why was it so much easier for things to go wrong than to go right? Is that what Sal had realised about him, how useless he was? Maybe if he'd waited in Australia until she was ready to leave, or found something better to live in once he was over here...

He didn't know how long he sat there before he heard a vehicle pulling up outside. What on earth...? Oh, the digger man. Right. Drains and foundations, they were what he needed to concentrate on just now. He stood up and took a deep breath. Better, and far more rewarding, than thinking about bloody women.

Chapter Four

Ellen slowly climbed the four broad stone steps to the solicitor's office. She hadn't been looking forward to this meeting, and Angus's words as he left for school that morning had made her dread it all the more.

'I'm not leaving Craigallan,' he had hissed at

her, eyes wide and angry in his thin face. 'I know that's what you're going to see the solicitor about, but you can't make me leave. Tell Gran and Grandad.'

'I'm just going to talk to him,' she had said, but he didn't trust her and she didn't blame him. Ellen and this unknown man were going to be talking about Angus's future. She had no idea what those decisions would be, but she was pretty sure he wouldn't like them. 'We'll have a discussion when you get home,' she had promised. He had hitched his school bag on to one shoulder and set off to catch the bus without another word.

The solicitor's office was in Dumfries. He had offered to come out to Craigallan to see Ellen, but she had decided it was about time she started taking the initiative herself and had announced she would drive in. So now she was here, in good time, wearing the out-of-date black suit because it was still the only smart item of clothing she had with her, trudging up the thickly carpeted staircase behind Mr McNicol's broad back.

He ushered her into a large office. On another occasion she might have appreciated its sparse decor. 'Please have a seat, Miss Taylor. It's good of you to come in.'

'No it's not. I should have come sooner, I know.'

'No point in rushing things.' His voice was deep and with the dark eyes and heavy jaw, he had a brooding air about him that could have been threatening, but his tone was kind. 'How are the children? And your parents?'

They spent a little time exchanging pleasantries, as Mr McNicol seemed determined to do. Ellen

47

found, to her surprise, that this put her at ease.

Eventually the solicitor took a sheaf of papers from the folder he had ready and said quietly, 'Right, shall we start?' He paused and leafed through the pages. 'I'm sure you'll be pleased to know that Mr and Mrs Moffat had both made a will, which makes our lives a lot easier.'

'Oh. Good.'

'It's a fairly standard document. Firstly, you need to know who the executors of the will are. In this case Mr and Mrs Moffat named two co-executors – you and me.'

'Me?'

'That's right. I'm happy to do whatever you wish me to do, but obviously that will involve payment. If you want to take over most of the duties yourself I'm more than happy to act as adviser.'

'Er, no, I don't know.' Ellen was feeling confused, and they hadn't even discussed the contents of the will yet. 'I'm very grateful for your help.'

'Very well. Shall I go on?'

'Please do.'

He smiled at her with apparent sympathy, but that didn't prevent him from getting down to the crux of the business. 'The will. In the event of both parties dying, which of course was never expected, their entire estate is left to the three children.'

'That's what I assumed,' said Ellen, feeling this was something she could get her head around.

'The estate will, of course, be held in trust until the children are of age. And I'm pleased to say that my clients did, at my suggestion, nominate a guardian if this very unfortunate eventuality should come to pass. I find that people are often reluctant to do so, but it's always a good idea. Did they discuss this with you at all?' He looked directly at her from the deep set eyes, catching her unawares.

'Er, no. I don't think... Well, yes, maybe.' A memory came back to her of a long ago drunken evening, when Angus was a toddler. Sam's remaining parent had just passed away and Jess had been bemoaning their dearth of relatives. She had made Ellen promise that if anything should happen to them, she would take care of their baby. And Ellen had, of course, promised, and never thought of it again. You didn't expect your sister to die when she was in her thirties. Ellen swallowed hard. 'I think something was said when Angus was a baby. I didn't think it was serious...'

'According to these documents, you are the sole guardian of all three children. I have to ask you if that is acceptable to you?'

'I... God, I never thought... What do you mean, sole guardian?' Ellen tried to get her thoughts in order. 'I'd assumed it would be my parents.'

Rory McNicol glanced down at his papers, calm and composed. 'It's sensible not to nominate a guardian who is elderly. I recall suggesting that shared guardianship might have been preferable, but this was what they decided.'

'Sam was an only child,' said Ellen, feeling as though she had to excuse her brother-in-law. 'He had cousins. They were at the funeral, you might have met them, but they weren't close. And on our side there were just us two girls.' She gave a shaky sigh. 'No, if it's not going to be Mum and Dad, it's got to be me.' It was obvious, yet she'd never even thought of it.

It wasn't panic that she felt wash over her now, but cold fear. She, Ellen Taylor, determinedly unmarried thirty-five year old, was now solely responsible for three children. 'This is a bit of a shock. I suppose it shouldn't be, but it is.'

'I'm sure that a lot of what has happened recently has been a shock. It'll take time to sink in. We don't have to decide anything today, there's no hurry.'

'But ... but...' Ellen gave up trying to put her thoughts into words and sat in silence for a moment. When he offered coffee she nodded, glad of the respite. For the first time since she had received the awful news about her sister, the question in her mind was not *Why Jess?* but *Why me?*

After he had provided her with a cup of very good black coffee, he waited a few minutes before he spoke again. He couldn't wait forever, she understood that, he had other clients to think of, but she appreciated his patience.

'As I said, you don't need to make any decisions now, but you do need to know what it is you have to decide.'

'Yes, I see.' She took another sip. The caffeine helped.

'The first question is whether you are prepared to accept the role of guardian. You are not obliged to do so. If you feel unable, then the state has a duty to step in.'

'The state? Oh, no, I couldn't do that.' She wanted to say, *Where are my parents when I need them?*

'You need to think about this carefully. It's a big

decision, taking on three children of, what, twelve, ten and...?'

'Seven.'

'Yes. Seven. It's a lot to ask.'

'They're my nephews and niece.' The words resounded in Ellen's head. They were her nephews and niece. She was their only aunt. They didn't know her well, or she them, but there was no choice.

'Yes. Fortunately, the financial situation isn't as bad as it might be. I understand that the mortgage on the Craigallan property will be paid off, and there is at least one additional life assurance policy that will go some way towards covering the children's living expenses. It's a shame they didn't take out holiday insurance, but as your sister died while working for the NHS, albeit part-time, I understand there will be a small payment there.'

'That's good,' Ellen said dully. She hadn't got around to worrying about money yet.

'I'll make steps to arrange confirmation of the estate. Once that is sorted out you will have control of the assets, to be used on behalf of the children. Living expenses and so on.'

'I suppose the money should be kept for them, for later?'

'I am reliably informed that children aren't cheap,' he said, with the glimmer of a smile. 'I'm not sure what your own financial position is, but it isn't expected that you will support them.'

He studied her in silence for a moment. 'I hope you don't mind me asking, but do you have a partner who will want to have a say in any decision you take regarding the children?'

Ellen thought of Richard, who found his own children quite burden enough. 'I don't think... No.'

'I see. To an extent, that makes things simpler. If you do decide to accept the guardianship, and once we have resolved the financial issues, you will then need to decide where you and the children will live. Specifically, whether you will remain at Craigallan or sell it.'

Ellen wasn't sure how much more of this she could take. 'Can I have some more coffee?'

'Of course.'

Her hand shook slightly as she held out the cup, but that was probably just the caffeine on an empty stomach.

'I live in Edinburgh. I have a job there, I lecture at one of the colleges, in Business Studies. I've got sort of leave of absence just now, but I'll need to go back. But the children want to stay here. I know they do.' The words came tumbling out. It wasn't that she expected Rory McNicol to offer her a solution, just that she had to voice it all aloud. 'I don't know what to do.' Ellen hated not knowing what to do! She was known for her quiet self-control. And now...

'As I said, you don't need to decide anything immediately.' He considered her for a moment. 'One possibility is to ask for an extended leave from work. If your college is in the public sector – yes? – then they are often very reasonable about that kind of thing.'

'We'll need to move to Edinburgh,' said Ellen.

'Possibly. But as I said, you don't need to make any big decisions right now. You could ask your

52

employers for, say, three months' unpaid leave, while you sort things out down here. Or even six months. That would give you and the children time to get used to – whatever it is you decide to do.'

Ellen shook her head. And then nodded. Neither seemed the right response. 'Maybe. Yes, maybe I could do that.'

She simply couldn't take anything else in, never mind make a major decision. A delay of a month or two sounded very attractive. She'd ask for, say, eight weeks leave, and surely she would have worked something out by then?

Angus's day at Dunmuir Academy was worse than usual, which was saying something. Fat Jason Armstrong had a go at him about *little orphan Annie* whenever there wasn't a teacher within hearing, and the Dawson boys and their crowd kept jostling him out of the dinner queue until he gave up and decided he could do without food today. But none of that mattered compared to what was happening somewhere in Dumfries. He wished he'd insisted on missing school and going with his aunt. *She* didn't know what was best for him and Cal and Lucy. In fact, she probably didn't even care. Why was it left to her to find out everything?

He hadn't been that keen on grown-ups before his parents had gone away, and now... He made a dive into the boys' toilets and got himself into a cubicle before the tears came. He hated Mum and Dad, he hated them. Why did they have to go and get themselves killed? Why did they have to

53

go away at all? Four days of boring Auntie Ellen was more than enough.

He couldn't get the picture of a wrecked car out of his head. It was there in his dreams as well. No one would tell him exactly what had happened so he had to imagine it. Had they been hurt, lain there screaming in agony, waited hours for help? He held tissue paper tightly over his face to stop the sobs.

When he got off the bus in Kinmuir village he almost didn't go home. He knew he had to, because the cows needed feeding and the ewes and lambs checking, but sometimes the walk up the hill was just too much. He carried his school bag in one hand, letting it bounce along the tarmac as he walked. His mum used to hate it when he did that. Well, she wasn't here to stop him now, was she?

Lucy was sitting on the stile at the very end of their land. She wasn't allowed to go any further on her own. She was still keeping to the rules.

'Auntie Ellen's been crying again,' she said without preamble.

Angus thought about this, and couldn't decide if it was good or bad.

'An' two more lambs've been born. Callum helped Kit with one of them.'

'Lambing's my job.'

'You weren't here, were you? Kit said the second one might've died if he and Cal hadn't got it out.'

'That's good, then. Thirty lambs, so far, from twenty ewes. Not a bad average.'

'Dad'd be pleased.'

They walked up to the house in silence and

then Lucy said, just before they reached the kitchen door, 'Angus, what about my swimming?'

'Huh?' Angus squinted down at her.

'You know, my lessons. I've missed them for weeks now.'

'Have you?' He felt annoyed and sorry at the same time. Why did he have to worry about her swimming lessons? 'And Cal hasn't been to football or golf. And you've missed guitar.'

'That doesn't matter. But you need to learn to swim. Mum said. When's your lesson?'

'Tomorrow, after school. Shall I say something to Auntie Ellen?'

'I'll speak to her.'

'Thanks,' she said, very quietly, and he wished he could take her in his arms and cuddle her like Dad used to do. He knew that was what she needed, but he couldn't do it. He swung open the door instead.

Ellen made him change out of school uniform and then wanted him to help with another lambing ewe, and make sure the horses were all right, before she would even start to talk to him. He said nothing and got on with it all as fast as he could. He had a pile of homework in his bag but what did that matter? When they were all back in the kitchen and his aunt was starting to bleat on about what did they want for supper he could bear it no longer.

'I don't want anything to eat. Why can't you just tell us what the solicitor man said?'

'But I'm hungry...' Cal wavered and fell silent under Angus's glare.

Ellen smiled in that false bright way she had.

55

'Well, why don't you all get yourselves a packet of crisps and some juice and then we can have a little chat? No hurry about proper food if you're not hungry.'

Angus noticed she poured herself a glass of wine. His parents never used to drink like she did. She took a deep breath and smiled again. You could tell more about what grown-ups were feeling from how they breathed than their expressions. 'Well, where shall we start?'

'I want to know what the solicitor said.'

Cal and Lucy both looked at him. They probably didn't even know what a solicitor was. He wished he didn't either.

'Do you really want to talk about this now?' Ellen met his eyes, gestured very slightly with her head towards the younger ones.

'Yes. This is about them, too.'

'Of course.' She took another deep breath and looked at the door for a moment. 'Right. Well. I went to see your mum and dad's solicitor today, to find out how things stand. Your parents have done the best they could for you, as I would have expected. Everything they had is left to the three of you.'

Angus tested the words in his head. 'OK.'

'I'm not entirely sure what it consists of yet, but it's the farm here and all the animals, and the car, and whatever money they had in the bank.'

'Not much.'

'And apparently there'll be some money from the hospital where your mum worked, and the solicitor thinks there is a life assurance policy, which will bring in some more. But there's no

56

need for you to worry about any of that now. Mr McNicol will sort it out.'

'And who gets us?' It sounded odd, but he couldn't think of any other way to say it. 'To look after and that?'

She took another breath. 'I do.'

'Oh.' He felt winded. Aunt Ellen? Not Gran and Grandad?

'Or I suppose you could say that you get me. At least, that's the way your parents left things. I'm your legal guardian.'

Angus stared at her. She had put on make-up to go and see the solicitor and it made her look smart and distant, not at all like his mum. What had she to do with them all? 'I'm not leaving Craigallan,' he said, speaking more loudly than he had intended. 'None of us are, are we?' He frowned at his brother and sister. Callum was looking at the clock, clearly thinking of television. Lucy was sucking her thumb and twisting a lock of hair around one finger. She'd almost grown out of that, until four weeks ago. 'This is our home.'

'I know that. And my home is in Edinburgh. But things can change, can't they? Sometimes they have to.'

'You can go back to Edinburgh. We'll be OK. Someone will look after us, Kit or Clare or someone. They're always saying they'll help. Just arrange it so we can stay here, OK?' He could hear his voice rising but couldn't stop it.

'Angus, it's not that easy,' said Ellen in that soothing, superior tone his teachers liked to use. 'I wish it was.'

'You can go away. We'll sort something out. Or

57

I'll ask Gran. Gran'll come down and...'

'Gran has to look after Grandad just now. And their house isn't big enough for you all.'

'They can move here. I said I'm not leaving Craigallan!'

'No one's saying you have to go anywhere just now.'

'I mean it. I'm not leaving. This was Mum and Dad's place, they wanted to stay here for ever, that's what they said. We're not leaving.'

'Your Mum and Dad didn't mean...'

Angus felt himself jolt upright. 'You don't know anything about my Mum and Dad. You don't...'

'Mummy! I want my Mum-mee.' Lucy's cry shocked them both. Angus faltered and turned to stare at her, open mouthed. Why did she have to start this now?

The child began to cry with horrible, wrenching sobs. Ellen glared at him and drew Lucy onto her lap, rocking her. 'Hush, Lucy, hush darling. Don't cry. There, now.'

Angus wished he could think of something to say, but he couldn't.

After a while Lucy's sobs quietened to hiccups and his aunt turned back to the two boys. She seemed close to tears herself. 'Listen. I won't promise you that I'll make everything all right for you, because I can't. I'm really sorry, but I can't. But I do promise that I'll do my very best to work something out. And for the time being I'm going to move down here and live with you. So is that OK?'

'We can stay here?' said Angus.

'For the time being.'

Suddenly he felt too exhausted to continue. It would have to do for now. 'Good,' he said, his voice feeling hoarse and uncomfortable. 'That's good then. And you'll have to find out how we do things here. For a start, Lucy has swimming lessons on a Thursday. And there're other things. And... And I'm going to my room now.'

He left the kitchen with as much dignity as he could manage, and then ran.

Chapter Five

Ellen was nervous. She circled the kitchen for the third time, trying to make sure she hadn't forgotten anything. Hens were fed and eggs collected. Lambing seemed to have tailed off, and Angus had checked on the cows before he went to school. Perhaps this farming business wasn't so difficult after all. Kit Ballantyne would no doubt keep an eye on the animals during the day, as she had become accustomed to him doing. She really would have to stop taking advantage of his kindness, but not today. Today she was going up to Edinburgh and she should have been jumping for joy.

Jess's friend Clare was going to have the children after school so that she didn't need to rush back. Everything was in hand. She made a final circuit of the kitchen and tripped over Monty who whined but didn't move away. 'It's only for the day,' she said as she bent and scratched his head. 'Not even a whole day. Just a few hours.'

He whined again and pressed his head against her hand.

'You want to come with me? Oh, go on then, why not? You'll be company, won't you?'

He gave a low grumble, the ageing border terrier equivalent of a shout of delight. Once in the car he took up position on the seat beside her, occasionally leaning his paws against the dashboard and contemplating the road ahead. He looked completely at ease. Had Jessie used to take him about with her? Ellen couldn't remember. She felt the familiar sinking of the heart as she thought of Jess, of not knowing what Jess would have done, and determinedly pushed those thoughts aside.

Today she was going to have a good time, get a little bit organised, and she wasn't going to think about the children until she got back to Craigallan that evening.

Her spirits rose as she dropped down from the Pentlands into Edinburgh. Just seeing the silhouette of the castle in the distance lifted her mood. This was her home; a beautiful, vibrant place, and she was going to come back here just as soon as she could. She was early for her appointment at the college and went for a mocha latté to fill in the time. Bliss, although she couldn't take Monty into the café with her. She couldn't think what had persuaded her to bring him. Dogs and Edinburgh didn't go together.

This point was brought home again when she went to meet Richard for a late lunch, in an elegant little restaurant close to his office. She found herself hoping that Richard would have to get back to work early, so that the terrier wouldn't be on his own in the car (windows slightly open) for too long. If he didn't have to leave, she would need to make up some excuse herself. Richard wouldn't understand about Monty.

Richard was late, not a great start, but not too late, and he held her close in greeting and seemed genuinely pleased to see her. He looked smart in the dark suit and pristine white shirt, his short, dark hair glossy. Ellen wished she had gone back to her flat first to change into something more suitable, but with fitting in a walk for Monty there hadn't been time.

'Ellen. Good to see you.'

'It's good to be here.'

'You're looking tired. Come on, let's order, then we can talk properly. Make sure you choose a decent meal. You look like you could do with feeding up.'

Ellen felt nettled. Did she look that bad?

'Tell me how you got on at the college. Weren't they surprised you wanted more time off?'

'Not really. Actually, they were very reasonable.' Ellen had met with her head of department. She had already discussed options with Human Resources, and it appeared that her head of department had done so too. 'They've agreed to let me stay on compassionate leave until the end of the month, and then I can take some unpaid leave. They'll hold the post open for me until September.'

Richard frowned. 'September? But I thought you would only need a month or two?'

That's what Ellen had hoped, but the more she thought about it the more difficult everything seemed. 'It's not that easy. The kids don't want to move up here. I'll have to take things slowly. I thought it would be best if they realised for themselves that it's not practical to stay on the farm.'

'You're being too soft on them. Children react best to being told what to do. And what happens if they don't come round to your way of thinking?'

Ellen shrugged. Her salad looked far from appetising. 'Richard, they're not my kids. They've been brought up to be allowed to choose things for themselves. They've had enough of a shock without me trying to impose my wishes on them.'

'You mean they're spoilt.'

'Well.' Ellen had never understood Sam and Jess's approach to child rearing, but there was no point in going into that now. 'They're basically good kids.'

Richard steepled his hands and looked at her consideringly. 'Have you thought of boarding school?'

'Boarding school? Heavens, no. I haven't got the money, and anyway Lucy is only seven, Callum ten. I couldn't just send them away.'

'I was sent away when I was eight.'

And look what that created, thought Ellen. She didn't say it. This was one area in which she and Richard's ex-wife were in agreement, but she knew she wouldn't be able to explain. 'As I said, I haven't got the money.'

'Yes, how exactly are you situated financially? You realise that it'll be a struggle once you've had a month or two without pay? I take it your sister and brother-in-law weren't exactly flush?'

'No, not exactly.' Ellen smiled at the under-statement.

'So are you expected to pay for everything from you own pocket?'

'I have done so far. Not that there has been much to pay for. Just food and that.'

'I take it you haven't got probate sorted out yet?'

'These things take time.'

'No harm in having the property valued, mean-time. Bringing up children is expensive, believe me. You're going to need to get your hands on that capital.'

'Yes. Well, maybe. I'm OK for the moment.' Richard's common sense used to be one of the things that Ellen admired about him.

He glanced at his watch. 'Better eat up. Can't stay much longer, I've got a two-thirty meeting. I told you lunchtimes were never good.'

'I know. Thanks for coming to meet me.'

'My pleasure.' He leant over and kissed her cheek, more like a friend than a lover. 'Take care.'

Ellen went to let Monty out of the car. She should have been pleased that Richard had needed to dash off, saving her having to think up some excuse of her own for an early departure. Instead, she sighed and bent to rub Monty's wiry head with her hand. 'Looks like it's just you and me, mate,' she said. She took him for a stretch of the legs and then drove the car to her little flat.

Her original intention had been to spend some time looking around the shops, but now she didn't have the energy. She made a quick raid on her wardrobe and headed back to the farm. She was already out of the habit of city driving and didn't want to get caught in the rush hour.

Ellen stopped to pick up the children from Clare's on her way to Craigallan. She had intended to stay no more than five minutes, but she had reckoned without Clare's quiet concern which, mixed with a heavy dose of the local tendency to string any conversation out to its limit, meant that you could never be brief.

Twenty minutes later, and turning down the offer of coffee, tea, or something herbal for the third time, Ellen edged towards the door. Angus was hissing 'I need to check Melanie *now*' while Clare promised Grace that Lucy could come for a sleepover very soon. 'I'll see you at the school next Wednesday night, I suppose?' she added to Ellen, catching her unawares.

'Wednesday?'

'Yes. Didn't you get the letter? You have to check the children's bags every day, or you'll never know *anything*. Wednesday was always going to be a PTA meeting, but now with all this talk of threatened school closures they're starting off with a talk about that. It's quite a worry. It would be a disaster for the village if the school was shut. You will be there, won't you?'

Ellen wracked her brains, but could come up with any excuse. She couldn't even remember if Wednesday was a day for swimming lessons, or something similar. 'Perhaps. I don't know. What time is the meeting?'

'Seven o'clock. Bring all the kids down with you. There'll be whole crowd of them in the park, you won't need to worry.'

When Ellen arrived at Craigallan, she remembered what it was she should have done before she left that morning. She should have stoked up the Rayburn. The day had been mild, but it was cool now, and the house already felt damp. No hot water until she got the thing lit, nor for a few hours after that. And no time to sit for a moment and work out what needed doing first. Angus and Callum were arguing. Lucy was hungry. Her flat, which had seemed so dull and silent, was suddenly very attractive.

'Kit's here,' said Angus, looking out the window. 'He's with Melanie. I *told* you I should have come home before now.' He headed out of the back door.

'Angus, can you help me with this fire?'

'No. I said Kit's here. I think there's a problem.'

Ellen frowned. Who was Melanie? Oh, yes, that fat little Galloway cow. Silly name. She felt a sudden quiver of nerves. Was the calving starting? She had just got used to the lambing, but she suspected the cows would be another matter entirely.

Angus was already outside and over the wall into the field, Callum following more slowly in his wake.

'Can I go too?' said Lucy.

'I thought you were hungry?'

'I want to see Melanie.'

'Look, Kit is here. I'm sure...' But Lucy had disappeared and Ellen gave in and followed, at a somewhat slower pace. All this giving birth wasn't her kind of thing. She had watched Angus lamb one ewe, and had felt queasy at the sight of all the blood.

'Is everything all right?' she called out brightly, staying on the garden side of the wall.

Kit Ballantyne had a halter around the cow's neck and was coaxing her towards the farmyard. Angus was beside him and Callum had run ahead to open the gate. The cow was bellowing.

'Just – going to get her – in the byre.' Kit used his shoulder to nudge the cow in the direction of the farmyard, grunting with the effort as she tried to swing away. 'Need her inside – so I can – have a look.'

'I see. Lucy, you stay here with me.' Ellen held on to the child's thin arm so that she couldn't jump down from the gate. Up to now she had found Melanie a rather sweet-natured beast, but she had heard somewhere that cows could be dangerous when there were calves involved. Kit was tall and solid, but even he was struggling to control the animal.

'Get some feed in a bucket,' he shouted to Angus. 'See if she'll come for that.'

'Right.' Angus ran ahead and was back almost instantly with a pail of some kind of grain. The soft, straight hair was falling over his face, which was tense. 'Come on, Melly, come on girl. That's right, food here.' He rattled the bucket and the cow raised her head and looked. Kit took the opportunity when she wasn't pushing against him to nudge her two or three steps closer to the yard. 'Come on Melly,' said Angus, shaking the bucket again. 'What's wrong? Why do you want to bring her in?'

'I just think I need to have a look. The calf is taking a bit too long to appear.'

'I knew I should have come home,' said Angus.

'Lucy and I are going to try and light the Rayburn,' said Ellen. 'Give us a shout if you need anything.'

'But I want to see what's happening,' wailed Lucy. 'Melanie is Angus's first cow. Dad gave him her as a calf last year. Why can't I stay and watch?'

'Because I really need your help. Remember what we said about all helping each other? If the boys are out there with Mr Ballantyne, then I need you to get the kindling for me. Then we'll start on food for everyone. These things are important too, you know.'

'But it's not fair.'

'Life's not fair,' snapped Ellen. The strain of the day was getting to her. Edinburgh had not been the pleasant break she had envisaged. She felt wrung out and had been looking forward to a quiet evening, but there was no hope of that now. She closed her eyes. Life wasn't supposed to be like this. She prided herself on never getting into situations she couldn't handle.

Kit's expression was grim, and she could tell he was worried. What would happen if something went wrong? Might they lose the calf? Or, worse still, the cow? Angus was bound to blame her. His sullen silences were already difficult enough.

She turned to her niece. 'Just do as I say, OK?'

Lucy turned to stare at her in surprise. Her pale, freckled face and blue eyes were so like Jess's. She sniffed and went to do as she was bidden.

They had just got the Rayburn lit when Callum came running into the kitchen. 'There's a problem,' he said breathlessly. 'Kit said I'm to get his bag for him, out of the car.' He disappeared through the other door and headed towards Kit's car, parked part-way up the track.

Ellen followed him as far as the doorway, wondering if she should offer to help. Not that she would even know what a vet's bag looked like. He seemed to find what he wanted without too much difficulty and was about to turn back when something caught his attention. He looked at the car, then at Ellen.

'What is it?' she shouted.

'It's Kit's mobile. It's ringing. Should I answer it?'

'Pick it up, at least.' She hurried up the track towards him, just in time to hear the ringing stop. She took the handset from her nephew and read the message: '5 missed calls'. What now? Five calls must be important. But she needed Kit here!

She and Callum hurried through to the farm yard, he lugging the bag, she holding the phone doubtfully before her. 'Someone's been trying to phone you.'

'God, why now?' said Kit, looking up briefly. For the first time since Ellen had met him, he looked harassed. The cow was on her side on the floor and Kit and Angus were beside her. She realised that Angus was still in his school uniform.

'I heard the phone ringing.'

'It says there've been five calls,' said Lucy, not wanting to be left out. She edged backwards as Melanie gave a sudden convulsion. 'Is Melly OK?'

'She will be,' said Kit through gritted teeth. 'When we get this calf out.' He used his weight to keep the heifer from standing up and started delving into the massive black bag with his one free hand. 'Right, Angus, this is what I want you to do.'

Ellen backed away, still holding the phone.

'Shouldn't be a minute,' said Kit, not even looking up this time. His attention was entirely on Angus and the animal that lay between them. For some reason Kit seemed to be giving the instructions and Angus to be doing the work. Ellen stood in the doorway, fascinated and horrified in equal parts, as her nephew put his bony arm right inside the cow. He was frowning in fierce concentration. Kit was swearing and sweating as he tried to keep the cow still. 'That's right... Feel for a foot...'

Callum came closer to get a better look and the heifer twisted and pulled away in surprise. Kit protected Angus with his body and got a hoof in his ribs for his troubles. 'Bloody hell! Callum, get out of the way.' The cow had slumped back down and was now breathing shallowly. 'Look, we need to move quickly. OK, one last try, Angus, and then I'll have to... Well, we won't think about that now. Right, get your arm back in again. Good, good. Are you sure it's a foot? Do you want the noose? Keep going, you're doing fine.'

He carried on telling the boy what to do, sometimes repeating himself two or three times, never losing his patience although his face was tense and sweat was pouring down it. Then, suddenly, Angus sat back and the forefeet and nose of the calf appeared where his arm had been.

'Ah, that's better,' said Kit with a huge sigh. 'That's more like it.'

Ellen found she had been holding her breath

and let it out in a long sigh of her own.

Kit cleared mucus from around the calf's mouth and nose, gentle and businesslike, and then sat back on his heels. 'I think she'll do all right on her own now.' He wiped his hand on the straw and stood up. They all watched as poor Melanie gave another tremendous push, and the calf's head appeared. A few moments later, the whole body came slithering out. Melanie rose to her feet, determined but unsteady, and began to lick it roughly. The skinny wet creature wriggled and whimpered. It was alive.

'I'll take the phone now,' said Kit from right beside Ellen, making her jump. 'Can't think why the surgery would need me at this time... It's not the surgery.' He frowned.

'Do you want...?'

'Excuse me, I'd better call the number back. Just give me a minute, will you? Keep an eye on her, Angus.'

He went out in to the cold dusk and Ellen was left in the barn with the heavily sweating cow, damp new calf, and three excited children. 'Is everything all right?' she asked tentatively.

'Should be OK now.' Angus was almost smiling. 'The calf had a leg twisted back so the heifer couldn't push it out. Kit's hands were too big but he told me what to do and I did it. I pulled the leg round and then it was OK. Look, she's trying to get to her feet already. And it's a female calf, that's brilliant.'

Ellen watched but didn't move any closer. The calf, barely five minutes old, was already struggling to stand. The dark coat was thickly matted and damp. 'It's amazing.'

'She wants to start feeding. Let's hope Melly will stand still for her.' His smile faded and he met Ellen's eyes with a glare. 'Now do you see why I needed to come home sooner? She'd never have managed on her own and if the calf died we could've lost them both.'

'But Kit was here...'

'She's my heifer,' said Angus fiercely, putting one hand protectively on the cow's flank. 'Kit said he'd only just got here. *Anything* could've happened.'

A few moments later, Kit reappeared, his expression troubled again. 'A problem?' asked Ellen, heart sinking. She had been hoping he would stay around a little longer. Melanie was still breathing heavily, the calf looked shaky, and Angus's expression was fierce.

'It's my mother.' Kit pushed the thick hair back with his forearm. 'It never bloody rains, does it? Give me a minute and I'll think what to do.'

'Something's wrong with your mother?'

'She's had a fall. Not a bad one, but Mrs Mc-Iver thinks someone should be with her.'

'Is she close by?'

'Mum? She lives just the other side of Dunmuir. Deer Bridge. Do you know it? I should go, but I don't want to leave Melanie just yet...'

'The calf's OK,' said Angus. 'I think.'

'That's good. I'll just stay a few more minutes.

'We'll manage,' said Ellen without conviction. 'If your mother needs you.'

'Yes, but the heifer's had a bad time. She shouldn't be left, it's her first calving. She may well need an injection after all that effort.' Kit pushed back his hair again, frowned at his watch. 'If only...'

'I could go to your mother, if that was any help.' An old lady was a far less worrying prospect than an ailing cow and resentful nephew. Ellen hardly expected Kit to agree but he nodded immediately.

'Are you sure? It's probably nothing to worry about, it's not the first time it's happened. But I can't just not go. I'll be forever in your debt.'

She smiled back. It was good to offer to do something for him. 'Give me directions and I'll be on my way.'

Chapter Six

Deer Bridge was a couple of miles north of Dunmuir. It was rather a quaint village of pale pink sandstone. Ellen had admired the buildings more than once as she passed through. Mrs Ballantyne's house was rather grand, standing well back from the road.

The door was opened by a slight, tired-looking woman in her fifties. 'I'm that glad you've... Oh, I was waiting on Kit.' She looked disappointed.

'Kit's busy with a calving just now, so I said I'd come instead. I'm a neighbour of his.'

'A neighbour? Well, that's good then. I'm a wee bit pushed for time myself. Come in, come in. And do you know Mrs Ballantyne?'

Ellen hesitated. 'I'm a friend of Kit's. I'm sure everything'll be fine.'

'She's in the sitting room.' The woman lowered her voice. 'I tried to get her up to bed but it was no use. She's a lovely woman, Mrs Ballantyne, don't get me wrong, but these days she can be that contrary. Are you sure you'll be OK? I should really get back, my husband'll be wanting his tea, like, but I didn't want to leave her.'

She nudged a door open and Ellen peered in.

A large woman was sitting in an armchair with one leg raised onto a footstool. 'Good afternoon,' said Mrs Ballantyne politely. 'Or is it evening. Good evening?'

'I'll be off, then,' said the woman who had let Ellen in. She left before Ellen could protest, or even ask what had happened.

Ellen went and sat on the edge of a soft, fancy settee. 'Hello, Mrs Ballantyne. I'm Ellen, a friend of Kit's. How are you feeling?'

'I'm perfectly all right. It's nice to see you, dear.' The woman had the same broad face as Kit, and a lovely smile. But despite claiming to be fine, she looked tired, or in pain.

'Is your leg hurting?' asked Ellen. 'You had a fall, didn't you?'

'Just a little one, dear. These things happen when you get older. I'll be fine in a wee while. Would you like a tea or coffee?' She made to get up, and then realised she couldn't with her leg propped up like that.

'Probably best if you don't get up just now. Perhaps I can make you a drink?'

It took a little persuading, but Mrs Ballantyne

eventually agreed that as she couldn't get up just now Ellen should go to the kitchen and make a pot of tea.

'I'm sorry to put you to so much trouble,' said the elderly lady. 'That's all I seem to be, these days: trouble.'

'Of course you're not. This is no trouble.'

Mrs Ballantyne didn't look convinced, but she accepted a cup of tea and did her best to make polite conversation. 'It's been a lovely day, today, hasn't it? Warm for the time of year.'

They chatted in this vein for a while until Mrs Ballantyne said, 'Who did you say you were? Are you Kit's girlfriend, come over at last?'

'No, no. I'm Kit's neighbour.'

'That's right, you said. Sorry, dear, I get confused sometimes.'

'We all get confused,' said Ellen. She hoped Kit would get here soon. She wasn't accustomed to caring for elderly ladies – for anyone, actually.

Kit, on the other hand, was clearly used to his mother. When he arrived an hour later he took in the situation at a glance, checked her leg to make sure she wasn't badly injured, and managed to cajole her up to bed. There was something about his solid presence that calmed the atmosphere, put everyone at their ease. Ellen was impressed at how gentle he was. She helped as much as she could, but she was sure Kit would have managed very well without her.

Kit had brought Callum and Lucy with him and they sat quietly in front of the old-fashioned television while the adults were busy. As soon as Ellen returned downstairs, however, Callum burst out with, 'I'm starving. It's nearly eight o'clock and we haven't had a thing to eat.'

'We have been a bit busy,' said Ellen with a sigh. The last thing she felt like doing now was cooking.

'Can we get fish and chips?' said Lucy hopefully. 'As a treat?'

'Or how about Chinese?' suggested Callum, catching on to the idea. 'There's a really good take-away in Dunmuir. Can we?'

'Well...' Ellen seemed to remember Jess hadn't approved of take-away food, but the idea of something ready-made was too good to resist. 'I don't see why not. Callum, why don't you run upstairs and see if Kit will join us? He won't have had anything to eat either and I think he's planning to go home soon. Tell him we're having Chinese.'

'Kit says yeah, if you're sure,' the boy reported, reappearing at twice his normal speed. 'Come on, can we go now?'

Ellen had just poured out a glass of wine and the children were eagerly opening the little foil dishes when Kit arrived at Craigallan. She found a glass for him and as she took a sip, found herself relaxing for the first time that day. The food was surprisingly good, and somehow she had come through yet another harrowing experience. Even Angus seemed happy that the heifer and calf were fine and Ellen had, for once, done something to help Kit by going to see his mother.

By the time they had finished eating, Lucy was almost asleep in her chair and it was time for Ellen to take her up to bed. What she really wanted was to sit quietly in the kitchen, have another glass of

75

wine, allowing herself to unwind completely. But of course she couldn't. She had never appreciated how long it took merely to supervise a sleepy child through the bedtime routine and then to read the required story.

When she returned downstairs, she found that Kit, of his own accord, had done the last round of the animals with Angus (not unexpected) and then returned to clear up the kitchen (miraculous). If Ellen had been him, she would have taken the chance to retreat to the childfree sanctuary of his caravan. She made them both a coffee and tried to think of the right words to thank him. And to tell him that from now on she really was going to stop relying on him.

'I hope your mother's going to be all right,' she said.

He looked up, the brown eyes wary. 'I'm sure she'll be fine after a good night's sleep.'

'Yes, of course...' She wondered herself quite what it was that had made her say that. 'It must be a worry. She was very sweet to me, but she seemed a bit confused. I suppose the fall would have shaken her.'

'It would,' he said, still looking defensive. Then he sighed. 'To tell you the truth, it's not the first time. I don't know what's causing it, whether she trips or it's something else... So far she's not been badly hurt but who knows next time?' He rubbed his eyes. 'She seems to have deteriorated a lot since my father died, but maybe it's just that I'm here to see it. I haven't been around much for the last few years.'

'You were in Australia, weren't you?'

'That's right. I spent quite a few years travelling around, you know, the States, Thailand, Malaysia. But the last two years I was in Australia.'

Ellen couldn't help wondering how old he was. Not quite her age, but surely too old for that travelling bug, which had always seemed a bit too hippyish for her. It was the sort of thing she could easily imagine Clare doing. 'It must be strange, coming back here.'

'It's fine. I was always going to come back, my father's death just precipitated it. My mother was pleased, she's been wanting me to settle down for ages.'

'That's good.' Ellen hesitated. 'She was a little confused about me though. She seemed to think I was a girlfriend? Someone who had come over to join you?' Partly she wanted him to realise the way his mother's mind had been working, but partly she was curious. She had thought of Kit as a solitary person, engrossed in his work and his house.

'Did she really? That was Sal, my Australian girlfriend. Ex-girlfriend. I told Mum she was no longer coming over but she must have forgotten.'

Ellen tucked away this information for later consideration. So he really had meant to settle down, with a girlfriend. Perhaps he wasn't so flaky. 'Maybe she was extra forgetful, with the fall, and then a stranger like me turning up.'

'I suppose it's a good thing that I'm on hand now and can see exactly how she is.'

'Don't you have any brothers or sisters, someone to help?' said Ellen. How she wished she had a sibling out there.

'No, I'm an only child. I used to quite like that

but now... I thought it would be OK if I came back and lived close by. But actually, she needs someone even closer on hand than I am, doesn't she?'

'I can hardly judge from the one meeting.'

'But that's what you think. That's what I think, too. Either I should live with her myself or find some kind of live-in home help. Mrs McIver does her best, but a couple of hours a day isn't enough any more.'

Ellen shrugged. This wasn't something she knew anything about.

Kit sighed again, tapping his fingers restlessly on the table. 'Anyway, let's talk about something else. How are *you* doing?' He shot her a smile and she realised that of all the people who had been dropping by he was the only one who hadn't yet asked her that question. When he did, he seemed to want a real answer. He bent and lifted Monty onto his lap and stroked the dog's wiry head, waiting patiently for a reply.

'Struggling,' she said, looking around the kitchen. Kit might have cleared away after their meal but there was still a pile of washing to fold and put away, paperwork piled up at the end of the table, children's possessions everywhere. 'Sometimes I think I'm just about coping, but it's touch and go.'

'It's very sad,' he said. 'I miss Sam and Jessie and I'd only got to know them recently. For you and the children it's a hundred times worse.'

'It's awful for the children,' Ellen agreed quietly. 'Terrible.'

'And it's not just them. I imagine it has totally messed up *your* life, too.'

78

'Well,' said Ellen, feeling she should protest. It was so selfish to think about how her life had been affected when it was so much worse for others. But she was too tired to be polite. She shrugged and said, 'You're right. It's such a shock. Everything has changed so suddenly I don't know where to start.'

'Take it slowly. Always the best way.'

'It's a nice thought.' She smiled. There was a calmness about Kit that was soothing. And, un-like Richard, he actually seemed to think she was doing all right.

'One day at a time, that's my motto.' He smiled back. His whole face lit up. He had a very nice face.

They were both quiet for a while. Kit stroked Monty. Ellen was starting to let the peace sink into her.

Then she saw the clock and realised how late it was. She sat up straight. 'But how can I take one thing at a time? There's so much to do. And we really can't expect you to spend so much time looking after the animals. I don't think I realised quite how much you do. I've been taking advant-age.' She nodded determinedly. 'If you would show me what needs doing, I'll try and do it my-self.' Even as she spoke, her heart sank. All those lambs, and Melly and her weak new calf, and all the other in-calf cows.

'No way, you've enough on your hands.'

'No, really. If you give me a few instructions, I'll take over.'

'I'm more than happy to carry on helping out.' He frowned, looking put out.

'Just because you're a vet and know what to do, I can't let you carry on. And I should pay you for what you have done, especially the calving. Shouldn't I?' She felt embarrassed. It was the first time that she had realised she wasn't just taking advantage of his time, but of his professional skills too.

'Look, I said I'm happy to do it, OK?' Kit sounded almost angry. He was looking away from her at the shadows. 'It's the least I can do. I was the one who encouraged Jess to book that holiday, and look what happened.'

Ellen stared at him. 'This wasn't your fault. It was – it was pure bad luck. It wasn't anyone's fault, unless it was that stupid idiotic taxi driver.'

'But if I hadn't encouraged them to go...'

'Jess had been wanting to go away, planning this for months. If it comes down to it, I encouraged her just as much as you.' Ellen shook her head. She had told Jess a trip away for her and Sam would be a marvellous thing (that was before she realised she was going to be asked to child-sit).

'I told them travel was good for the soul,' Kit said, grimly. 'And I don't even know if they believed in souls.'

They sat in silence for a moment. Ellen wished she believed in souls, believed that Jess and Sam were still *somewhere*.

Kit shook his head. 'Anyway, that aside, I enjoy spending time with the animals. It's more or less what I wanted to do myself, have a small-holding, be self-sufficient, you know?'

'No,' said Ellen honestly. She didn't know, but

she was relieved that the hard glint was fading from his eyes.

'I'll show you stuff, if you want, but really, there's no hurry for you to take it all on.'

'It seems so unfair. I should at least pay you.'

'Consider you're doing me a favour. It takes my mind off worrying about my mother.' He looked up and smiled gently when he saw the concern on her face. 'I mean it.' He touched her hand.

She smiled back at him. It seemed that he really did mean it. 'Thanks. That's very kind of you.'

When he got up to take his leave, Kit gave her one of his quick, comforting hugs. She was sure this was instinct on his part, offering comfort, but again she was caught by surprise. And, even more unexpected, was how comfortable it felt to be in the circle of his arms. His touch sent a flicker of feeling through her she hadn't expected. She looked up into those sleepy brown eyes and the flicker quivered again. Kit seemed to notice nothing, patting her on the back as though she were a dog or one of the children. This was ridiculous. She stepped back, and gave him a swift smile.

Chapter Seven

It was a chill, damp morning. The brisk walk to school with Callum and Lucy had done nothing to dispel the cold that had settled deep inside Ellen. The grey sky seemed to weigh down on her and the faint, persistent drizzle was soaking her hair and dripping down her neck. The feeling of connection which she had experienced briefly with Kit had passed. The cloud was so low she couldn't see the top of the hills. Even the dog seemed depressed, walking sadly along behind her.

Missing Jessie hit her unexpectedly at times like this. The pain of loss was like an ache right through her, no muscle would work, she just wanted to lie down and cry. It took conscious effort to put one foot in front of the other. Her face felt numb with the battle to keep back the tears. She would start to think she was getting over it, and then it all came swamping back. Jessie, her only sister, was gone, gone forever. No one to fight with, to resent, to trust. She can't have gone, she can't, Ellen wanted to scream to the still, green hills, but common sense prevailed, and she trudged on home.

She should be making the most of these weeks away from work. In her old life, she would be arriving at work just now, and the idea of a few weeks in the country would have seemed wonderful. But this wasn't a holiday and no matter how hard she tried she couldn't pretend it was any fun.

As she reached the last corner, she paused to survey the home that had been her sister's pride and joy: the long, low, white-washed building, with tiny dormer windows in the slate roof. It was attractive, in a quaint sort of way. Which was a good thing, if it came to selling it. A shiver of anxiety went through her at the thought, and she hurried inside.

She was just about to switch the kettle on when

her mother phoned. During the trudge home Ellen had wished her mother was there so they could discuss *things*. Now her mother was at the end of the phone she found that she couldn't.

'Is Dad OK?' There was something in her mother's tone that was worrying.

'Yes, dear, he's fine. He's been a bit depressed, but the district nurse said that happens sometimes. He seems brighter today.'

'That's good.' It wasn't too bad, at least. 'And how are you, Mum? Are you looking after yourself?'

'I'm perfectly all right. It's you and the children I'm concerned about. I just wish I was down there doing something to help. Do you think I should have them for the Easter holidays?'

Ellen's heart rose, but only momentarily. 'No, Mum. Not if Dad isn't well. He's taking up most of your time and energy. I know the kids want to see you but, well, I think they'd want more of your time than you could give them just now.' Ellen remembered her father as he had been. A calm, composed, reserved background to her mother and sister's loquaciousness. She had felt rather than been informed that she had his cool approval. He, like her, didn't get involved. His illness seemed to have made him withdraw even more.

Her mother sighed. 'I suppose you're right. But I do miss, well, all of you.'

Of course. Why hadn't Ellen thought of that? Jess was forever dashing up to Stirling, keeping in touch.

'Perhaps we could all come and see you during

the Easter holidays. Just briefly. We wouldn't want to be in the way...'

'Do you think you could?' Her mother's voice was raised in hope.

'I don't see why not.'

'Well, that would be lovely. Just lovely. But I wish there was something *we* could do to help *you*.'

'Don't worry about it, Mum.' There was no point in saying anything else.

'Actually, there is one thing. Dad and I have been thinking we should give you some money. It's not right you having to pay for everything and I doubt the solicitor has sorted Jess and Sam's finances out. I'll transfer some into your bank account this very afternoon. How would that be?'

Ellen was touched. 'That's very kind of you Mum. I am managing at the moment, but...'

'We're pleased to do it. If we can't help physically, the least we can do is give you money.'

'Thanks, Mum,' said Ellen bleakly. She was grateful. The only problem was she would far, far rather have had some of their time.

'We're glad to help. And now, tell me, how is Angus?'

'Angus?' Ellen rubbed her face, searching for a reply that was both truthful and comforting. 'He's not saying much.'

'Poor, poor boy. He'll be taking this hard, he takes everything hard, does our Angus.'

'Yes.'

'But he's a good boy underneath. Sam found him a real help around the farm.'

'He's certainly that.'

Her mother paused, so Ellen knew that the next words were important. 'You know that Jessie was worried he was being bullied at school, before – before all this happened? She didn't think he was happy.'

'No, I didn't know.'

'But she might have been wrong. Has he said anything?'

'Not about school.'

'Is he willing to go?'

Ellen tried to think. Mornings were always such a rush. None of the children were exactly eager to go to school, but she had assumed that was normal. 'I think he'd rather stay here, because of the animals. But he's never actually tried to avoid going.'

'That's good.'

Ellen didn't know if it was or not. She now had another thing to add to her list of worries.

'Ellen, I don't mean to nag, but have you had someone in to look at that kitchen roof yet?'

'The kitchen...? No, no, I haven't. But I will. I'll look in the Yellow Pages and phone someone.' Another thing for the list.

'That's good. I do wish I was closer and could do more to help.'

'Mum, don't worry about it. You just concentrate on looking after yourself and Dad, I'll manage down here.'

'You're a good girl, Ellen.'

Ellen made a noncommittal noise. If her mother knew that what she really wanted to do was throw all her things in the car and hightail it back to Edinburgh she wouldn't be so complimentary. But giving her even an inkling of that would only trouble her more, so Ellen kept that thought to herself.

She made herself a coffee and then wandered slowly through the house. When she returned to the kitchen she paged through the most recent *Solicitors Property Guide*. She needed to get a feel for property prices around here. It was only sensible, wasn't it? And as she turned the pages, she realised with surprise that Craigallan might be worth quite a lot. When Sam and Jess had moved to this area one of the attractions had been the ridiculously low prices. They had got the house and a couple of hundred acres of land for a very reasonable sum. Now property speculation, or rich southerners, or both, had reached Dumfriesshire and Craigallan could provide a tidy sum to invest for the children.

She wished she felt happier about that fact. She had to get her head around what they were going to do in the future, and that meant what was best for them and not necessarily what *they* thought was best. With Monty at her heel, she wandered through the large, if scruffy, downstairs rooms and the quaint, old-fashioned rooms upstairs, avoiding as always the master bedroom. With a little effort the place could be made rather attractive.

But that wasn't something she could do today. Today, she was going to take care of those things she never managed to get on top of, like the washing and ironing, the cooking and cleaning. She was beginning to realise just how much work was involved in looking after a house and three children.

When the children arrived home the house immediately descended into chaos again. A whole day's tidying undone in minutes. With the three of them all having their different agendas Ellen could never quite keep up. It was after six when she heard Angus come into the back kitchen and she hurried through, determined not to lose track of him again. 'Angus, do you need to do that now?' He was filling a bucket at the sink. 'I'm worried you haven't done your homework yet.'

'Don't call me Angus.' He kept his thin back to her as he spoke, his tone sullen.

'But...?'

'My name's not Angus, it's Sam. Call me Sam.'

'Sam?'

'It is, you know,' said Callum conversationally, coming in with a football under his arm. 'Samuel Angus Moffat.'

'And Angus is a bloody stupid name. It was too confusing to call me Sam when – when Dad was around, but now he's not, so you can. I've told the kids already.'

'I...' Ellen could feel herself floundering. 'I suppose we could call you Sam if you wanted, but I think Angus is a lovely name. And so did your Mum and Dad, or they wouldn't have chosen it.'

'They only chose it as a second name. Samuel is my real name.'

'Yes, but.' Ellen's heart ached as she looked at the hunched shoulders. 'Actually, I think they put the names in that order 'cos it sounded better. You know, Angus Samuel doesn't run off the tongue quite so well as Samuel Angus, does it? I really think that was the only reason.'

Angus shrugged. 'I don't believe you.'

She stopped herself snapping, telling him not to be so rude, and said carefully, 'OK, we'll talk about it over supper. And I really think you should come in and do your homework now.'

'After I've done the sheep. Someone's got to do them, haven't they?'

'And then we'll have to go down to the village,' said Callum. 'Can I take my football? We'll play with it in the park while you're at that meeting.'

'What...?' And then Ellen remembered the meeting about school closures. She didn't know why people expected her to be interested in that, but the kids seemed to want to go down to the park, and it was good to see them keen on something. And maybe it wouldn't be such a bad thing to find out what was happening with the school. If, coincidentally, it was to be closed down, that could be another good reason for moving them all up to Edinburgh, wouldn't it? 'OK, but that means eating your tea *quickly*. And if you want to come too, Angus...'

'Sam.'

'...Sam, then you'll need to do your homework when we get back. I hope you haven't got much.'

He shrugged, his back still facing towards her.

Ellen sat silently through the meeting later that evening. She let the discussion drift over her head. What did village politics matter to her? She had so many other things to worry about. Not just Angus, but the next cow that was due to calf, and Lucy's clinginess, and whether or not to sell Jess and Sam's old car.

The school meeting felt as foreign to her as if it had been in another language. All this talk of investment in rural communities, the pros and cons of single-teacher schools, the importance of a new playing field, why did they think it was so important?

'You'll do the bric-a-brac stall with me, won't you?' said Clare suddenly.

'Er ... what?'

'At the coffee evening. We always have a bric-a-brac stall. OK to help out?' Without waiting for an answer she waved her hand to attract the attention of the Chairperson, 'Ellen and I will take care of that.'

The woman, who Ellen thought was possibly the school head teacher, nodded her neat, grey head approvingly and noted down their names. A number of people turned and smiled, nudging each other as they whispered her identity.

Just what Ellen needed. Yet another job.

The last day before the Easter holidays found Ellen waving a bottle of milk temptingly in front of the newest calf and trying to remember if Angus normally warmed it first. The calf certainly didn't seem very interested and the mother was taking exception to Ellen's interference. Didn't the stupid animal realise she was trying to help? She was glad there were metal railings protecting her. She stuck the enormous rubber teat into the calf's mouth once more, and it spat it out.

'Bugger,' she said, and put the bottle down with a bang. She would have to come back to that later. She checked the water and hay and then went outside to have a look at the sheep. She knew she was supposed to be checking that the lambs were 'pairing up' with their mothers, but how were you supposed to tell one sheep from another?

She wished she had thought to leave Monty in the house. He was a liability when it came to counting sheep. He thought it was a great joke to scatter the lambs, after each foray he returned to Ellen with a stupid grin on his face.

'No, you haven't been a help,' said Ellen, bending down to pat his wiry head. 'You're an idiot, did you know that? Old men like you should be sensible.'

He butted her ankles gently, pleased with the attention.

The ewes and lambs were in the two fields nearest the house. Ellen walked among them twice, and decided that as far as she could tell nothing was ailing and every lamb seemed to have a ewe it considered to be its mother. Now, what else was there to do? She tapped one of her new wellies against the gate and went through the list in her mind. Dog fed, mash, and corn put out for the hens, cows and calves not in dire need although she'd have to have another go with that bottle. Sheep all fine and ... ah, yes, the horses. Angus and Kit had moved them into one of the upper fields. She opened the gate and let herself and the Monty through. She would go and look them over.

She could see Kit's caravan as she climbed higher, and the dark scars in the ground where digging had begun. There was no sign of activity there now, so she supposed he must be at the vet practice today. She hadn't yet worked out when he did and didn't work. She knew he was employed by the Dunmuir practice, but sometimes he seemed to be around for days on end.

He spent quite a bit of time with Angus, and she was grateful for this. The boy seemed happier around him, about the only time that he was. He was still insisting on this ridiculous change of name and she and the children were trying, not very successfully, to comply. She wondered if Angus was bright enough to try for vet college himself. He certainly had the animal skills. She tried to picture herself discussing future careers with him, and failed. Perhaps she could get Kit to sound him out?

Now, where were the horses? Ellen was sure that they were supposed to be in this field somewhere. It was a sloping, hummocky enclosure, far larger than the neatly dyked paddocks beside the house. Then, as she climbed higher, she thought she heard something. A whinny or a neigh, low and intermittent. She quickened her pace, her breath catching in her throat. Somehow, it didn't sound right.

Jess and Sam had had two horses – or rather, one pony for the children to ride and one old mare to keep the pony company and for Jess to ride in her very occasional spare time. The pony was a rather pretty tan gelding called Tony. Lucy adored him and was always asking to be allowed to ride, but Ellen usually tried to avoid the issue. She wasn't keen to get close to Tony's strong yellow teeth, which had already given her a nip. Bridget, the mare, was a far calmer animal, but much too big for the children.

It was Bridget who was in trouble. As Ellen breasted the last rise she saw both horses at once. Tony was circling round and round the larger sloping field, clearly upset. Bridget was down on her side. Then the mare tried to get to her feet, slipped in the mud and fell heavily, with another faint whinny. Ellen ran, at the same time thinking, 'Not something else going wrong. What am I going to do? And what will Angus say if I don't do it right?'

As she drew closer she saw what the problem was. The mare had her front feet entangled in a wire fence and her back ones were sinking deeper and deeper in the mud as she tried to free herself. The ground here was marshy. The twisting and wrestling of the horse had pulled one of the wooden fence posts out of the earth, but it hadn't freed her. The thick wire was caught between a shoe and hoof, and the more Bridget struggled the more tightly it became trapped.

Ellen stepped cautiously up to the horse's head, pushing Tony back so that he wheeled and galloped off.

'Poor Bridgy,' said Ellen, patting her head shakily. 'Tony! No! Away from there.' She jumped back as Bridget struggled to get to her feet again. She didn't succeed. There was no way she could do so until she was freed from the wire. Ellen edged closer, took hold of the muddy metal, and gave a tentative tug. Nothing happened. She pulled harder. The mare's leg jolted, but the wire was as firmly stuck as ever. Ellen retreated a few steps. What on earth could she do? She'd have to cut the fence, but for that she needed metal clippers. Where would she find those?

'It's OK, girl,' she said, keeping an eye on Tony, who was prancing close again. 'It's OK, just give me a minute.' At that moment Monty tried to greet Tony, causing him to panic and buck, and Bridget made another mammoth effort to get to her feet and out of the way.

Ellen was caught by one flailing hoof and went over in the mud. Bridget fell back on her side, and Tony wheeled off down the field. Ellen scrambled to her feet, muddy and shaken, but she didn't think she was hurt. She backed away from Bridget who was breathing heavily, her eyes were wide with fear.

'Oh God. Right. I'll get something, someone. I'll be right back.' Ellen began to run down the field. She slipped on the damp grass but managed somehow to keep to her feet. She had to get help.

She went first into one of the outbuildings where her brother-in-law seemed to have kept his tools. There were rows of implements laid out, a complete mystery to her. How was she supposed to find wire cutters when she didn't even know what they looked like? Her training had been in economics and accountancy.

Eventually she grabbed a couple of things that looked like possibilities and then ran across to the house. In the kitchen she came to a stop. The one person she knew would be able to deal with this was Kit Ballantyne, but he was presumably at work, and did she have the nerve to call him there?

As she stood there, undecided, she heard the sound of a car on the road. It slowed as it approached and Kit's muddy estate car turned in. A miracle! She pulled open the door and ran out, waving wildly.

Kit stopped immediately. 'Are you all right? What is it?'

'I'm fine. I mean, sort of. It's the horses, can you come? I really need your help.'

He climbed out and looked her up and down, taking in the mud and torn trousers. 'Are you sure you're OK?'

'Yes! But Bridget has got herself caught in a fence and I can't get her free. I didn't know what to do. I'm so glad to see you. Will you come?'

'A fence? Yes. Hang on a minute.' He pulled his bag from the car. 'Still in the top field, yes? Can you show me?'

Ellen considered herself fit but she had difficulty keeping up with Kit. She followed, panting, giving brief directions. As they breasted the hill they saw Bridget lying where Ellen had left her, now totally still. Tony was standing beside her, pawing the ground. 'Oh no. Is she...?'

'She'll be fine.' Kit covered the last few yards and knelt beside the stricken horse, one large hand on her chest. 'She's just resting. Having a bad time of it, aren't you, old girl? No, don't try to get up yet.' To Ellen he said, 'Can you open my bag and take out some of the tools? I'll tell you which one I need.'

'Won't these do?' She held up the tools she had brought from the shed.

He didn't even try to hide his smile. 'Ah... No. Those are for sheep shearing.'

She looked down at the heavy rusty scissors in disbelief, then dropped them and began search-

94

ing through the bag he had brought.

'No, not that. No. Yes, pass that one, I'll try with those. Keep looking for something similar but bigger.' He stretched out an arm to take the cutters from her, keeping a pacifying hand on the mare. He adjusted his position so that he could see the wire more clearly, talking softly. Then with a couple of grunts he clipped through the wire and sat back. 'Excellent. That's the first part done. She's not tied down by the fence any more, but I'm worried about all this mud. She'll struggle to get a foothold. Is there any straw nearby?' He stood up and looked around, but they were high on the hill and all they could see was grass, reeds, and rock.

'Is she going to survive?' asked Ellen in hushed tones. Lucy had told her proudly that Bridget was over twenty years old. An accident like this couldn't be good for her.

'She should survive. I can't say if there's any damage 'til we have her back on her feet, but... There, there, girl. No, don't try...' But Bridget was kicking wildly again. Once she realised that she was no longer attached to the evil fence, she tried and tried to right herself. She only succeeded in pushing her back hooves further into the dank mud.

'Reeds,' said Kit. 'Best we can do just now. See if you can gather some up and we'll put them around her, might give her a grip.'

Ellen hurried to follow his suggestion, thankful he was there. She ripped up the slippery green-brown vegetation so frantically that she tore her skin. Between them they made a carpet around

95

the mare's front legs, then Kit dug out some of the mud at the back and forced vegetation down in its place. He was now nearly as muddy as her, and had to jump back twice when Bridget went through her flailing and whinnying performance.

'It's awful,' said Ellen, nearly in tears now. 'What if...?' And then the mare gave an extra lurch, got a reasonable grip with one leg, hovered for a moment so that they thought she would fall back again, and then rose, muddy and shuddering, onto all four feet. She gave a series of great snorts and shook herself violently.

'Bridget! You did it.' Ellen flung her arms around the horse, smelling the sweat and mud and feeling the violent beat of her heart. 'You're a star.'

Kit grinned. 'She'll be fine now. Stand back, I think she's off.'

At that moment Bridget gave a huge shrug, sending Ellen staggering, and limped off towards Tony. They sniffed and rubbed noses, then Tony set of on a mad, celebratory gallop.

'Not very appreciative, animals, are they?' said Kit. He had put an arm about her shoulders, grinning down at her. 'You were really worried about her, weren't you?'

'Of course I was. I thought she was dying.'

'Take more than an hour or two on her side to put an end to old Bridget. She's tough. Look, she's having a drink now.' Sure enough, the muddy brown mare was drinking from one of the bigger marsh pools. 'I'll give her a few minutes to settle down and then check her over, just to be sure. She might have twisted a leg, but I don't think so from the way she's moving.'

'Thank goodness for that.' Ellen moved away and wiped her hands down her filthy jeans. After watching the way Kit had managed the situation, so competent and knowledgeable, she was feeling rather silly. Why had she panicked? He must think she was a fool.

As he didn't need her help now, she decided to leave him to it. 'I'm going back down,' she said. 'I'll put the kettle on.'

'Good idea. Get yourself out of those wet clothes.'

She walked heavily down the hill. Part of her was elated that Bridget had been successfully rescued, but another part was now feeling absurd for over-reacting. And not being able to cope on her own. She didn't want Kit putting his arm around her and patting her like some amusing younger sister.

As she reached the farmyard she heard the cows lowing and remembered she still hadn't given the calf her milk. She collected the bottle and took it into the kitchen with her. She could heat it up in the microwave while she made some coffee. Suddenly, after all the excitement, she felt cold. She huddled against the Rayburn as she waited for the kettle to boil. What she really needed was a shower, but coffee came first.

She had just put Kit's mug on the side of the stove to keep warm when he arrived, knocking briefly on the back door before letting himself in. 'Bridget's fine. She gave herself a wee bit of a fright, but there's no damage done.' He went to wash his hands, completely at home.

'Thanks goodness for that. Is there anything I

should do for her?'

'Keep an eye on her. When the kids come home you could get them to bring her in and groom her. Hose her down first. Do you think you'll be able to get them to do that?'

Ellen frowned, suspecting criticism. 'I think we can just about manage it between us.'

'Lucy's fond of the horses, she'll like doing it, but she'll need help from one of the boys. And then maybe she could have a ride on the pony, he's putting on a bit of weight, could do with the exercise.'

'I know that.' Ellen was definitely feeling more annoyed than grateful now. Of course she knew Tony Pony was overweight. 'You might not have noticed, but there's rather a lot to do around here, and horses aren't my forte.'

'Get Callum to do them. He and Angus are perfectly capable, but Angus is busy enough with the farm animals.'

'I'll think about it.' Ellen resented his advice. If he knew so much why didn't he just take over the horses himself? Except that was just what she couldn't ask him to do. He was doing far too much already. She sighed. 'Here's your coffee.'

'Thanks. I could do with that. It was going to be my first priority when I got back to the caravan.'

'I'm sorry.' Now she felt guilty as well as annoyed. 'I was in such a rush I never even asked if you had the time to spare. And I should pay you for your help. I can't keep taking advantage...'

'Rubbish. What are neighbours for?' He seemed relaxed, but his tone was firm.

'That was all very well at the beginning. But we

can't go on and on accepting favours from everyone.'

'Why not? Accept them as long as they're offered. I would.'

Ellen shrugged. She leant back against the Rayburn, seeking comfort from its warmth. Automatically she checked the heat gauge and then tossed on a couple more logs.

'Getting to grips with that wood burning monster, are you?'

'Yes, I think so.'

'It's not the most efficient thing in the world. I told Sam they'd be better off with something more modern.'

'You mean like gas central heating? It'd certainly be my preference.'

'Well, actually, I meant one of these new German stoves that burn sawmill off-cuts and keep going by themselves for days on end. I'm looking in to getting one of those myself. They heat the water, too.'

Ellen could see the attraction of something that didn't need feeding every few hours, but she felt too protective of Jess and Sam to agree with him. And something else had just occurred to her. 'What on earth do you do for a bath or shower at the moment? Is there one in the caravan?'

'Well, they say there's a shower, but between you and me it's more like a leak in the roof. If you're lucky you catch the occasional drip. But don't worry about me, it gives me a good reason for popping in to see my mother.'

'How is she?'

He pulled a face. 'Much the same.'

'I'm sorry. Look, if I can't pay you for all your help, how about you feel free to use the facilities here, if you need?' Why on earth hadn't she thought of that before? 'There's usually hot water and the shower's pretty good. The bath's a bit odd-looking, but it's massive and great for having a soak.'

He looked surprised and she felt embarrassed, wondering if she was speaking out of turn. She wasn't used to this neighbourly thing.

'That's very kind of you. I'll bear it in mind.'

His cool tone made Ellen all the more determined to do him a favour. Why should he always be in the superior position of giving? 'Why don't you have a bath right now? After all, it's my fault you're covered in mud. Don't worry about me, I need to try and get this milk down the calf before I start to think about getting into clean clothes.' She took the bottle of milk from the microwave.

'Do you always warm the milk for the little dears?' He was laughing at her again.

'Of course. And I tuck them up in their hay at night. Actually, Angus-Sam usually does it and I couldn't get the stupid thing to take it cold.'

'You were probably too gentle. You go and have a bath and I'll do it.'

'No.' She glared. 'You go and have the bath and I'll do it.' And before he could disagree, she headed out of the door. 'Towels in the airing cupboard. Help yourself.'

Chapter Eight

During the Easter holidays Ellen insisted on the children going with her to Edinburgh. She was never going to get them to consider moving to the city unless they spent some time there, saw it for themselves. So she encroached on Kit Ballantyne's good nature once again and asked him to look after the animals for a couple of days. He agreed easily, but she didn't feel she could impose on him for too long, which made the trip a bit of a rush. A day and a night in Edinburgh, then on to Stirling for a quick visit to their grandparents, and back home.

It was a squash with the four of them in her one-bedroomed flat, but she was determined to make an adventure of it. 'Right, who gets the sleeping bags and bed-settee and who gets the bedroom?' she demanded as they dragged their luggage up the two flights of stairs.

'Can I sleep in the double bed?' asked Lucy, bouncing on it excitedly. 'You can share with me if you want.'

'Well.' Ellen pushed open the window. The place smelt as though it had been empty for too long – which it had. 'I have to say I'd rather sleep on my own.'

'But it's a really big bed an' I would stay on one side. I wouldn't be any bother.'

'Don't believe her,' said Callum. 'She used to

get in bed with Mum and Dad and she drove them mad.'

'Did not.'

'That's what they said. You kicked all the time.'

Lucy's lip began to tremble as she remembered. Ellen said quickly, 'Well, you probably wouldn't like sleeping with me at all. I kick, and even worse, I *snore*. But if you want to give it a try for one night, I don't see why not. And that leaves the boys to share the bed-settee in the sitting room. That OK?'

Angus shrugged. Callum dashed through to set up the bed there and then. It didn't seem a good idea to Ellen, given the size of the flat, but she didn't stop him. She was pleased to see him excited, and hoped that he might spread a little of his enthusiasm to his brother.

She squeezed past them into the tiny kitchen, dumping carrier bags of food onto the work surface. It took only a few minutes to put away the provisions, switch the fridge back on, wipe the dust of weeks off the counter. But the place felt all wrong after the space of Craigallan. What had once been her cool, quiet retreat now seemed small and colourless. Far too small.

She stood in the doorway and watched Lucy and Callum rolling around like puppies on the bed-settee, cushions and pillows everywhere. It hadn't taken them long to create havoc, and she might not even have minded if Angus had joined in. But he was standing near the window, looking silently at the buildings beyond. She clapped her hands and shouted above the racket, 'Right, who's for fish and chips and a walk up to the park? We'll sort everything else out later.'

What the children needed was other children. That became clear to her as she pushed Lucy on the swing in the park, watched Callum and Angus on the climbing wall. In Kinmuir they knew everyone, were immediately involved in the games and conversations. She had to find a way of making that happen here, of making them want to be here. But who did she know with children in Edinburgh? All her friends were friends precisely because they shared Ellen's interests and lifestyle, which had to date been almost entirely childfree. Richard's girls lived down south with their mother. He was away just now, which was probably a good thing.

She thought of phoning a couple of colleagues from work, but found she couldn't even remember which ones had girls and which boys, let alone the children's ages. There wasn't enough time on this visit, but it was something she really must organise for their next trip.

In the afternoon she walked them past a couple of local schools, and then wished she hadn't. The solid Victorian architecture might appeal to an adult, but the children's attention was drawn to the high windows and lack of playing fields.

'Why don't they have windows you can look out of?' Callum asked.

Lucy looked intimidated, and took Ellen's hand.

Ellen bought them ice creams and they walked up towards the castle, watching the crowds of shoppers and tourists. It was overcast, and the grey sky only made the dark stone of the buildings the more overpowering. Ellen was glad when they entered the gardens below the castle and were among greenery. She pointed out some of the landmarks and explained how this had been the 'Nor' Loch' before it had been drained to make way for the railway.

'I would've left it as a loch,' said Angus dourly. 'That's the natural thing to do. Can we go back to your flat now and phone Kit? I want to know if the next heifers have calved.'

'When are we going to see Gran?' asked Lucy. 'Can we go today?'

'No. Tonight we're going to the cinema, remember. We'll look it up on the internet when we get home and you can choose what you want to see. Tomorrow we go to Gran and Granddad's.' She turned to her younger nephew. 'What do you think of Edinburgh, Cal?'

'It's OK. It's very big.'

'Yes, I suppose so. But you get used to it.'

'I wish we'd brought Monty,' said Lucy.

'And your flat's too small,' said Angus.

'Then it's lucky we're only staying the one night, isn't it?' snapped Ellen before she could stop herself.

Lucy took her aunt's hand once again as they began to walk back along the busy pavements. She wasn't used to so much traffic. And Ellen found that she didn't like it much, either, but she certainly wasn't going to let Angus know that.

The visit to Ellen's parents was equally unsettling, although in a different way. They were delighted to see the children, and they began to relax in a way they hadn't done in Edinburgh. This house was familiar to them from frequent visits, and even their grandfather's frailty didn't put a dampener on their high spirits. Their grandmother spoilt them and they went to bed that night so full of chocolate and cake Ellen thought they might be ill.

It was when the children were safely out of the way that Ellen began to notice other things. Like how much her father's health had deteriorated since she had last seen him, and the lines of worry on her mother's face.

'The children are enjoying being here,' she said, settling on the settee with a mug of cocoa. 'But I hope it's not been too much trouble for you.'

'Of course not,' said her mother. 'We're delighted to see you all, aren't we, Frank?'

Her husband nodded, shakily, and pulled himself slowly to his feet. 'Time I was in bed myself,' he said, his voice soft and muffled by his illness. He said to his wife, 'No, don't come with me. I'll manage this once. You and Ellen have a nice chat.'

Mother and daughter watched in silence as his edged his way out of the room with the aid of a walking frame.

'He has enjoyed having you all here, but he does find it tiring.'

'I can see that.' Ellen sighed. Suddenly it seemed that wherever she looked there were difficulties ahead.

'Tell me how the children liked Edinburgh,' said her mother. 'Lucy certainly seems very taken with the new clothes you bought her.'

'Yes.' Ellen sighed again. 'Lucy isn't the one that is difficult to please.' She wished she could take back the words as soon as she had said them. She wasn't here to complain to her mother.

'Angus might come round to the idea,' said her mother, but doubtfully.

'Yes, I've got plans to take them up to Edinburgh again soon,' said Ellen with more enthusiasm than she felt. 'I'll organise it better, arrange for them to meet some of my friends' children.'

'That's a good idea.'

The silence lengthened. Ellen struggled for something to say, to keep her mother from asking questions, but she was suddenly too exhausted. She swallowed the last of her cocoa and put her mug aside. 'I'm pretty tired myself, I think I'll head on up...'

'I'm worried about you, Ellen,' said her mother.

Ellen forced her face into a smile. 'Look, I'm fine.' She sounded like Angus. 'Really.'

'You've taken on a lot, with the children. Don't think your father and I don't realise that.'

'We're managing. It'll take some time for us all to adjust, but we'll get there.'

'Can't Richard do more?' Ellen's mother shook her head sorrowfully, clearly prepared for a long discussion of the woes of the situation.

Ellen shrugged. 'Richard's busy.'

'Friends help each other out when they have difficulties. You know your father and I aren't sure he's the right person for you...'

'I'm fine,' said Ellen again, her voice harder now. This really wasn't the time to list Richard's bad points.

'I wish you had someone to help you, this is such a lot for you to take on, on your own. If only you were married, had someone to support you...'

'But I'm not, and I don't want to be, so what's the point of thinking about it?'

'Is that Miss Taylor? Miss Ellen Taylor?'

At the words, the official tone of voice, Ellen felt a chill run right through her. 'Yes? How can I help?'

'A moment, please. I have Mr Fletcher on the line for you. The rector of Dunmuir Academy.'

There was a click as the call was transferred.

'Miss Taylor?' A man's voice spoke, pleasant and controlled. 'I'm so glad we managed to get hold of you. I wonder if I could trouble you to come down to the school?'

'Yes, yes, of course. But why? What's happened?'

'We've had a ... little incident involving Angus. Nothing serious. He's perfectly all right, if a little bruised in spirit. I think the best thing would be for you to come here and we can discuss things.'

Ellen wanted to demand all the details right there and then, but the man's calm, self-assured tone brooked no questions. She checked the clock. One thirty. Plenty of time to be back before Callum and Lucy came home from school.

'I'll come straight away. It won't take me more than fifteen minutes.'

Ellen had been to the school once before, to meet Angus's guidance teacher in the wake of his parents' death. She tried to remember where they had met or what they had said, but couldn't. This time she took more notice. The building was of 1960s construction, brick, concrete and glass, mostly on three floors. It looked in need of some attention and when she made her way into the entrance hall she noted a bucket catching drips in one corner. It reminded her that she still hadn't found anyone to fix the kitchen roof at Craigallan.

Mr Fletcher was a brisk, balding man in his fifties, who shook her hand and ushered her into his office. Angus was sitting on a chair pushed back against one wall. He didn't look up.

Ellen glanced doubtfully from the boy to the teacher and back. Angus looked so sorrowful, that straight hair flopping over his face, skin deathly pale. But if he was in trouble she wanted to know what had happened before she started offering sympathy. She compromised by laying a hand briefly on his shoulder.

'Please take a seat.' The rector sat down himself, beside rather than behind the desk. 'Now, I can tell you what I understand to have happened, but I would much prefer it if Angus explained for himself. Angus?'

Ellen held her breath. Was her nephew going to demand his 'real' name?

He didn't. He raised his head, but didn't look directly at either of them. 'It was nothing. Just a … misunderstanding.'

'And what caused this "misunderstanding"?'

'I, erm, can't remember. It was nothing.'

'It may or may not have been a misunderstanding, but I beg to differ when you claim it was nothing.' Mr Fletcher didn't raise his voice but his tone was firm. 'Miss Marshall came upon you and three other boys having what appeared to be a full-scale fight outside the dining hall. I'd like you to tell your aunt and me what started this.'

Angus shrugged very slightly and shot Ellen a quick glance, as though to judge her level of sympathy. Ellen felt a lump rise in her throat. Poor Angus. Why hadn't she listened to her mother's warnings?

'I'm sure it wasn't your fault,' she said gently. 'But you'll need to tell us what happened so we can help.'

'Why don't you ask the others?'

Ellen let the rector answer that. She was wondering herself where the other boys were.

'I have already spoken to Jason, Paul, and Ryan. They have all three been suspended from school for the next week, as you will be.' Mr Fletcher waited for a reaction, but Angus had gone back to looking at his feet and said nothing. Ellen noted that his trousers were frayed and rather short. When had that happened? Was she supposed to notice when the kids needed new school clothes on top of everything else?

'Angus, your aunt and I are waiting to hear what you have to say.'

Angus let the silence drag out as long as he dared. 'We were just messing about in the dinner queue. That's all.'

'A normal amount of pushing and shoving is something we have to live with. One boy on the floor being punched by another is absolutely not. I would like to know what started this.'

'Nothing. We were just messing about.'

'I don't recall that Jason and his friends are boys you normally go about with. Am I correct in that?'

'I suppose.'

'So it was three against one?'

Angus shrugged again.

'Where were your friends?'

Angus let out his breath in a rush. 'I don't have any friends, do I?' He spoke so quietly Ellen struggled to hear his words. She moved towards him, wanting to touch him, comfort him, but he shrank back into the chair. She thought he flinched slightly, as though something was sore.

Mr Fletcher waited a full minute. When the boy offered nothing more he said, 'Is there anything else you would like to tell us, Angus?'

The boy shook his head. Ellen suspected he was close to tears.

'Very well then. Your one-week suspension starts from today, and I don't expect to see you back in school until a week on Monday. This will of course be confirmed to you by letter.' Mr Fletcher left a pause, but Angus said nothing. 'Please go and wait in the corridor for a few moments, while I have a word in private with your aunt.'

Ellen felt shaky with anger, guilt, and fear. How could the school let this happen? Why hadn't she noticed there were problems?

'Perhaps you won't agree with me, but I have to say that I don't think this is all Angus's fault,' she said, as soon as the boy had left them alone.

'It is rare that the fault is all on one side.'

Ellen glared. She was getting a bit fed up of this measured tone. 'Actually, I disagree. I think Angus is being picked on.'

'Has he told you that?'

'Well, no. But I know my sister had ... concerns that he might be being bullied.'

110

The headmaster was sitting back, apparently relaxed, listening with irritating patience. 'I don't recall her saying anything to me about that. I'll check with Angus's teachers.'

'I don't know if she had been in contact with the school about it or not. How would I know? I was in Edinburgh, they were down here. No one thought for a moment that I was going to end up responsible for the children. I just know she had her worries.'

'As I said, I'll look in to it. I have always had the impression that Angus Moffat is rather a solitary boy. Not exactly friendless, but somewhat aloof. I gather that this has become more pronounced since his parents' unfortunate death.'

'It's hardly likely to make him more outgoing, is it?' Ellen felt criticised. She hadn't thought Angus was any different to usual, but what did she know about usual?

'And perhaps it wouldn't be a good idea to let Angus spend time on his own in Dunmuir just now.'

'So you do think he's being bullied?'

'I couldn't say,' he said, carefully. 'But my advice would be to keep an eye on the boy. You know how silly twelve and thirteen year olds can be, don't you?'

Ellen knew practically nothing about children of any age, but she decided not to share that fact.

Chapter Nine

'Did they hurt you?' said Ellen as Angus slid into the car seat beside her.

'No. I'm fine.' He shrugged and she was pretty sure he flinched again. She wanted to insist, to push back his fringe, make him open his shirt so she could see for herself. But natural reticence stopped her.

'I can't believe this has happened. And the school...'

Angus just turned to look out of the side window and said nothing. Once they reached Craigallan he took himself of to change and disappeared outside. By the time he came in for his evening meal, a faint colour had returned to his cheeks. Ellen decided to see that as a positive. She didn't have the energy to tackle him right now.

She rustled up a stir-fry and said that as it was Friday she didn't see why the children shouldn't eat their pudding – yoghurts – in front of the television. With a glass of wine and the local weekly paper, she curled up in the chair beside the Rayburn and tried to relax.

But she couldn't. Angus wasn't just being bullied, he was being beaten up! And she hadn't done anything to stop it.

Oh, Jess, I'm sorry, she thought. For not realising how hard it is. For not getting it right. Jessie, Jessie, where are you? She let the tears well up in her eyes then dabbed them away before they fell. She didn't want the children to know she had been crying. As far as she knew, they hadn't shed any tears themselves for a week or two, and she wanted to keep it that way.

She leafed through the newspaper, amazing herself once again at the minutiae that appeared to interest the local people. How many school fetes and charity appeals could one person take? Which reminded her that there was that coffee evening for the primary school coming up right after the holidays. Hadn't Clare talked her into volunteering her services? She was pretty sure there was something, but couldn't quite remember what it was she had promised to do.

She raised her eyes to the ceiling for inspiration. And didn't at all like what she saw there.

'Shit.' She let the paper fall to the floor. Was that a drip? She went over to the corner and squinted upwards. Yep, it was definitely a drip. She looked down. There was already a small puddle forming at her feet. It had been raining hard since late afternoon, and this time the rain seemed to have found a way in. Why now? Richard had finally agreed to visit for a weekend and was arriving tomorrow. She had been so looking forward to a break. A leaking roof was not the sort of thing to put Richard in a good temper.

She turned helplessly in a full circle. What did one do in situations like this? Her flat in Edinburgh had a service agreement and all you needed to do when a problem arose was to ring the factor. Nothing was that easy at Craigallan.

She pulled out an old washing up basin from

beneath the sink and placed it under the drip. If that was what they did at Dunmuir Academy, why not here? The irregular 'plop' of water echoed around the kitchen and made her feel even less at ease. She went to the back door and peered out. The rain seemed to be tailing off. So perhaps the leak would resolve itself? If she was really, really lucky that might even be before the plaster ceiling caved in.

This was ridiculous. She had to do something.

Lucy appeared in the doorway at that moment and paused doubtfully, looking at the ceiling. 'Auntie Ellen, it's dripping.'

'It's OK, sunshine. I'm going to get it fixed.'

'Oh.' Lucy looked at the bowl on the floor with interest. 'Will it be all right like that?'

'Yes. Absolutely fine. For the moment.'

'What's happened?' said Angus, coming up behind his sister.

Lucy skipped over to the basin and watched with interest as the drops fell. Angus's gaze followed her and then he looked at Ellen. 'The roof has started to leak,' he said. 'I knew we shouldn't have just left it.'

'Yep. So let's see what we can do about it, shall we? Is there a ladder about somewhere so I can get up in to the roof space and have a look?' Ellen had noticed the hatch into the loft only a few days ago, and wished she had investigated at that point.

'Dunno. There might be one in the shed.'

'Can you and Callum go and look, please?' Ellen spoke calmly and firmly. If he thought she expected nothing but obedience, perhaps she would get it? This time, at least, it worked. The two boys

114

trooped outside.

Lucy had transferred her attention from the drip to her aunt. 'Are you going to fix it?'

'I'm going to try.'

Lucy considered this. 'Mum didn't like ladders,' she said at length. 'Shouldn't we get Kit to do it?'

'No we should not.' Ellen was all the more annoyed because that was exactly what she wanted to do. She knew nothing about buildings, whereas Kit clearly knew a great deal. She reminded herself yet again that she had decided to stop relying on him so much.

At that moment the front door bell rang and for a second Ellen wondered if her thoughts had actually summoned Kit to help. It was about this time he occasionally dropped in if he wished to use their washing facilities. Then she remembered that he never used the front door. No friends did. With a *tsk* of impatience she went to answer it.

It was Mrs Jack, the lady who lived with her invalid husband in the bungalow opposite Clare. She bestowed a bright smile on Ellen and held out a small envelope. 'So glad you're home. I was beginning to wonder, although with the car parked out on the road like that one would have thought someone was in.' She paused for breath and tried to see over Ellen's shoulder. 'I hope I'm not interrupting? I'm just doing my little bit for the greater good.' She gave a tinkling laugh and thrust the envelope so far out that Ellen had to take it. 'Collecting for the Red Cross, such a deserving cause. You don't need to fill it now, but it'll save both of us time if you do. Shall I just step inside and wait for a minute?'

'I'm not really sure...' said Ellen.

'I don't hold with supporting some of these new-fangled charities, but the Red Cross is an excellent organisation, very well established, everyone agrees. I like to do my little bit to help, which isn't easy with Mr Jack the way he is. I feel this collecting is my little contribution, so to speak.'

It occurred to Ellen that Mr and Mrs Jack were the only people in the village whose first names she didn't know. And although she had never met Mr Jack, she could have done with seeing a little less of his wife.

'I'll come in, shall I? I shan't mind waiting.' Mrs Jack bared her teeth in what Ellen suspected was supposed to be a smile.

Ellen decided that it was easiest just to acquiesce, and led the way through to the kitchen. 'I'll just find my bag...' Angus and Callum had clearly found the ladder, for it was now propped up in the gaping hole in the ceiling. The handbag was forgotten. 'Angus? Callum?'

Two faces appeared in the gloom above.

'Do you think it's safe for them to be up there?' said Mrs Jack.

'Angus! What are you doing?'

'Looking for the leak,' muttered Angus. 'You weren't here.'

'Are both of you up there? Honestly, I thought you had more sense...' Her heart rate picked up, just at the sight of them so high above. 'Come down at once!'

It didn't help having Mrs Jack as a fascinated witness to the events. But then, if Mrs Jack hadn't come calling she would have been in the kitchen to stop them climbing up in the first place.

'There is absolutely no reason for you to go up there.'

'I'm holding the torch for Angus,' said Callum, oblivious to her tone. 'Have you ever looked up here? It's so cool.'

'Can I see?' said Lucy, putting one foot on the ladder.

'No you can not.' Ellen could see the boys weren't going to come down without an argument, which she really didn't want to have in front of Mrs Jack. 'Angus, Callum, stand back from the opening and don't move any further. I'll be with you in just a minute.' She grabbed her handbag and pulled out the first note she could find from her purse. It happened to be twenty pounds, but she didn't have time to look further. She stuffed it into the envelope and handed it back to Mrs Jack.

'Oh, so generous, thank you.' Mrs Jack was still staring upwards in great interest. It was as if she wanted the boys to fall down in front of her. She reluctantly transferred her attention to Ellen. 'Of course you'll need to fill out your name and the amount on the envelope, I do like to do every-thing properly.'

'You do it. I trust you. Now, I'm really a bit busy...' She ushered Mrs Jack back to the front door, pushing her almost bodily to keep her mov-ing.

'I think you need to keep a better eye on those two boys,' said Mrs Jack. 'I don't like to tell tales, but living where I do you can't help seeing things you'd rather not. A little wild at times, aren't

117

they, and to think they would go up a ladder on their own like that...' She paused and turned to see Kit striding down the track, a towel slung over one shoulder and wash bag in his hand.

'Good evening,' he said politely. 'Is everything all right?'

Ellen groaned. This was all she needed to get the village gossips started. Mrs Jack's eyes were positively bulging from her head as she looked from Kit to Ellen and back.

'I need to get back to the kids. Mrs Jack is just going. Thank you so much for calling.' Ellen let Kit in and shut the door in her unwanted visitor's over-eager face.

'What on earth...?' said Kit, but she didn't wait to explain. She dashed back to the kitchen and he, of course, followed her.

'Look, you go and have your shower. I'm just...'

This time she checked the ladder was correctly positioned and then climbed it herself, two rungs at a time. For once Kit forbore to give advice, but dropped his towel and bag on the floor and held the ladder in place.

Ellen's heart was in her mouth. She had no idea what sort of floor covering there was up here, whether the boys risked falling through the ceiling at any moment. Amazingly, they had done exactly as she asked and were standing a foot or so from the opening, balanced on the wooden rafters.

'Don't tread on this stuff,' she said, gesturing at the insulation that was laid thickly between the wood. 'You'll go straight through.'

'We know that,' said Angus. 'We're not stupid. Now, can we get on with this?'

Ellen paused to catch her breath and recover from her fear of a calamity that wasn't. 'You two need to go back down. At once.'

'But who's going to help you...?'

'I'll help her,' said Kit, appearing through the trap door and considerably reducing the light in the loft. 'What on earth are you boys doing up here?'

'I can manage on my own,' said Ellen untruthfully. 'If you can help the boys back down.'

'I...' began Angus.

'Now!' said Ellen, uncompromising. She didn't mind raising her voice in front of Kit. She angled the torch so they could see what they were doing and waited in silence until they had complied. It was only when the boys were back at floor level that she felt able to breathe again. She peered around by the light of the torch, trying to see where the water was coming in and realising, although not admitting it, that it would have been easier with someone to hold the torch.

She wasn't even surprised when Kit's head reappeared in the hatch and he levered himself easily onto the rafters. He was agile, for all his bulk. 'I see we seem to have a little leak,' he said cheerfully. 'Want me to have a look?'

'Would you take no for an answer?' said Ellen ungraciously, and then sighed. She shouldn't be ungracious. It wasn't Kit she was annoyed with, it was circumstances that were constantly wrong-footing her. 'It's up here, I think.' She pointed the torch and he examined the roof in silence for a while.

As it turned out, they weren't able to fix it,

although they positioned a second basin on the rafters to catch the worst of the drops. The problem was with the slates on the outside, and that was definitely beyond Ellen and she refused to involve Kit further. 'You're not a roofer, are you?' she said firmly. What she needed was to get in a professional.

She insisted Kit go for his delayed shower and sent the children back through to the sitting room. Then, armed with the Yellow Pages and the cordless phone, prepared to do battle. It was just a question of being persistent. And if that didn't work, she would play the helpless female. One way or another she was going to get a roofer out to Craigallan the following day.

'Yes!' she yelled, an hour and countless phone calls later. 'Eureka!'

The children came back through at once. They must have been listening.

'Someone's going to fix it?'

'Yes indeed. A very nice man called Mr Kirkpatrick is coming out tomorrow morning. Right, what are you lot up to? Need more food? How about fruit?'

'But I don't like fruit,' said Lucy. 'Can't I have another yoghurt? Please?'

'I'm not hungry,' said Angus, looking at the fruit bowl which contained a couple of bruised apples and a blackened banana.

'Suit yourself,' said Ellen, her brief good mood evaporating. Where did all the food go? She could have sworn she'd bought enough to feed a small army. 'Oh, go on, have yoghurts, if there are any left.'

120

'Or maybe an ice cream?' said Callum hopefully.

'Yoghurts or nothing. And then it's your bedtime, Lucy. Goodness, how did it get to be so bl ... so late?'

Kit came to say farewell before departing to his lair. He declined her half-hearted offer of a drink, seeming a little offended that she hadn't let him do more on the roof. Well, if he was annoyed and stayed away over the weekend, it wouldn't be a bad thing. Ellen couldn't somehow see Kit and Richard getting along.

Chapter Ten

Ellen was looking forward to Richard's visit. The thought of his sensible grown-up presence cheered her. She wouldn't be alone with the children. She would have someone to share her concerns with. She found herself glancing down the road at least half an hour before he was due to arrive.

Lucy had been invited to spend the day with Clare's daughter Grace, and Callum and Angus were out in the fields.

They embraced warmly when he arrived, only slightly late. 'Come in, come in. Good drive down? Shame it's raining but I'm sure it'll clear. April showers seem to be the order of the day.' The roofer had already been and put a temporary patch on the kitchen roof, so at least she didn't have to worry about that.

Richard followed her into the kitchen and looked around. He had been here only once before, after the funeral, and it had probably looked different then. Tidier, definitely. Ellen felt defensive. 'Cup of coffee? Want to put your bags in the bedroom? Shall I show you around?'

'Coffee would do for a start. And then I rather fancy a look over the property. It's certainly strikes me as a place with potential.'

Potential wasn't one of Ellen's favourite words. It implied there was something wrong with the here and now, but she smiled and nodded. It was strange seeing Richard here. He looked so smart. All his clothes looked new, and clean. They were country wear, sure enough, but not as Jess or Sam or Kit would have known it. She hoped he'd taken her advice and brought some Wellingtons.

Over coffee Richard brought her up to date on their Edinburgh friends, and his progress at work. Ellen was just starting to relax and get back into the swing of this kind of conversation when the back door burst open and Callum came flying in, holding one hand with the other.

Couldn't they have stayed outside just a little longer?

'My hand. Oh. Ow. My hand.' He stopped short when he saw Richard.

Ellen stood up and tried to make her tone sympathetic. 'What is it, Cal? Are you OK?'

'Angus made me do the gate for the top field and I told him I couldn't do it and he said I had to 'cos he was carrying the feed and I caught my finger. And it's so-ore.'

'I told you to be careful with those gates,' said

122

Ellen, pushing his hand under the cold tap and holding it there despite his protests. It was bleeding from under a flap of skin on the thumb.

'Can't you stop now? It's sore.'

'OK. Hold it over the sink while I get some kitchen towel.'

Callum did as requested, wiping his tears away with his other hand and leaving dirty streaks down his face. He sniffed.

'Hello there,' said Richard.

'This is my friend Richard, remember I told you he was coming for the weekend?'

Callum dipped his head. ''Lo.' The children didn't seem to be too good on the social skills front. Something else for her to think about.

Ellen dried the injured hand and wrapped a clean piece of kitchen towel around the thumb. 'Keep that on until it stops bleeding. It shouldn't be long.'

'OK.' He sniffed again. 'Can I go on the computer for a bit?'

'I don't see why not,' she said, giving him a quick hug. He looked so sorrowful. Perhaps he had had a bit of a shock. 'Just until the bleeding stops, then we'll put a plaster on it and you can go back out and help Angus.'

'You're going to have to learn not to be so soft on them,' said Richard when they were alone once again. 'I thought you said they all had to help out? Are you sure he wasn't just looking for an excuse to get out of his chores?'

'As it happens, yes I am. That was a nasty cut, there's no way he would have done it on purpose.'

'You don't know how manipulative children can be. Take my word for it.'

'Hmm,' said Ellen. She didn't want to start arguing yet.

Kit was careful to keep away from Craigallan over the weekend. He didn't want to intrude, although he wouldn't have minded seeing what Ellen Taylor's boyfriend looked like. It wasn't even Ellen who had told him the man was visiting. He had heard of it, along with many other odd bits of information, from the children.

Those poor motherless, fatherless children.

Why had Jess and Sam gone away, to that city, taken that taxi, been in that accident? He remembered once again the delight on Jessie's face as she had told him she had booked. He went over the memories tentatively. Was Ellen right, that it was no one's fault? That he couldn't have stopped them, even if he'd wanted to? He kicked savagely at a lump of soil left by Robbie's digger, scattering the dirt. Even if it wasn't his fault, but he couldn't stop the regrets.

He checked on the sheep with Angus on the Saturday evening. Walking in the fields wasn't intruding, was it? They circled the field a couple of times, in what Kit hoped was a companionable silence. One of the second batch of ewes was clearly starting to lamb and they hunkered down to watch. She looked all right, it wasn't her first time and he doubted she'd have any trouble, but it was good sometimes to see a normal, healthy birth. And he guessed she was carrying twins. As there were sometimes complications with the second lamb, it was worth hanging around to check.

Half an hour later the ewe was licking clean her new offspring, and Kit was feeling that things couldn't be all wrong with the world when you could witness something like that.

'You going to overnight them in the byre?' he said to Angus. 'Want me to give you a hand moving them down?'

The boy looked doubtful. 'Dad said he was going to leave the blackies out this year...'

'Well, and no reason why not, as long as the weather doesn't turn and you don't have a particularly sickly lamb.'

'You think it'll be OK?'

'More than likely. They're sturdy animals. You don't need to worry about them, Angus. Now, if it was those soft Suffolk crosses...'

The boy smiled faintly, seeing the joke. 'I'll put them inside when their time comes.'

'Good lad. Well, I'd best be off now. And perhaps you should go in too?'

'I'll go in in a bit.'

Angus glanced at the lighted window of the kitchen, and Kit could feel his animosity. He was finding it difficult enough to adapt to life with his aunt. The boyfriend made it even worse. Kit wondered if Ellen would move the children to Edinburgh, take them to live with this man. He didn't like the idea. But it really wasn't his problem and even if it was, there was absolutely nothing he could do about it.

He had a very brief spruce up and then headed into Dunmuir, where he'd agreed to meet Deb and Alistair for a drink.

'You're looking bright and cheery,' said Deb as they settled at a table by the fire. 'Not.'

'Bloody Building Control.' Kit would rather talk about that than Jess and Sam, or Ellen and the kids. And it was true, things weren't going as well with the house as he would have liked. Either the weather was awful, or the digger driver had other commitments, or that irritating man from the Council needed to come out and tick some boxes before they could move on to the next stage.

'Ah.' Deb nodded sympathetically. 'What is it this time? Foundations too shallow? Septic tank not in the right place?'

Kit gave a faint smile. He'd clearly moaned about this quite a lot already. 'No, those things are sorted now. But they don't like the design of the porches. And they want me to change the cement mix. It's a special one, low environmental impact, and it makes so much sense...'

Even if Alistair and Deb didn't share his enthusiasm for environmental issues, they were sympathetic. The evening progressed and his mood was improving nicely until Deb said, 'And how's your mother doing?'

Kit grimaced. 'Not great. I took her to see Dr Gilmour last week. I'm getting really worried about these falls.' Kit ran a hand through his hair. 'She thinks Mum may be having some mini-strokes and that's what's causing them. She's referring her to a specialist at the hospital.'

'That's good, then,' said Alistair, but it sounded more like a question than a statement.

'She's lucky to have you so close,' said Deb.

'Probably not close enough.'

'It's never easy when your parents get old.' Deb patted his hand sympathetically. 'And your mother is such a dear.'

'She has her moments.' Kit suppressed a shudder. The word *stroke* still made him quail. He wasn't sure his mum had even taken them in. She'd just nodded and smiled, even when Dr Gilmour had mentioned it might be time to think about getting her more help in the house. Or even for her to move elsewhere...

Kit rose to his feet and offered to buy the next round. After that he'd make sure they talked about something else. He'd rather spend a whole week doing small animal clinics than break the news to his mother that she was no longer fit to stay in her own home.

'Angus. I mean Sam. We need to have a chat.'

'Mmm.'

It was Sunday morning and Ellen still hadn't managed to talk properly to him about what had happened at school. She needed a time when they were alone and when his mood wasn't one of outright antagonism. Not easy in that constantly busy household, and Richard's visit only made it worse.

Ellen knew the child didn't want to talk, and she could sympathise. She didn't particularly want to have this discussion herself. She had left Richard reading the Sunday papers and Callum and Lucy playing upstairs, and followed Angus out to the byre. She had expected to find him busy as usual, sweeping or putting out food, but

127

instead he had been standing perfectly still, with his head resting on the neck of Melanie, his favourite cow, his face averted. He stood upright when he saw her.

Ellen turned over a metal bucket and sat down on it. 'How are you doing?'

'OK.' The cow put her head over the top of the stall and nudged him, and he patted her absently.

'I can see that things aren't that great at school. That's what I wanted to talk about.'

'It's all right.'

'Your mum didn't think so.'

He shot her an angry look, tossing back the flopping fringe. 'How would you know?'

'I know she was worried about you. She'd spoken about it to Grandma. But I don't know any details, so I'm hoping that you might be able to fill me in.'

Over the last few weeks Ellen had learned that Dunmuir Academy was considered to be a 'good' school. It was small enough for the teachers and pupils to know each other reasonably well, and most of the children came from Dunmuir or the surrounding villages, not an area known for social problems. Which didn't mean things couldn't still go wrong.

'Angus?'

He eyed the door out into the farm yard with longing. 'It's... I'm OK. I'll go back next week. It'll be fine. Now I need to...'

'No, it's not OK.' Ellen rose slightly and pulled open the collar of the muddied shirt he wore. She touched the bruises on his neck. She'd heard him telling Callum he got them in rugby, but she

128

didn't believe him. 'Those boys really hurt you. I don't know what you did to provoke them, but I'm not having this.'

'I didn't do anything. I was just standing in the...' He stopped and glared.

'You were standing in the dinner queue and they picked on you?' He didn't deny it. 'Has this been going on for long?'

'A bit.'

'You should tell your teachers. Or me. Angus, you can't let them bully you.'

'It's nothing.' He tried to sound bored, but she saw the slight quiver of his lip.

'I'm trying to help, Angus. I really care about you. I want what's best.'

'Then call me Sam, not Angus.'

'Sorry. Sam. Now the school are aware there's a problem I hope they'll keep an eye on things. Do you want me to come up to school more often? Drop you off and pick you up? I could do that for a while, if it would help.'

'No!' He looked so horrified she had to smile.

'Well, we've got a few weeks to think about it. Which reminds me, what are we going to say to Cal and Lucy?'

'I've told them I've been suspended.'

'When?'

'This morning.'

Ellen must have been too preoccupied with Richard to notice. 'Did you tell them why?'

'I said it was a fight.' His expression brightened fractionally. 'Callum thinks he should get a week off school too, 'cos he's always getting into fights.'

'Is he?' Ellen was worried. What sort of problems

did Callum have that she didn't know about?

'Just normal stuff. Playing, like. He used to love play-fighting with Dad.'

Ellen remembered the riotous rough and tumble evenings, when Sam finally relaxed and all three children climbed over him like puppies. That was something else they were missing out on.

'There's something I'd like you to think about,' said Ellen as she rose to her feet. 'You don't have to stay at that school if you don't want. There are at least three secondary schools in Dumfries if you wanted to change.'

'Go to school in Dumfries?'

'It's a possibility. Another possibility is...' Ellen took a deep breath. She'd never said this in so many words before. 'If we move to Edinburgh, you would go to school there. You could choose one for yourself.'

'I'm not moving to Edinburgh!' His expression, which had been interested at the mention of Dumfries, was now pure horror. 'This is our home. We live here. I'm not leaving!'

'We haven't decided anything yet. It was just something I wanted you to think about...' She put a hand on his arm, but he shrugged it off.

Richard spent the morning indoors, reading his way steadily through the mass of Sunday supplements. Ellen was surprised, and a little disappointed. He was normally the one up early and planning the route for the day's climb, having organised someone else to make breakfast for him. She had hoped that that sort of interest

130

might translate into helping around the farm.

After a light Sunday lunch he stretched out long, Rohan-clad legs and suggested, 'How about a walk? Any good hills around here?'

Ellen could feel her spirits sinking further. The children weren't keen on 'walks', and would never manage the sort of hill that Richard would have in mind.

'There isn't anything very challenging nearby,' she said cautiously. 'Criffel is the nearest big hill and that's the other side of Dumfries, and not exactly difficult.'

'We went up Criffel once for Dad's birthday,' said Callum, bringing a third slice of toast back to the table. 'It took for ever. Dad had to carry Lucy.'

'That was ages ago. I was a baby then.'

'I thought we were going to chop wood this afternoon,' said Angus.

Ellen sighed quietly. 'That was a possibility,' she said. It had been Angus's suggestion. They were running short of firewood and it had seemed a good idea to tackle the problem while Richard was around. She knew next to nothing about saws and axes, but surely he would help? She turned to him now and said, 'Any good at chopping wood?' Kit would have known exactly what to do.

He frowned. 'Not really my idea of a fun Sunday afternoon. I'd rather stretch my legs, get a bit of fresh air before heading back to Old Reekie.'

'You're only going back tomorrow morning, aren't you?'

'No, I thought I'd get the driving over with today. And from what you said of school mornings here, I thought you'd rather have me out of the way.'

'Oh.' Ellen tried to smile. She was going to be on her own with the children again. 'But you'll stay for supper? I've got a joint of beef, I thought I'd have a go at a proper Sunday dinner.' But not roast chicken. That brought back too many awful memories.

'Perhaps. It would have been easier if you'd cooked it at lunchtime. I really don't want to leave here too late.'

'Well, thank you very much,' said Ellen sharply. 'Suit yourself, why don't you?' She suddenly realised what a strain it was having Richard and the children making their different demands on her. It clearly hadn't occurred to him that he was here to help. All four of them reacted identically to her tone, pausing to stare and then looking away.

Richard said, conciliatory, 'Sorry. Is that a problem? I suppose we should have discussed it before.'

Ellen sighed, not even trying to smother the sound, and stood up to begin clearing the table. 'Look, you go for a walk if that's what you want to do. There's an Ordnance Survey map around here somewhere. There aren't any very exciting hills but I'm sure you can pick out a reasonable route. Angus and I will have a go at the wood pile. Cal and Lucy can bring the horses in and groom them'

'Aw, why can't I do some chopping...?'

'Because you're helping Lucy with the horses.'

'But...'

'Get her started, at least, OK? And then you

can maybe have a go with an axe.'

'And can I ride Tony Pony?' asked Lucy, bouncing in her seat.

'Yes, if Cal will help you tack Tony up. Now, clear your places and off you go.'

The children did as they were told, not with enthusiasm, but at least they did it. She hoped Richard noticed.

He was tapping his fingers on the table and looking out of the side window at the hills. She thought he might be planning a route, but when he spoke it was to say, 'You've got a lot of animals here, you know.'

'I know.'

'When would be the best time to sell them?'

Ellen shot a look towards the back porch, where the children were still pulling on coats and boots. She shook her head warningly at Richard.

'What?' he said, making no effort to lower his voice. 'Have you still not told them you're going to sell up? Come on Ellen, spring is by far the best time to put a house on the market, you'll need to get a move on.'

'We're thinking about it,' she said coolly. She was still watching the back porch and saw Angus glance towards them. His face was expressionless but he went out quickly and closed the door with a bang.

'And what about that old wreck of a car you've got parked out there?' said Richard, oblivious. 'It's just losing value sitting there, not to mention getting in the way. I can't understand why you haven't sold that, at least. You don't need it, do you?'

'No.' Ellen had been reluctant to do so much as

133

open the door, let alone drive it. It was still Jess and Sam's car. 'Yes, you're right, that's one thing I can do. I'll get in touch with a garage this week.'

'That would be sensible. Not that you'll get much for it.'

Ellen didn't really need to have yet another depressing fact pointed out to her. She said, 'Perhaps I'll start using it myself and sell my car. Jess and Sam's is bigger, more practical with the kids.' She smiled at Richard's look of horror. How could she want to swap her shiny hatchback for that wreck?

She began to stack dishes in the sink, wishing yet again that Jess had believed in a dishwasher. Maybe if she sold the car she could invest the money in one?

After a while Richard said, 'Now where's that map? I suppose I might as well get going.' He sat and waited for her to bring it to him. She didn't know why she had been so keen for him to visit.

The walk cheered Richard and he returned looking more lively than he had done since his arrival. He even agreed to stay and eat with them, as Ellen had gone to the trouble of getting the roast ready early, but the meal wasn't exactly enjoyable. Angus said nothing but glared a lot, and Richard's glow of self-satisfaction diminished steadily as the normal bickering of the younger two grew in volume.

She went out with him to the car, to say goodbye in private. He held her close, the once-familiar arms encircling her. She felt nothing at all. 'You'll come up to Edinburgh soon?' he said.

'On your own?'

She kissed him softly on the cheek and withdrew. 'No.'

'But Ellen, it's your turn now.'

'It's not so much about turns, is it, as about what's possible.'

'Anything is possible when you want it.' The words sounded familiar to Ellen, but they no longer meant the same thing.

'I'll phone you,' she said, compromising. 'Take care.'

As he drove away she didn't even feel sad. It had certainly been a change having another grown up in residence, but it hadn't actually made life easier. And she was sure that the children hadn't liked it. And just at the moment, she had to think of them. For the first time in her life she was putting other people first.

I'm doing my best, Jess, she said silently. I might not be doing it right but I am doing my best.

Chapter Eleven

Angus's week of exclusion from school passed quickly, and he seemed happier than at any time since his parents' death. He was definitely a solitary child, quite content to spend the whole day outside, scarcely exchanging a word with anyone. As far as Ellen could see, the only person he sought out voluntarily was Kit, and whether this was for his company or his advice about the animals wasn't clear. He was a good worker, competent and conscientious. Surely a twelve year old shouldn't be that conscientious? At times the tense set of his shoulders and concentration on his face made her want to weep.

One day she made him go into Dumfries with her and bought new school trousers, jeans, and T-shirts. He was a thin child, but had definitely shot up in the last couple of months, and the old clothes only added to his forlorn air. He thanked her, but without enthusiasm. She didn't know if that was typical of a boy on the verge of his teens, or another sign that her nephew was unnaturally withdrawn.

On the drive back to Craigallan, she said, 'Well, what am I going to tell that head teacher of yours?' She found it easier to talk to him when she was driving, so they weren't forced to look at each other. 'He's going to phone me tomorrow and he'll want to know how you feel about going back to school.'

'Fine. I said.'

'Are you worried about those other kids picking on you again?'

'No, I'm not scared of them.'

'I'm certainly going to ask him to keep an eye on them. Little thugs.'

Out of the corner of her eye she saw the boy shrug, his favourite response when he didn't want to speak.

'I wondered, are there any kids that you would like to invite up to Craigallan?'

'No.' He sounded horrified.

'There must be other farmers' children at the

school, people who are interested in animals like you.'

'Mmm.'

'Well, are there?'

'They're not like me.'

Ellen saw that as a chink in his implacable refusal to discuss his life with her. 'What do you mean? Why aren't they like you?'

There was a long pause. She thought he wasn't going to answer, but he seemed to have been working out a response. 'They're interested in – other stuff. Football and computer games.'

'You play football with Callum.'

'Yeah, but I'm not interested in it.'

'What are you interested in?'

No answer. Ellen decided to give up for now. In some strange way, she felt she had made progress. She would tell the rector that she was sure Angus had learnt his lesson and that she hoped the other boys had, too.

Ellen wasn't normally a coward, but she had delayed and delayed phoning Richard. She knew she had to end things, and yet she hesitated. They had been together, in their way, for over five years.

It was Richard who phoned, eventually, more than a week after his visit. They exchanged pleasantries for a while, and Ellen felt that already he was a stranger.

'How's work going?' she asked, thinking – why am I asking this? Do I care? She was procrastinating again.

'Rather well, rather well. We've just landed ourselves a new contract which will keep me busier than ever.'

'That's good.' Ellen knew that Richard loved to be busy. She realised that she didn't have any idea how he would react to her finishing their relationship.

'And how are you and the children?' he asked heartily.

'Fine. Well, as fine as can be expected.'

'Excellent.'

Ellen took a deep breath to steal herself. 'Richard, you know when you were down here?'

'Er ... yes? I'm afraid I won't be able to get away again for a while, it's a very difficult time just now. One of the other partners is on leave and with this new contract, you can imagine.'

And that was a lie. New contract or not, Richard had always been able to make time for those fun weekends in the country. This made Ellen feel better. 'I wasn't going to suggest you come down again. More the opposite. I was thinking that perhaps you and I should, well, ease things off a bit. I'm down here with the kids and they have to come first and...' She didn't mean ease off, she meant finish, but suddenly she didn't know how to say it.

'You mean you're going to stay down there?'

'No. No, I'm planning to bring them back to Edinburgh. But it won't be for a while and, well, I feel I've got to concentrate on them just now. I don't have time for, for, for...' she wasn't quite sure what she didn't have time for. 'I'm sorry Richard.' She wanted to say it was nothing personal. That was how it felt. She had never been attached to him on a personal level; they had just had two lifestyles that complemented each other. And now they didn't.

'I see,' said Richard. 'I see.'

'I think it's for the best,' said Ellen.

'Very well,' he said. It seemed he wasn't going to put up any protest. She wondered, briefly, how much he really cared. He would no longer have a partner for socialising, but she didn't think it would take him long to find someone else. Good-looking, well-off (if selfish) single men were at a premium in Edinburgh. He would be all right. 'Do keep in touch,' he said politely.

She mouthed something similar in return. And that was that.

On a long weekend in early May, Ellen wandered down to see Clare.

'I thought you might have taken the kids to Edinburgh again.'

Ellen sighed. 'It wasn't exactly a stunning success last time.' She settled down to watch Clare battering a massive lump of clay.

'You can't tell anything from one visit,' said Clare tossing the long, dark hair over her shoulder with a flick of her head. Ellen wondered why she didn't tie it back. 'They might come round. Want a coffee?'

'No, I'm fine. I should get back to Cal and Sam soon.'

'Is Angus still being difficult about his name?'

'He's still insisting on Sam, if that's what you mean. I'm trying to get used to it.'

They sat in companionable silence for a while.

'I don't know how you can work with the kids

about,' said Ellen, looking around the studio, which was a less-than-weather-tight shed beside Clare's cottage. The broad windows meant you could see the girls running around in the garden, and the thin walls allowed you to hear their screams too. 'I'd be totally distracted.'

'You get used to it. I kind of tune out unless it sounds like serious trouble. In fact, sometimes silence is more worrying than noise.'

'I suppose. I get a lot of silence from Sam.'

'He's nearly a teenager. I'm sure it's normal. So, have you done any house-hunting?'

'I've been checking websites for places in West Lothian. But prices are horrendous. I know I'll do well on my flat, but it'll still be a struggle to find something big enough for all of us within commuting distance of Edinburgh.'

'Not that I want to sway you or anything, but that could be a good argument in favour of you staying down here.'

Ellen grimaced and ran fingers through her hair. She still hadn't managed to have it cut. 'Don't think I don't realise that. But...'

'But your job is in Edinburgh, as well as your boyfriend.'

'Boyfriend no longer,' said Ellen lightly.

'Oh.' This time Clare paused, holding grey-coated hands carefully away from her and she turned to study Ellen's face. 'I'm sorry. What happened?'

'I decided to break it off. It's not a big thing. If it couldn't survive the pressure of the kids then it wasn't meant to be, was it?'

'It's a shame though,' said Clare gently. 'It can

be good to have a man around.'

Ellen was surprised. She expected that from her mother, but not from Clare. As far as she knew, Clare hadn't had a long-term relationship since Grace's handsome, unreliable father had moved out four or more years ago. 'You manage without.'

'I've had to. But, you know, I think it might be time for a change. Time I made an effort.'

Ellen was happy to be distracted from her own problems. 'Have you got your eye on anyone at the moment? How about Kit Ballantyne?' Ellen wished Kit hadn't been the first man she thought of. 'He's single, isn't he? And a very kind man too.'

Clare went back to her clay. 'Kit's a friend. And not really my type.' She paused and raised an eyebrow at Ellen. 'Although my sources tell me that you and he are pally enough for him to use your bathing facilities.'

Ellen hoped she wasn't blushing. 'Who told you that? Not that it means anything, of course.'

'Mrs Jack, who do you think? You didn't expect her to keep quiet, did you? Anyway, I think that pretty vet nurse has got her eye on Kit. Devon, I think her name is. I hear she's talked him into going to the Dunmuir ceilidh with her.'

Ellen felt surprise and disappointment, on Clare's behalf, of course. 'That's nice. I suppose.'

'Are you going?' asked Clare.

'No. Who would I go with? And who would look after the kids?' It was months since she had had an evening out, and a good ceilidh was just the thing to raise her spirits.

'Take the kids with you, everyone else does. And you don't need a partner, that's why it's all the more impressive that Devon has got Kit to go *with* her.'

'When is it?' Ellen could feel her interest growing.

'A week on Friday.'

'Are you going yourself?'

'Of course. We could share transport. How about it?'

Ellen set off back up the hill with a swing to her step. While she was here she should make the most of what was on offer. It was odd how her spirits were raised by the idea of going to a small-town ceilidh.

Chapter Twelve

'This is the second time this has happened! Cows all through my garden! It really isn't good enough. I said last time, if I was inconvenienced like that again I would do something about it!' A large woman with grey-blonde hair stood on the Craig-allan door step, hands on hips, fury in her eyes.

'The second time?' said Ellen, faintly, rubbing sleep from her eyes sufficiently enough to recognise Mrs Jack.

'Exactly! The last time was just before Christmas. They trampled the lawn and ruined the special wreath I had made for the front door, not to mention knocking down one of my garden ornaments. Some of us like to make an effort with our gardens, you know.' She cast a disparaging glance at Craigallan's weed-filled flowerbed. 'I told Mr Moffat that it simply wouldn't do.'

'Oh,' said Ellen. Surely the woman realised that Ellen hadn't been responsible for the cows last December – and Sam Moffat was no longer around. 'I'm really sorry this has happened. Er, where are the cows now?' And how was she supposed to get them back?

'I couldn't possibly say. Halfway through the village no doubt. Creating a major road hazard. Why is it farmers these days can't keep their gates closed and their fences in good order? I could claim compensation, you know. It's not good enough, people have no consideration...'

'Thank you for letting me know,' said Ellen, interrupting the flow. It would have been far better if the stupid woman had phoned, but no, she had to come and harangue Ellen on her own doorstep, and at six o'clock in the morning. No wonder Ellen's brain was struggling to get in to gear. 'I'll get dressed and be straight down there.'

'I knew it was a ridiculous idea, a woman and three children trying to run a farm. The sooner you see that for yourself, the better for all concerned. Especially your neighbours. I could have gone straight to the police, you know.'

'I'm very glad you didn't. Thank you for letting me know...'

'Hrrmph,' said Mrs Jack, and turned and marched back to her car. Clearly, she had no intention of helping round up the animals.

A small part of Ellen's brain felt grim satisfaction that she was seeing Mrs Jack in her true colours. She had known that caring attitude was just a front.

'Angus!' she shouted, as she closed the creaking front door. 'Angus, get up now! In fact all of you, I need your help.' Cows were such enormous animals and she really preferred it when they were on the other side of a fence to her.

The children, on the other hand, seemed rather to enjoy the occasion. They grumbled about being woken up, but once dressed they began to giggle about past break outs and how lucky it was they didn't still have that bull, he was a real escapologist and a nightmare to get back in again. Ellen hoped the cows weren't going to start getting bolshie, she didn't want any more damage. She had only just had the car's front wing repaired.

They drove down the road and caught up with the herd milling round in the centre of Kinmuir village. Ellen quailed at the sight of them but Angus took in the situation at a glance. 'Stop here. I'll go through the church yard and cut them off before they go further. Come on, Cal, you can come with me. Aunt Ellen, all you and Lucy need to do is get the car out of the way and walk on ahead of them back to Craigallan. Make sure there are no gates open into other fields, and stop them going back into that woman's garden. Or Clare's.'

He and Callum had jumped out and disappeared before Ellen had time to protest that it surely wasn't that simple. She shifted the car and gave Lucy what she hoped was an encouraging smile. Five minutes later, Angus and Callum appeared around the corner, driving the cattle in front of them. The cows were heading more or less in the right direction, but their calves kept doubling back, panicking at a rustling branch or banging gate. That would set the cows into a swirl of indecision and stop any progress up the road. They were such brainless beasts. The only good thing was it was so early no one else was about.

Then, when they had progressed less than a hundred yards back up the lane, Ellen heard a car approaching. Wasn't it just typical that today of all days some idiot would decide to get up at the crack of dawn and need to get by? She turned around, trying to put a pleasant, placating smile on her face, and saw Kit Ballantyne leap out of the vehicle.

'Goodness me,' he said cheerfully. 'Do we have a bit of a problem here?'

She had been determined not to call him for help, but she couldn't deny it was good to see him.

'Kit!' shouted Angus, the relief clear in his voice. 'Have you got some rope in the car? I was thinking we'd get on better if I could lead one of the cows, but I don't have a harness.'

'That boy's got brains,' said Kit approvingly, and swung back to his car.

Kit found a rope to sling around the neck of Angus's favourite, Melanie, and agreed she would probably walk better for him than Kit. He then moved his car on to the verge and took Angus's place at the back of the herd. Progress was now steady, if not exactly orderly.

Not to be outdone, Ellen went to help him, but all this achieved was to make her feel silly as she

145

flapped her arms about. The animals seemed to respond twice as quickly to Kit as to her.

Eventually they closed the Craigallan gate firmly behind the last miscreant. 'Thank you so much,' said Ellen. 'I really appreciate your help. Again.'

Kit smiled his lazy smile. 'Always a pleasure. Which reminds me, I was off out to a call. Something about a sick llama, as if I know anything about llamas...' He raised a hand in a vague farewell and loped off down the road to where he had abandoned his car.

Ellen felt nervous about visiting Kit in his caravan. She realised guiltily this was the first time she had ever been to visit him. He had been so helpful to her, but she had never really made an effort in return, never been to see how his life was progressing. She had resented rather than appreciated him. And now here she was, about to ask for his help again.

It was a cool, still late afternoon in early June. There had been rain during the day (when wasn't there?) but at the last moment the sun had appeared and the rays picked out all the different greens of the hills and the valley. She was knowledgeable enough now to see that the brighter fields were the ones not currently being grazed, and to wonder why the farmer who owned the land adjacent to Craigallan hadn't put his stock on it yet. She would never have thought of things like that a few months ago.

The track to Kit's plot of land was steeper than she expected. It climbed up beside the copse and then swung round suddenly to the flat area where the house was to be built. It was a good position. Being slightly higher, the views were even better than those from Craigallan. You could see the shape of the valley, a long oval saucer, with the good grassland along the sides of the burn, and the narrow tarmac road on one ridge. Not a car in sight.

While Ellen waited for the caravan door to open, she tried to place the music that was resounding within. American. Kind of rock. She hadn't brought any of her own music down from Edinburgh, and hadn't felt inclined to try out any of Jess and Sam's. It felt suddenly good to hear the thud of a good baseline once again.

'Well hello.' Kit looked surprised by her appearance on his doorstep. He wore muddy tracksuit bottoms and an unbuttoned fleece shirt. His feet were bare. He wasn't expecting visitors. 'What brings you up here?'

'It's a lovely afternoon. Monty needed a walk.'

'Excellent idea. You want to come in?' He stood back and gestured her inside. 'It's a mess.' Which it was, but a pleasant one. The caravan was bigger and scruffier than it looked from afar. Inside it was mostly one room, with bench seats, tables, and work surfaces all littered with clothes, books, mugs, and papers. He turned down the music with one hand and cleared a pile of books from one bench with the other. 'Have a seat. D'you want some coffee? I might just be able to find two clean mugs. Or there're beers in the fridge if you prefer.'

'A beer'd be brilliant. I didn't know you had a fridge.'

'All mod cons here.' He flashed her a grin. 'As long as it doesn't rain, it's great.'

'Steve Earle,' she said with satisfaction, as she took a first long drink of beer from the can. Glasses weren't offered.

'Steve...? Yeah, d'you like his stuff? Some of it's a bit rough but the man's got talent.'

Ellen hadn't heard the music for years, and hadn't realised until that moment that she did like it. 'It's got a certain something.'

'D'you want me to switch it off? Something quieter?'

'No, no, it's fine.' She took another drink and made room for Monty beside her.

Kit said, 'Cows all recovered from their outing? And have you heard any more from our good friend Mrs Jack? Callum said she was threatening to complain.'

'The cows are fine. And Mrs Jack doesn't seem to have gone to anyone in authority. Thank goodness.'

Kit pulled a face. 'I wouldn't put anything past that woman.'

'Nor would I.'

Ellen remembered the way the stupid woman had spread stories about him using the washing facilities at Craigallan. Maybe that was why he wasn't coming down so often.

They chatted for a while. It would have been nice just to relax and forget she had come here for a reason.

Eventually she shifted in her seat and decided to get to the point. 'I wanted to ask you something. A couple of things, actually.'

'Go ahead.'

Now she had the opportunity, she hesitated.

'It's about Angus. You know he was suspended from school last month?'

'Yes.'

'Did he tell you himself?'

'No.' Kit pulled a face. 'One of the others mentioned it.'

'I'm worried about him. He won't really tell me what happened. In fact, I can't get through to him at all. He's back at school but I don't think he's any happier. I get the feeling that he trusts you, likes you, more than me, and I wondered if he had said anything...?'

Kit said cautiously, 'He's a good lad.'

'I know that. But he's got his bad points too. It's driving me mad, his never talking.'

'He's had a rough time recently.'

'You think I don't know that?'

'Of course you do.' His tone was gentle, sympathetic. She should really stop over-reacting. It was just so hard not to feel criticised, when she herself felt she was so useless.

'I'm really worried about him, or I wouldn't ask.' Ellen paused.

Kit narrowed his eyes and looked at her over the top of his drink. 'Ask?'

'Whether you could try and have a word with him. See if you can find out what is worrying him, if there's anything I can do about it.'

'I don't know if he would talk to me.' He took a swig from his can. 'I mean it when I say Angus, Sam, I mean, is a good kid. But I don't know that he's an easy one.'

149

'You can't expect it, after what has happened.' Now Ellen was the one jumping to Angus's defence.

'I know. But even before, was he an easy kid? I'm not saying losing his mum and dad hasn't affected him, it's bound to have, but I don't think it changes your personality overnight, you know? He's got a lot going for him. He's bright and conscientious. But don't you think he's a bit, well, snooty with it? He's got something about him that puts other kids off.'

'Cal and Lucy think the world of him.'

'That's different.'

'He's being bullied at school. I'm absolutely sure of that, even if he won't admit it.'

Kit mulled her words over and said, 'Aye, I can see that might happen.'

'You just said he was snooty. That seems to imply he is superior.'

'Maybe I should have said reserved. That kind of thing doesn't make you so popular.'

'But it's so awful. I don't want it to happen. How can I stop it?'

He shrugged. 'Aren't you a teacher yourself? Don't you have experience of it from your work?'

'I'm a college lecturer. The youngest kids I deal with are seventeen, most are older. I don't know anything about youngsters.'

'And Angus hasn't said anything to you since going back to school?'

'He says it's fine. But I'm sure he's worried. I'd really appreciate it if you could sound him out.'

'I'll see,' Kit said, but he didn't sound hopeful. She wondered if he thought she was being underhand. But what else could she do? The direct approach hadn't worked. 'I'll try,' said Kit, which seemed a little more positive.

'Thanks.'

Ellen paused. This next topic was one she felt even more nervous about. She took a deep breath. 'The other thing I wanted to ask you about was the animals. Selling the animals.'

There was a sudden stillness. Kit said nothing, he didn't even move, but the feeling of withdrawal was definite. Monty butted her arm and whimpered quietly, as though he too disapproved.

Ellen hurried on, 'I know Angus-Sam is adamant that he wants to stay here, but it's really not possible. My life is in Edinburgh and... Anyway, I just wanted to know when the best time would be to sell *if* we do decide to go down that road. I need to know these things, don't I? And how much the stock is worth, things like that.'

'I'm probably not the best person to ask.'

'I thought, being a vet, you might have some idea...'

'It's not really my field of expertise.'

The tone of the conversation had changed.

'I'm just taking soundings at the moment. I suppose I'll have to go to a stock auctioneer, or something, but I thought you would have some idea.'

Kit was silent for so long she thought he might not answer at all. He sat tapping his fingers on his thigh, not looking at her. Then he said abruptly, 'I'm really not sure this is the right thing to do.'

'What?' Ellen hadn't expected enthusiasm, but the outright opposition took her by surprise. 'I

151

beg your pardon?'

Kit frowned at her. 'Listen, do you think it's wise to decide something so serious so soon? Sam and Jess spent a very long time building up Craigallan, and as you know, Angus is very attached to the place. Aren't there other options?'

'I don't consider this soon,' said Ellen coolly. 'I've had over three months to think about it. And it's not getting any easier. You saw the hassle we had with the cows.'

'I never think it's a good idea to rush into things.'

'I am not rushing into this. Never mind, forget it. There are other people I can ask.' She could feel her temper rising. Why was he being so negative? The fact she had her own doubts made it all the more infuriating.

'I'm sorry, I'm doing this all wrong.' Kit ran his fingers through his already ruffled hair and sighed. 'What I meant to say was, have you definitely made up your mind?'

'Yes,' said Ellen firmly, raising her chin. 'Yes, I have.' She didn't tell him she hadn't yet discussed it with the children. 'Running a farm, even a small farm, is far too much for me and the children. You know that better than anyone.'

She narrowed her eyes, daring him to deny it. Helping out as he had done over the last few months just wasn't sustainable.

He let out a long, slow breath, suddenly deflated. When he did speak, it was in business-like tones. 'OK. Obviously, it's best not to sell the lambs quite yet, they'll fetch a far better price if they're fat lambs, which means another month or so. You'll get a good price then, first lamb of the year. As for the calves, better to hang onto them for a while. But other stock it doesn't make a whole lot of difference. You won't get much for the hens, or the horses. The horses you'd do best to advertise in a specialist paper.'

Ellen said hesitantly, 'You wouldn't be interested in buying any of them yourself?'

'Me?'

'I don't know how much land you have, but you once mentioned you'd like to go into small-holding.'

'I've only got a couple of acres. And I don't have the time.' Which begged the question of how he had managed to help them so much up to now. 'Angus lives for those animals, you know.'

'There's more than just Angus to think of,' she snapped. 'And moving to Edinburgh would solve the school problem, at least.'

'Solve it or displace it?'

She glared but didn't answer.

He looked at his watch. 'Well, is that everything? I really should pop down to see my mother.'

Ellen was sure that was just an excuse. She put down her empty can. She could take a hint, and anyway she had to go and collect the kids. She rose and Monty immediately followed her. At least someone liked her.

She was hurt by Kit's disapproval. Did he think this was easy for her? That she was looking forward to separating Angus from everything he loved? But someone had to be sensible around here.

She could feel tears rising to her eyes, which was ridiculous. It had nothing to do with Kit –

she was an independent woman who did what *she* wanted. She grinned wryly at the thought and wiped away the tears. Ha! That was a bit of a joke now, wasn't it? She had to do what the children needed her to do, and that took away her independence more than she could possibly have imagined.

She continued to fume as she arrived back at Craigallan. What was it to Kit, anyway? Did he think she could uproot herself, learn to run a farm, find a job in Dumfries, just like that? She didn't even know if there were any Further Education establishments in Dumfries.

Later, as she lay trying and failing to get to sleep in the uncomfortable spare bed, it occurred to her that it wouldn't do any harm to find out if there were any possible employers in the area.

Chapter Thirteen

Ellen was getting ready for the ceilidh and Lucy was sitting on the bed in the spare room amidst the mounds of clothes, watching preparations with interest.

'Are you going to wear that?' she said, looking Ellen up and down with pursed, disapproving lips. She reminded Ellen of Jess.

'What's wrong with it?' Ellen tried to see herself in the tiny mirror. She had put on loose black linen trousers and a short-sleeved pale pink top. She thought it would be comfortable for dancing.

'You've got so many pretty things.' Lucy fingered a silky dresses that lay on the bed. 'I like pretty things.'

Ellen dropped a hand briefly on the soft blonde hair. Lucy was such a girly girl, it was easy to forget her amidst the needs of boys and farm. 'I'm glad you do, darling. But I don't think they're quite the right thing for a ceilidh, surely?'

'Grace's mum is going to wear her green and gold party dress, Grace said so. And her new sparkly sandals. And you're much prettier than her, even if you do have short hair. You should wear a dress, too.'

Ellen stood looking down at her niece, trying to decipher her words. Ellen was pretty, short hair wasn't pretty, she should be keeping up with Grace's mother Clare. She touched her hair, which she had finally managed to have cut. She really wasn't used to this girly talk.

'I prefer trousers.'

'You always wear trousers. This is a party. You should wear a dress.'

'Mmm.' Ellen wasn't convinced. It was so long since she had dressed up, and then it had been dinners in smart Edinburgh restaurants, or even a visit to Richard's favourite, discreet nightclub. She didn't think those sort of outfits would look right in Dunmuir. She'd rather play it safe. 'Maybe I'll dress up another time. But what about you? Haven't you got a special party dress you want to wear?'

Lucy was easily distracted. She bounced off the bed. 'I've got some things. Come and see. You can help me choose.'

155

Ellen still felt she was trespassing whenever she went up the steep stairs to the upper floor of the house. True, she had to go there to tidy the children's rooms, sort out their clothes, muck out the bathroom. But she kept these tasks to a minimum. She hadn't been able to face the ordeal of emptying Jess and Sam's room, and until she did perhaps she would never feel at ease up here.

Lucy glanced at the door to her parents' room at the end of the corridor, but she said nothing. Her expression didn't even change. She had got over the tears, the crumpling every time she remembered. Ellen wished she knew what was going on inside that small head.

And as if on cue, as Lucy pulled a filmy, three-layered white lacy dress from her wardrobe, tears began to well up. She held the material against herself, watching her reflection in the mirror. 'Mummy and Daddy bought me this for Christmas.' She sniffed. 'Mum bought me a bigger size, 'cos she said it was really a summer dress. I really really loved it.'

The dress was long and sleeveless, with a bodice embroidered with tiny pink flowers, and the layered skirt floated as she moved. Ellen could remember just enough about being seven years old to imagine how like a fairy princess it could make you feel.

'It's beautiful. Do you want to wear it tonight?'

Lucy's face was solemn, the hint of tears still in her eyes. 'Do you think Mummy would have said yes?'

'I think this is exactly the sort of occasion Mummy would have bought it for. Why don't you

156

try it on and we'll see how it looks?'

Thankfully, the tears receded. Once Lucy had stripped off her leggings and sweatshirt and slid the filmy garment over her head, her excitement returned. She twisted and turned, preening herself in front of her mirror which was a lot more useful than the tiny one in the guest bedroom. 'It fits me now. I must have growed.'

'Yes, darling, I think you have.' Ellen swallowed the lump in her own throat and said determinedly, 'Now, what about shoes? Have you got anything pretty enough to go with it? Ooh, those are nice. And then you better start getting the tangles out of your hair while I go and see how the boys are getting on.'

The ceilidh was in the Dunmuir Community Centre, a drab 1970s building that saw constant use, Dunmuir being that sort of active small town. The band consisted of drummer, accordion player, and fiddler, fronted by a jovial man to call the dances. He knew most of those present by name, and according to Clare wasn't afraid to use this fact if he thought there weren't enough people on the dance floor, or the dancers weren't taking the steps seriously enough. Ellen tried to picture Richard in these surroundings, and failed.

'Good crowd,' said Clare, busily arranging seats for their party at one end of a long table. 'OK, kids, this is our base. You can wander off but if you go outside stay in the car park. If you want us, you know where to find us. That OK with you, Ellen?'

'Er, fine,' said Ellen. She still found it difficult

to remember she was the one in charge of the children. She noticed Angus looking around with lowered head, and cursed herself for forgetting that not everyone in Dunmuir was friendly. She determined to keep an eye on him, to see how he interacted with the other youngsters – if at all. 'Remember what Clare said,' she repeated to the Moffat children, but mostly for Angus's benefit. 'Don't wander off.' She took their shrugs for agreement, and turned to the more interesting topic of what everyone wanted to drink.

The hall had rows of trestle tables down each side, with the central area cleared for dancing. A bar was being run from the kitchen hatch at the rear. It was doing very good business even before the band had tuned up.

Callum and Lucy stayed nearby for the time being, sipping the cokes which they still considered a luxury. Ellen felt guilty for going against her sister's wishes every time she gave in to them, but couldn't bring herself to believe that fizzy drinks were the fount of all evil. It hadn't escaped her notice that Angus had asked only for water. She looked around for him now and saw, to her surprise, that he was talking to the man with the fiddle.

'Who's Angus ... Sam talking to?' she murmured to Callum.

'Dunno.'

'That's his guitar teacher,' said Lucy. 'Don't you remember?'

Ellen vaguely recognised the man, although she had only met him fleetingly. Usually she dropped her nephew at the gate, and was in such a hurry when she picked him up that she did no more than pay and depart.

'I get the impression Angus is quite musical,' said Clare, twirling her hair through her fingers. 'Jess always said he was keen.'

'Yes, I think so,' said Ellen doubtfully. She had to remind him to practice, but once he started he could play the guitar for ages. Whether he was any good, she couldn't have said. She tried to recall whether her brother-in-law had been musical. She would have to ask her mother.

'I'm going to learn the clarinet when I'm eight,' said Lucy. 'Mum said.'

'Did she? And what about you, Cal, don't you want to learn something?'

'No way.' Having finished his drink, Callum slid off his seat and departed to join a crowd of his friends near the door. Ellen wondered why she didn't worry about him. Somehow, his answers always seemed disarmingly honest. He didn't want to learn a musical instrument be-cause it was hard work, and he wasn't interested. That was all there was to it. There weren't many things that interested Callum – football, golf, computer games and television. Ellen felt a rush of affection for him. He wasn't a difficult boy to please.

'There's Kit,' said Clare, raising a hand to wave with a jingle of bracelets. She gestured to the empty seats at their table, but he merely raised a hand in acknowledgement and moved on. Ellen wondered which of the girls in his group was Devon, and decided it was probably the one with shoulder length dark hair and heavily-made-up

159

eyes, who kept herself glued to his side. She was pretty, but very young. She giggled a lot.

Ellen found herself glancing over at Kit's table more than once. It was only natural to be interested. She presumed the rest of the group were from Kit's vet practice. There was another man about Kit's age and two older men, both wearing the ubiquitous tweed jackets of the rural over-fifties. She presumed the women with them were their wives.

Despite what Clare had said there seemed to be an awful lot of people paired off, and Ellen felt self-consciousness at having no partner of her own.

Angus knew as long as he saw Jason Armstrong's gang before they saw him, he was OK. They didn't scare him. They'd mocked him from afar at school the last couple of weeks, but they hadn't dared come near. Old Fletcher must've put the wind up them, they were cowards really. In a crowd like this they couldn't do him any serious damage, but he knew better than to let them corner him. Even as he chatted to Grant McConnell, his guitar teacher, he kept a wary eye on the hall.

'I keep telling you, you should have a go,' said Grant, proffering the fiddle. When Angus didn't take it he put it to his chin and played a short jig, then held it out again. 'See?'

'Naw, I think I'll stick with guitar.'

'You should try both. Nothing ventured, nothing gained.'

Angus shrugged. He'd love to try the fiddle, but what was the point of starting now? His Aunt

160

Ellen was going to drag them off to Edinburgh soon, and the way she kept going on about money there was no way she'd buy him a violin even if he asked.

'Hey, Simon.' Grant accosted a gangly, curly-haired youth who was moving past. 'Si, this is the boy I was telling you about.' Grant turned to Angus. 'Simon's set up a band and he's looking for someone who can actually play guitar, not just pretend to.'

Angus looked down, letting the hair flop over his eyes. He vaguely recognised the older boy from school, and was sure he wouldn't want anything to do with a lowly first year.

'Are you Angus Moffat?' said Simon. 'I've been meaning to look you out but you know how it is.' He smiled. He had a round, friendly face, only slightly marred by acne. 'Don't suppose you've got your guitar with you now?'

Angus felt a stir of excitement, and for the first time in weeks didn't even notice that someone wasn't calling him Sam. All he said was, 'Naw, haven't.'

'Never mind. How about we set up a time...'

'I've got an old acoustic guitar in the van, if you want,' said Grant McConnell, off hand. He dug into his pocket. 'Here're the keys. I'd better go, looks like I'm wanted on stage. And don't forget to bring those keys back!'

Before he had time to think, Angus found himself following Simon out of the hall.

'Now, which is his van?' asked Simon cheerfully, looking around the car park.

'I think it's that white one,' said Angus. He

wondered how Simon knew Grant, but didn't like to ask.

Grant's van was an ageing transit, useful for carrying about all his musical instruments. He was the sort of person who could play just about anything, which he did when and where he liked. Angus envied him bitterly.

The two boys settled themselves in the back of the van, with the doors ajar, and Simon began to explain about his band. 'We've been going a couple of months. Three of us. You'll know Ed and Mark from school. I've been doing lead guitar and vocals but it isn't working, it's difficult doing both. That's what I was telling Grant and he said you'd be able to take over the guitar, if you were interested. What do you say?'

'Don't know,' said Angus, fingering the acoustic guitar nervously.

'You're a bit young, like, but Grant says you're good. Why don't you play something for me?'

'Like what?'

'I dunno. How about "Word Up", d'you know that? Thought you would, it's one of Grant's favourites.'

Angus started slowly, but once he got into the rhythm he forgot his nerves and let the music take over.

Simon grunted. 'Not bad. D'you know the chords for "American Idiot"? Good. Right, I'll sing it and we'll see if you can keep time.'

Angus was amazed at the teenager's confidence, that he could start singing just like that. He had a good, strong voice, too. It was great to play along to him. Angus never liked singing himself, for all

Grant's encouragement. To his surprise, he realised he might really be able to do this.

They had worked their way through four or five songs when the rear doors of the van swung open with a bang and three pale faces peered in. 'Oooh, look who it is, thought I saw little orphan Annie creeping oot the hall.' It was Jason Armstrong.

'Who are you? Get lost, we're busy,' said Simon, scarcely looking round. Angus followed his lead and ignored the boys, but he knew he wouldn't be able to play now. His hands weren't quite steady.

'Found yourself a bum chum, have you, Annie?' continued Jason. His cronies laughed hysterically.

'I said get lost,' said Simon.

Jason swung on the door, not caring when it veered back and jarred the hinges with a crash. His friends sniggered. 'Come on, give us a tune then. How about a nursery rhyme, isn't that your level?'

'Go away,' said Angus, through clenched teeth. How had he been so bloody stupid as to get himself stuck out here? What happened if Simon went off and left him? Even if he stayed, Jason had a big enough crowd with him to take them both on. And there was hundreds of pounds worth of equipment in this van. He could feel the sweat breaking out.

'We just want a little tune, come on, you were happy enough to play for your boyfriend, weren't you?'

Simon tried to stand up but was hampered by the low roof. 'Clear out,' he said, advancing to the door. 'Go on, scoot.'

'Oooh, think you're a fucking tough guy, do you? Just 'cos you're in Third Year doesnae mean shite.'

Jason stepped back from the door with surprising agility for his bulk, and swung it in as Simon leant out. It hit him on the head and he sat back, stunned. The gang needed no further invitation. They swarmed forward, one elbowing Simon as they passed, another pulling out a keyboard and dropping it on the tarmac. Jason himself advanced on Angus.

Chapter Fourteen

Ellen sank back into her chair with a sigh of relief. Three dances in a row was about her limit. She fanned her face and took a long drink of lager. She had persuaded a mightily embarrassed Callum to do the Dashing White Sergeant with her, and after that she had had no difficulty finding partners. Clare had been right. Everyone was friendly, all they wanted was to have a good time.

Clare returned to the table after the next dance, her face as pink as Ellen's felt, and threw off the lacy cardigan she had been wearing, showing the bangles and rather a lot of bare flesh. Her party dress, as Lucy called it, consisted of two tiny straps and tiers and tiers of green and gold silk. She made Ellen feel very plain in her pink and black.

'I'm not fit enough for this,' shouted Clare happily. 'Didn't used to need to take a breather.'

'You're doing better than me.'

'Hardly.' Clare gazed around the room, checking up on her daughter and taking in the new arrivals. Lucy and Grace were doing what they considered to be a Gay Gordons in one corner, Callum was drinking more coke and eating crisps with his friends in another. Ellen couldn't see Angus, but he had been talking to an older, curly-haired boy not long ago. She had been pleased to see him mixing.

'I thought Kit might have come over and said hello,' said Clare.

'I'm sure he will,' replied Ellen, although she was far from sure. Since she had visited his caravan to ask his advice on selling the Craigallan stock, they hadn't spoken. He still helped Angus morning and night, but he didn't approach the house. She presumed he was holding it against her, but what on earth did he expect her to do? Her heart sank as she remembered what she had lined up for tomorrow.

An agricultural specialist was coming to value the property in the morning. A cattle auctioneer was coming out to look over the animals in the afternoon. She hadn't dared mention any of this to Angus. Even the thought of that made Ellen's good mood evaporate.

They sipped their drinks in silence for a while. When the band took a break Clare said, 'Reasonable turn out, isn't it? All leading lights of the town, as well as plebs like us.'

'Are they?'

'Yeah. That table over there is teachers from the school, and you see that pretty blonde woman, that's Eilidh Gilmour, one of the local doctors. Mmm, and it rather looks like she's pregnant. I hadn't heard that. Suppose we shouldn't be surprised, she and Patrick have been married over a year. And then there's the vet contingent. And the two tables over there are local farmers.'

Ellen glanced across and thought she saw Mrs Morton, the head teacher at Kinmuir. She turned away quickly. Mrs Morton had thought it was an excellent idea for Ellen to join the Parent Council and she was still trying to work out a good reason why not.

She said, 'Mrs Jack's not here.'

Clare pulled a face. 'Thank goodness. Stupid woman came and asked me if I knew Grace had been playing out in the rain last week. Of course I knew! I encouraged her, she's not going to melt, is she? I just hate the way that woman talks to you, so sincerely, because she's *really* got your best interests at heart. What does she know about children?'

Ellen smiled grimly and recounted her problem with the cows.

Clare giggled and said, 'She's a silly cow herself. She should spend more time worrying about that husband of hers and leave us alone.'

'What's her husband like?'

'Don't know, nobody ever sees him. I suppose Dr Gilmour must have done, I've noticed her going in and out of the house. He must be really ill.'

'That's a shame.' Ellen wondered if she felt most sorry for Mrs Jack or the unknown husband.

'Kit says it can't be easy for her. That was when

I criticised her fat little dog. Ugly overfed beast. Kit never has a bad word to say for anyone.'

Except me, thought Ellen, but didn't say it. She knew he didn't approve of what she was doing. She sighed.

Clare changed the subject with a suddenness that was typical of her. 'See anyone who takes your fancy?'

'Er, no,' said Ellen.

'Come on, you should make an effort. Didn't I tell you I think the time is right for a change for me? And I rather like the look of that fiddle player. Don't suppose you know if he's married?'

'No, I don't. All I know is his name's Grant and apart from Kit Ballantyne he's the only person on this planet that Angus likes talking to.'

'Grant, is it? Seeing he's at the bar just now I might just get us another round. Same again, is it?'

'Clare! He's only a babe, can't be more than thirty.'

'But sweet with it,' said Clare, heading off.

Ellen laughed. She wouldn't have had the nerve herself, but it was fun to feel like she was part of the wider world. She gave Kit another covert glance and was embarrassed when he turned and caught her eye. She looked quickly away.

Kit knew that he should never have let Devon talk him into bringing her to the ceilidh. He was under no illusions about her intentions, nor about his own, but sometimes he was just too damned soft to say no. Now he had her stuck limpet-like to his side, and everyone was leaving the two of

167

them alone, as though he wanted to keep her to himself. He tried to catch Alistair's eye as he and Deborah went off to chat at another table, but to no avail. His friend just winked and departed. Some friend.

'Tell me more about this house you're having built,' said Devon, smiling invitingly. She really did have the most stunning eyes, and a lovely, voluptuous mouth.

Shame it was all too ready to pout, which it did when he said, 'Some other time maybe. Talking about houses, that reminds me I really must go and have a quick word with my neighbour about, er, shared access. So if you'll excuse me, I won't be a moment...' He made a quick getaway, before Devon decided to join him.

He had seen Ellen and Clare sitting on the far side of the room and thought how much happier he would have been with them. Clare in her bright gypsy dress, and Ellen so cool and neat in a plain blouse and trousers, there was no similarity between the two, except that they were both good company. He started to think about how lucky he was with his neighbours, (as long as you forgot about Mrs Jack) but that brought him all too quickly to the memory of Jess and Sam. He didn't want to go there.

'Are you on your own?' he said to Ellen, finding that Clare had disappeared by the time he made his way across the room.

'Yes.' She smiled at him, a little wary. 'Clare's gone to get drinks, were you looking for her?'

'Not really. Just for some adult conversation.' He slumped down in one of the empty seats and

168

wished he had brought his drink with him. He waved and caught Clare's eye and gestured her to bring him a pint.

'I hope you're not thirsty, she might be a while,' said Ellen.

'Why? The queue's not too bad.'

'She's trying to chat up that cute fiddle player. The trip to the bar was just an excuse.'

He groaned. 'And there was me thinking I'd timed it just right for a decent drink. Only wine at our table.' He stretched himself back in the seat and prepared for a long chat. He didn't really mind about the beer. Ellen gave him another small smile. 'I'm surprised you came over at all,' she said. 'I get the feeling I'm out of favour.'

'Why should you be?' Kit was surprised. He had been upset at the thought of her selling Craigallan, but after all, it wasn't his business. Who was he to give advice to others?

'We haven't really spoken since I asked you about selling the stock, so I thought...'

'I'm not saying I think you'd be doing the right thing if you sold, but it's your decision.'

'Yes, it is.'

Kit sighed. So she hadn't changed her mind. He said lightly, 'Well, at least if we're friends again I won't feel bad about using your bathroom facilities occasionally.'

'You're more than welcome.'

Kit couldn't tell from her cool tone whether he was welcome or not. He decided to leave that topic for the moment. 'How's Angus getting on at school? I've been trying to sound him out, by the way, but no luck so far.'

'Thanks. He says he's all right, but I'm still not sure. I've got an appointment with the head teacher next week.'

Kit looked around the ugly hall with its high-level windows and scuffed walls. 'And how are you enjoying a night out Dunmuir-style?'

'I'm having fun.'

'Good.' He nodded approvingly. 'And perhaps when the band starts up again you'll give me a dance?' He hadn't thought that was the reason he had come over here, but now it seemed that it was.

Ellen blushed very faintly. She said lightly, 'That's very kind of you. Although there's someone looking daggers at me over there who might not be too pleased.'

'Sssh, don't look, if you give her any encouragement she'll be over here like a shot.' Kit knew it was bad manners to criticise your date, but it was important that Ellen knew it hadn't been his idea to bring a partner. 'Next time I'll be more careful about what I let myself be talked in to.'

Now Ellen looked amused, thin eyebrows raised in question. He saw that she, too, had made an effort for the evening. She wore more make-up than he had ever seen on her, but hers was tasteful and low key, the way everything about Ellen Taylor seemed to be. Kit put his head on one side and met her questioning stare with a smile. He was just wondering why it had never occurred to him to invite Ellen along as his partner when there was a commotion at the door.

Callum came racing in, shouting, 'Auntie Ellen, Auntie Ellen, you've got to come *now*. There's some boys and Angus and...'

Neither Kit nor Ellen waited to hear more. They shot out of their seats and were through the swing doors into the foyer before he had even drawn breath.

'Where...?' said Ellen, pausing as they burst out into the cool night-time air.

Shouts and a crash directed them to a white van with a crowd of youths around it. Kit set off at a run, but before he had reached it the alarm had been raised and four or five boys disappeared over the fence and into the night. Only two girls were left, laughing and chewing gum. When he pulled back one of the doors, he found Angus and another youth inside.

Angus had blood coming from his mouth and his shirt was ripped, the other boy was holding one hand to his head. Around them were scattered instruments and sheet music. 'What's going on? Are you OK?'

Ellen appeared at his elbow. 'Angus. God, are you all right?'

Angus rubbed his hand across his mouth, smearing the blood. 'I'm fine. But...' He gestured at the mess around him. Slowly he picked up what was left of a guitar, its neck broken, strings adrift. As he moved forward Kit felt his foot touch something on the tarmac and stooped to pick it up. It was a keyboard.

'What the hell happened?' he asked.

'It was those same boys, wasn't it?' said Ellen. 'Jason someone or other and his pals? I saw someone run off. Bloody little cowards.' She wasn't calm and collected now. 'Bastards! How dare they...'

'It was nothing,' said Angus, staring in horror at the broken instrument.

Kit touched the older boy on the arm. 'Are you OK?'

'Aye, I think so.' The boy rubbed his head again and gave a tentative smile.

He seemed the more forthcoming, so Kit addressed him. 'Can you tell us what happened?'

'I'm not really sure, it was all so fast. Some kids came up and were calling us names and then ... I think I banged my head. Not sure.'

Kit swung round to the girls who were still eavesdropping. 'You can tell us what's been going on, can't you?'

'Naw...' said one, beginning to drift away. 'We only just got here, like. And, you know...'

They were gone. Kit wasn't even sure he would recognise them again. All teenage girls looked this same these days, too much make up and midriff, not enough sense.

'Whose van is this?' asked Ellen.

'Grant's,' said Angus quietly. 'He's going to murder me.'

'No he's not. This time we go to the police, this is assault and wilful damage.'

'It was an accident,' said Angus.

'We'll see about that. Come on, let's go back inside.'

Kit didn't think he had ever known Ellen look so furious. Frozen with shock, befuddled with grief, struggling to cope – those were sides he had seen before. But this purposeful stride and white anger were entirely new. He followed on behind, intrigued.

172

Grant was dragged out to see the damage and the police were called. Ellen couldn't believe this had happened. Dunmuir seemed so quiet, so safe. And Angus still refused point blank to give any details.

'It was nothing,' he said time after time.

Which of course meant the police just shook their heads and murmured something about boys will be boys. Not much they could do, when both Angus and Simon were intent on belittling the affair. Ellen said she was sure the attackers had been Jason Armstrong and his gang, but Angus claimed it had been too dark to see and Simon said (seemingly honestly) that he didn't know the boys.

So, once again, those little bastards were going to get away with it.

The thing that really upset Angus was the damage to Grant McConnell's instruments.

'I'll pay for them,' he said, his lip so swollen now it hardly moved. 'Just tell me what it costs and I'll save up.'

'You'll do no such bloody thing,' said Grant. 'It was an old guitar, and the keyboard is just scratched. And it wasn't you did the damage. Wait till I lay my hands on those fuckwits...'

Ellen backed up Angus's offer to pay for the damage, but Grant refused again.

'Then I'll get the children home,' she said. The ceilidh no longer seemed like a fun place to be. People were looking at them, mostly sympathetic, but she knew Angus was mortified by it and she didn't exactly enjoy it herself. 'Simon, are you sure you're OK? Shouldn't you see a doctor? That was a bad knock you had.'

'I'll be fine. I'll head back home, too.'

'I could give you a lift,' said Kit, who was still standing nearby. It was he who had looked at Angus's injuries and decided they were 'a mess but not serious'.

'No. You go back and join your party,' said Ellen firmly. She was glad now she had brought her car, and hadn't yet had more than one drink. 'I'll give Simon a lift. Come on, kids, let's get going.'

She tried to seem calm, because she could see Lucy was upset by the whole thing, but inside she was seething. The little bastards! How could they do that! Her recent annoyance with Angus was replaced by a fierce protectiveness.

Chapter Fifteen

The rest of the weekend passed quietly. Monday was the day the agricultural agent was visiting Craigallan. Ellen didn't even know if she wanted to do this any more, but it was too late to change the arrangements. As they inspected the house, and then the farm buildings and fields, she was focussed more on the anger still fizzing inside her than on plans for selling.

'Sorry?' she said, realising that the agent was waiting for a response.

'I said, do you have the deeds for the land? Going through those will be a lot easier than surveying it again from scratch. Two hundred and thirty acres, you say?'

'Or thereabouts.' Angus had once mentioned that his parents had owned two hundred and thirty-five acres, before they sold off that chunk of land to Kit. She hadn't dared ask him outright for more details.

'Fine. Well, you look out that paperwork and I'll do my sums and get back to you with a valuation. The place isn't in as good a nick as it might be, but it should still fetch a tidy sum. The sooner you get it on the market the better. We're almost in summer and spring is really the best time to sell.'

Ellen knew that already. Wasn't everyone always telling her so?

After the man had left she dawdled in front of the house, trying to concentrate, see it as others might. Monty pushed around her ankles, hoping this was the beginning of a proper walk, and she bent absently to pat him. Then she walked around the side of the house into the farm yard, and looked about here, too.

The house was a decent place, although it could do with a lick of white paint to give it that cared-for look so sought after by home-buyers. It was quaint, with its dormer windows and dark slate roof. She crossed her fingers mentally as she thought of the roof. The patching job *seemed* to be holding.

The farm buildings were of a piece with the house, the same white-painted stone walls and low slate roofs. She could imagine some soft southerner falling in love with the place, turning the buildings into a workshop or holiday homes. Why didn't the idea please her? Such possibilities would make the place easier to sell. Wanting to keep the farm as a going concern was a pipe dream, only someone as young and unrealistic as Angus would think it could happen.

Angus thought he had got school down to a fine art. He moved around when a crowd moved, kept his head down in class, did just enough work to get by. The thing was to survive by not being noticed, and then get back to his real life of Craigallan.

This meant the bruises on his face were a real disadvantage.

'Heard you had a bust up with Jason Armstrong,' said Martina McCulloch, one of the prettiest girls in his class, who normally acted as though Angus didn't exist. She examined his face in fascination. 'So it's true?'

Angus mumbled something and turned away, only to find two of the football stars eyeing him from the other side. 'The police went round to Jason's house. His dad's fuming,' said one helpfully.

'I didn't tell the police anything.' Although Angus had a feeling Kit had made his own enquiries, and passed what he knew on to the police.

'You should have done. He's a pig,' said Martina unexpectedly.

'How many of them were there?' asked one of the footballers. 'I bet he wasn't on his own. He never does anything on his own.'

'I dunno.' Angus swung his bag onto his shoulder and made to turn away again, but more of the class had arrived and the questions kept on coming.

He was surprised they were mostly sympathetic, but he just wished they would leave him alone. The fight and its aftermath, the mess in Grant's van, the fact that Simon Scott had been dragged into it, they were all best forgotten. He made sure he sat at the back of his classes and kept his head down. He didn't need questions from the teachers as well.

He forced himself to brave the queue in the canteen, and although he saw Jason and his gang scowling at him from a distance, they didn't come near. They were probably still wondering what he had said to the police. Let them worry a bit longer.

And then Simon Scott came over to him, sauntering away from a group of youths his own age. He bent to study Angus's injuries.

'You look a mess,' he said cheerfully.

Angus tried to smile in an off-hand way, which hurt his lip. 'I'm OK. How're you? I'm really sorry about – you know–'

Simon shrugged expansively. 'Not your fault. Bunch of bastards.' He had survived the fight better than Angus, with only a bruise on his forehead. He touched this now. 'Still, gives you a kind of kudos, doesn't it? I hear they're claiming we hit them first. I hope you throw a good punch, can't remember I did much damage myself. Hitting my head kind of slowed me down.'

'I didn't do much,' said Angus, but was flattered all the same.

'Anyway, what I came over to say was, are you

still up for joining the band? I hope so, but if not we'll need to start looking for someone else.'

'Me? Er, are you sure...?'

'Dead sure. You play great.'

'Well. Thanks.'

'That's fine then. I'll set up a practice and let you know.'

Simon wandered back to his own friends and the girls behind Angus in the queue nudged him to move forwards.

'Ooh, aren't you the big boy, friendly with the Third Years,' said one of them, but for once he didn't mind.

After the auctioneer's visit, Ellen took the car down to pick up the younger two from school and drop them at dancing and golf. Then she went to collect Angus. He wouldn't be pleased, he seemed to prefer getting the bus, but she didn't care. She wanted to make sure he was all right.

She parked outside the school gates, in a place Angus would have to pass on his way to the bus stop. She waved him down and he climbed into the passenger seat. He didn't complain, but he didn't look in the least bit grateful.

'How was school?' she said brightly as she pulled away from the kerb, avoiding the hordes of teenagers who seemed to find it impossible to walk on the pavement.

'OK.'

'Did anyone say anything about Friday night?'

Angus did his thin-shouldered shrug. Sometimes it made her want to shake him. And if he hid behind that fringe one more time she was going to cut it off herself.

They drove to the golf course which was on the northern edge of the town. They had fifteen minutes to wait so now was as good a time as any to ask a few questions.

'Ang – I mean, Sam – are you happy at the school? You know what I said about changing schools – we can still organise that. If you want?'

'It's all right.'

Ellen sighed. She changed tack. 'Simon Scott seems a nice boy. Did you see anything of him today?'

'Mmm, sort of.'

'How is he?'

'Fine, he said.'

'And is this band thing going ahead.'

'Maybe. He said he'd fix something up.' Angus tried to sound as though he didn't care, but Ellen was delighted.

'That's great. Just let me know when, and I'll take you into town if need be.'

'It probably won't happen.' He looked at her briefly from beneath the pale hair. He had a large bruise down one side of his face as well as a burst lip. He looked a mess. 'Look, don't make such a big thing of it, OK? What does it matter anyway, if we're moving to Edinburgh?'

'Sometimes you sound just like a teenager,' she said, trying to make a joke of it.

Angus turned to look out of the side window, and didn't answer.

It was only when she spoke to her mother that evening that she realised another reason why he might have been upset by her words.

'I was thinking of coming down next week, if your father is still doing all right.'

'That's good,' said Ellen, although she wasn't sure that it was. Now she would have to think about where her mother would sleep, and how to distract her from talking endlessly about Jess or, still worse, asking questions about Ellen.

'I thought I'd come down on Thursday and stay for the weekend, although of course that depends on what you have arranged for Angus's birthday. Thirteen in just over a week. I can't believe it. Such a landmark.'

'What?' said Ellen faintly. She had forgotten entirely about Angus's birthday. Her mother had mentioned it when they visited Stirling at Easter, but it had seemed so far off she hadn't given it a moment's thought. And now it was a week away and she had arranged nothing. Worse, Angus knew she had arranged nothing. No wonder he felt unloved.

'I can't help thinking how excited Jessica would have been,' her mother was saying sadly. 'She did like a good party, do you remember the one she arranged for our ruby wedding anniversary? All of you came here and we had that lovely garden party. She was so good at that kind of thing.'

'Yes,' said Ellen quickly. Her mother had started this sort of reminiscence more and more, and Ellen wasn't sure she could stand it. 'We haven't quite decided what to do for Angus's birthday, although of course it would be lovely to have you here, whatever happens. I'll phone you at the weekend, shall I, and we can sort out details? Now, tell me how Dad is.'

When she finally drew the conversation to a close, Ellen took herself outside with Monty. She plodded through the upper fields. The sun was sinking and already there was dew on the lengthening grass. It was a beautiful evening.

Unfortunately, it wasn't only the grass that was growing now the warmer weather and longer days had arrived. She could already make out patches of nettles and thistles, and what looked distinctly like young bracken. She remembered all too well the endless battles Sam used to fight with the bracken – it had been his pet hate and was one of the few things about which he could become quite loquacious. Ellen kicked at one of the young stems and sighed. It was her problem now.

She stopped suddenly and turned that thought over in her mind. Her problem? When had it become *her* problem? Wasn't she just about to put the place on the market and get shot of it? She'd had more than enough of leaking roofs, ailing animals, and broken gates. She was a lecturer, she wasn't meant to deal with situations like this.

But she wasn't meant, in her own plan for life, to be left with three children to look after, either.

She turned in a slow circle, taking in the rising hills, the darkening sky above, the misty green of the fields sloping down towards the copse, with Craigallan tucked away in the shadow at the bottom. The only sounds were the sheep, the trickle of the myriad small streams, and the panting of Monty as he returned from rabbiting to check on his pack leader. He looked doubtfully up at Ellen, wiry head on one side. Why have you stopped, he seemed to be asking. What's going on here?

This is ridiculous, Ellen told herself. There is no way on earth you can cope with running Craigallan. Forget it.

Later, when she was putting Lucy to bed, she asked her in a whisper what she thought they should do to make Angus's birthday special, as though she had been planning this secret approach all along. Lucy giggled delightedly and agreed to think of possible treats.

Kit Ballantyne considered himself a patient man, but even he was growing frustrated with the lack of progress on the house. He was wasting the best months of the year for outdoor work due to on-going delays from Building Control, and he was sure they were doing it on purpose. Some people just seemed to adore the little bit of power bureaucracy gave them.

He wasn't in the best of moods when his latest phone call to the council offices had ended in a vague promise of something 'by the end of the week, probably'. They had pointed out once again that if his proposed house had been of 'a standard construction' it wouldn't have taken them nearly as long to process the paperwork.

He realised he was going to have to bring in outside contractors if he wanted to make decent progress before the autumn. And, after all, it was just a wooden house. Anyone could throw it up, couldn't they? As long as you paid them.

But even if he did give in and get professionals to do a lot of the work, he still needed to be on hand to supervise. That was the reason he gave people for not wanting to move down to Deer Bridge and live with his mother. He didn't mention Craigallan and the animals.

Later he went out into the soft evening to review again the half-dug foundations and septic tank. Recent rain had made them little more than ugly, unnaturally shaped ponds, but if he tried he could see them for what they were. The beginning of something special. Tomorrow morning he would get on to a couple of local building firms and see when they could let him have a team of joiners. And he would give the timber merchants a definite delivery date. That would give him something to aim for.

He watched Ellen as she walked up the hill behind Craigallan with the dog in her wake. Seeing her put his own problems into perspective. He hadn't lost a dearly loved sister, nor had to uproot a perfectly planned life. The fact that he had never had a perfectly planned life was beside the point.

Sitting talking to her at the ceilidh had made him realise something. He wasn't sure what, yet, but it would come to him. He waited to see if she would turn in his direction, whether she might even come and talk over that awful incident with Angus, but she carried on, walking slowly up and over the ridge to where the horses were. Disappointed, he turned back to the caravan.

Chapter Sixteen

Angus had been looking forward to seeing his gran. He hadn't told anyone he missed her, because they wouldn't be interested. And then, when he came home from school early, he overheard his aunt on the telephone and everything else was forgotten.

'Yes, I would definitely like you to put it on the market,' she was saying. 'I'm happy enough with the particulars you've e-mailed me, and we can talk about the viewing arrangements later. I'd like you to go ahead immediately. Yes, yes, of course. Yes. Thank you.'

Angus slid slowly out into the yard and headed for the byre. He had to get away before she knew he had heard. He had to get away before he killed her. All this talk of discussing things and children having the right to their opinion too. It was all rubbish, absolute bullshit. She was putting Craigallan on the market. How could she do that? It wasn't fair! She couldn't just do that. Could she?

The calves were out in the fields now but the byre still smelt of cow, and he sank down on a bale of hay, breathing it in, *not* crying.

How could he stop her? What could he do, at almost thirteen, against a grown up? He thought of going to Kit, to try and get him to make her change her mind, but what could Kit do? He wasn't family. And he knew, he just knew, that she would already have talked Gran round, she wouldn't have dared do this without discussing it with her first. He'd planned to persuade Gran of a few things of his own over the weekend. But he had left it too late.

He had visions of himself uprooting the For Sale sign and burning it, of petrol-bombing viewers' cars, of catapulting stones at them as they toured the fields. It made him feel very slightly better, just to imagine the satisfaction it would give him. He pushed his fringe back from his eyes. Stupid hair, always getting in his way.

After half an hour or so, when he heard Callum and Lucy's voices and knew he wouldn't attract particular attention, he slipped back into the house and up to his room.

When Angus came down stairs, Ellen stared at him, aghast. 'What...?'

He scowled at her, his face pale and set. And his hair shaven to the scalp.

'What have you done to your hair?' she said, stupidly.

He put up a hand and touched the stubble that was left. 'I cut it.'

'But...' Ellen had thought she could no longer be surprised, but she was wrong. He looked, quite frankly, awful. The stark, uneven cut did not suit his bony face and made the bruises all the more prominent. 'How did you do it?' And why?

'Used that razor thing Mum had. It was easy.'

Ellen remembered, vaguely, that Jess used to cut Sam and the boys' hair, but she would never have dared herself. She hadn't even known where

185

the electric cutters were, but Angus clearly had. 'If you wanted it cut, I could have taken you to a hairdresser's.' She remembered how the fringe had irritated her, but she hadn't got as far as suggesting doing something about it. Had he suspected?

'I don't need a hairdresser's. Mum said they were a waste of money. You're always wasting money.'

'What will your grandmother say?' said Ellen. It sounded feeble but it was the only thing she could think of just then. They were just about to leave for the station.

Angus was slinking out of the back door when Callum and Lucy burst in. 'Auntie Ellen, can we... Jesus, what have you done?' This was Callum.

'Angus has cut his hair,' said Lucy in awe. She put a hand protectively to the blonde locks that now reached to her shoulders, and were a nightmare to keep tidy. 'Did you do it all by yourself?'

'Cool,' said Callum, walking slowly round his older brother. 'Makes you look really tough. Can you do me too?'

'We haven't time to discuss this now,' said Ellen, more calmly than she felt. 'You need to finish all your chores before we go to collect Gran. So scoot!'

'I don't need to go to the station,' said Angus, not looking at her. 'There's a lot to do. I'm old enough to stay here alone now.'

Ellen shook her head, both a negative and an indication of despair. She thought Angus was looking forward to seeing his grandmother. She didn't think she would ever understand him.

Kit was pleased to be invited to Craigallan for Angus's birthday tea. It would take his mind off his mother, who he had taken on a depressing and inconclusive visit to the hospital earlier that day. He hadn't seen Ellen properly since the ceilidh. Now he had the afternoon off work, and was determined to make the most of it.

Ellen had told him the tea – a traditional afternoon tea, to be held when the children came home from school – was to be a secret and not to mention it to Angus. He wasn't sure that it was the sort of secret a thirteen year old would appreciate, but what did he know? He did as he was told and appeared at the kitchen door at four o'clock, clean if not smart, in moleskin trousers and a denim shirt.

He entered to find Ellen and Angus mid-argument.

'You've what?' said the boy. 'You've invited Simon Scott here? What made you think he would want to come? And why couldn't you ask me first? Why...?'

'We thought it would be a nice surprise,' said his grandmother, who was hovering anxiously in the background. 'Someone your own age.'

'He's not my age. I hardly know him. Who else have you invited?' Angus was shouting now.

Kit made a gesture to Ellen that perhaps he should retreat, but she shook her head. 'Here's Kit. We invited him as well. I suppose that's all right?'

Angus swung round and whatever else he had been about to shout died on his lips. He was too

187

polite, or shy, to have a tantrum in front of neighbours. 'Hullo,' he muttered, dropping his head. He had done something very strange to his hair. It made him look older and more vulnerable at the same time, especially along with the quite spectacular bruises.

'Happy Birthday,' said Kit cheerily. He thrust out a parcel which he hoped to goodness was suitable. 'Here.'

Angus took the present but gave his aunt another murderous glare. He stood with the package in his hands, as though he didn't know what to do with it. None of the ripping of paper and whoops of joy or disappointment that Kit recalled from his own childhood. But Angus wasn't a child any more, wasn't that what he was telling them?

'Open it then,' said Ellen.

'Here's Clare,' said her mother, glancing out of the front window. 'It's just a few neighbours, Angus, that's all.'

Kit cringed, waiting for some complaint about the name, but Angus didn't bother. He stood as near the door as he could without actually leaving the room. When Clare handed him her present he held both packages in his hands, still refusing to open them. Kit wanted to kick him. Ellen had gone to a lot of trouble.

He saw exactly how much trouble when she led them nervously through to the dining room a few minutes later. It was a dark room that Kit had never seen in use, but this afternoon there was a white cloth on the old wooden table, laden with plates of sausages, scotch eggs, sandwiches, crisps, and cakes. On the wall above the mantel-piece was a banner that Lucy had obviously been involved in making. It said HELLO TAENAGer and HApPY BIRThDAY SAMUEL ANgUS. There were balloons everywhere. Kit tensed, waiting to see how Angus would react. Ellen looked equally anxious.

Angus said nothing at all, but at least he didn't walk straight back out.

Ten minutes later the front door bell rang. It had to be the boy, Simon, as anyone familiar with the house would have gone to the kitchen door. The desultory conversation halted. Angus made no move to go and answer it. If anything, he hunched himself lower and smaller.

Callum, however, had no reservations. He put down his glass with a bang and leapt up. 'I'll go.' At least he and Lucy seemed to be enjoying the occasion.

Kit recalled Simon Scott vaguely from the fight at the ceilidh. He was a tall boy with curly hair and a ready smile. He followed Callum back into the room, looking about with interest.

'Hi there,' he said cheerfully, thrusting another parcel towards Angus. 'Happy Birthday and all that.'

'Thanks.' Angus had managed to shed his other parcels, unopened. He looked around for some-where to put this one.

Simon continued breezily, 'I'll tell you what it is if you like. It's the guitar book I've been using to practice. It's in my own interest to give it to you, like, so you can practice the same stuff. That is, if you're still interested in joining us? I haven't had a chance to arrange anything yet 'cos all the Third Years have been doing work experience. God, what a waste of time...

The adults melted away towards the window and left the two boys to themselves. For the first time since Kit's arrival, Angus didn't look like he was about to scream or burst into tears. He didn't say much, but with Simon that didn't seem to matter. He opened the parcel slowly and held the music book in his hands as though it was something fragile.

'Have some more tea,' said Ellen's mother to Kit. 'And tell me how you're getting on with your house. Frank and I always thought it was such a fascinating idea...'

Ellen wished that it was appropriate to have wine with a high tea. She was shattered and desperately needed something to buck her up. Coffee would have to do. She escaped to the kitchen to make another pot. While the kettle was boiling, she sat down at the table and rested her head in her hands. She was doing this all wrong, but she didn't know where to start to try and do it better.

'Are you OK?' said Clare, coming quietly into the room, and making Ellen sit quickly upright.

'Yes, fine.' She began spooning filter coffee into the pot. 'I love the smell of fresh coffee, don't you?'

'Heavenly,' agreed Clare, but she was still examining Ellen closely. 'You've arranged a really great party here.'

'I got it wrong,' said Ellen crisply. 'It would've been more suitable for Lucy. I should've realised that when she was so excited about it.'

'She loved the idea of a secret.'

'Yes.' Ellen shuddered. They had kept the party so secret she had been afraid that Angus wouldn't turn up at all. She had had to tell him in advance that Simon was coming to stop him storming out into the fields straight after school. She hadn't been able to speak to him at breakfast as she had hoped because he had spent all the time before school outside. His grandmother kept saying how worried she was about him, which didn't help.

Ellen poured boiling water onto the coffee grounds and breathed in the delicious fragrance. She said brightly, 'Right, best get back through before they start throwing sausage rolls at each other. Isn't that what teenagers do?'

'Not these ones,' said Clare. 'I'm glad to see their wounds are healing. It was a horrible fight, wasn't it?'

'Yes,' said Ellen shortly, and headed back towards the laughter and happy voices. At least it was starting to sound like a party.

'Why don't you show Simon your new guitar?' Ellen said to Angus, a little later. She had tried so hard to find an appropriate present, and had hummed and hawed over this. Electric guitars didn't come cheap. So far, Angus hadn't even taken it out of its box.

'It's an electric,' said Callum enviously. 'A Fender something. Ang ... Sam's been wanting one for ages but he hasn't played this yet. Maybe he's scared he won't be able to?'

'I've got a Fender,' said Simon. 'They're great. Can I see?'

191

'If you want,' said Angus. The three boys left the room, Angus easily the least enthusiastic.

'What's wrong with him?' said Clare. 'I thought he'd be over the moon. And music is one thing you can do in a city or the country.'

'Maybe that's the problem,' said Ellen. Yes, maybe that was the problem. Angus was very tense about something and she still hadn't told him of her decision. The sooner they got that out of the way the better. She wished she hadn't arranged for Simon to stay all evening.

'Ooh, look, six o'clock,' she said. 'Time for a proper drink. Who's for wine? Beer? A double whisky?'

Angus remained in his room when Simon's parents appeared to collect their son. It was one of the many things Ellen found irksome, the children's inability to say a proper hello or good-bye to visitors. Angus had grunted something from the door of his bedroom. The fact that Simon seemed to find this perfectly acceptable didn't make it any better. On top of everything else that day, she was ready to explode.

'I'll go up and see how he is, shall I?' said her mother. She was tired from the journey the previous day, the lines of worry seemed permanently etched on her face. Did Angus think he was the only one with problems?

'I'll go,' said Ellen grimly.

She knocked on the door and entered without waiting for an invitation, just in case none was forthcoming. That was another thing she was unfamiliar with – the etiquette of entering teen-

192

agers' bedrooms.

'We're all tidying up the dining room. I know it's your birthday but you could come and keep us company, at least. Your Gran has come down specially to see you and all you do is hang around outside or hide up here.'

Angus put a hand to his shaven head. Ellen had made an attempt at tidying it, so that it was now short all over. It still looked awful. 'I thought you wanted me to play my guitar.'

'I thought you might *want* to play it while Simon was here. And you seemed to be having fun. Were you?'

'It was OK.'

'Good.' Ellen took a deep breath, battling to keep her temper. 'Are you going to join his band?' Angus shrugged. She wanted to slap him. 'Simon seemed keen on the idea.'

Angus hadn't met her eyes since she entered the room, but now he dropped his head right down. 'What's the point?'

'The point is to have fun, do something, not mope around here on your own the whole time.'

'I mean, what's the point if we're leaving Craigallan?'

'What?' said Ellen. 'Who said anything about leaving?'

'Oh, you didn't. Not to us, anyway.' He raised his head long enough to shoot her a venomous look from pale eyes.

'Actually, I've been wanting to talk to you about that, but it's difficult when you're never there.'

'It's OK, I know already. I heard you on the phone. When do we have to move?'

193

'You...? What are you talking about?' Angus was sitting on the one chair in the room. Ellen dropped onto the carelessly made bed. This wasn't how she had planned the conversation, but you had to take whatever opportunities arose. 'What did you hear on the phone?'

'You've put this place on the market.' He scuffed his feet on the carpet. 'You've put Craig-allan up for sale without even telling us! I thought you said Mum and Dad had left Craig-allan to me and the kids? So how can you go and sell it? I suppose you want the money, that's what it is, isn't it? You're fed up of forking out for us all the time and you want to go back to your nice life in Edinburgh and...'

He paused to draw breath and Ellen said loudly, 'Actually, I haven't put Craigallan on the market.'

'I told you, I heard...'

'I've put my Edinburgh flat on the market. I thought if what you all really wanted was to stay down here, then that was what we should do. So you're getting what you want, all right?' She had raised her voice so much that it ended in a shout. 'All right?'

The silence that followed was total. Angus slowly raised his head. His shoulders unclenched. He swallowed. 'Stay here?'

'Yes. If that's what you want.' The anger was still surging through Ellen, although all opposition had gone from her nephew. 'Or perhaps you feel we should discuss it first? As you say, I shouldn't make all these decisions on my own. Perhaps Cal-lum and Lucy want to move to Edinburgh. Shall

194

we ask them? As you're so good at discussing things, Angus.'

He didn't respond to her tone. After a long pause he said, 'Why didn't you say anything?'

'I haven't had much chance, have I?' She had struggled so long to be patient with him, now she didn't care. 'Your Gran and I were going to break the news over breakfast this morning, a sort of extra birthday present. But you weren't there. You're never there, are you?'

'I've got work to do.'

'We've all got work to do. Life's difficult for everyone. Try thinking of someone other than yourself for a change.'

'You don't understand...'

'No, I don't! And how am I ever going to, when you hardly speak to me? You need to make some effort too. You're forever sneaking off outside.'

'There's things I have to do,' said Angus, but his tone was no longer belligerent. He still seemed in shock.

'We've all got things to do! But at least some of us tell others what we're doing and where we're going to be. I think it's time you started showing a little more consideration.'

Angus seemed hardly to hear her. He sat back and put his guitar aside. 'We can really stay here?'

She sighed, the fight seeping out of her. 'That's what I was thinking, but there are a lot of things we still need...'

He didn't wait for her to finish. He grinned suddenly. 'We should go and tell the kids,' he said, jumping up. 'We don't want them to feel left out.'

Ellen opened her mouth to say more. There was

195

still an awful a lot to discuss. But he had already gone, leaping down the stairs two at a time.

'Cal and Luce where are you?' he shouted. 'Come here. I've got something to tell you. Cal!'

Ellen followed reluctantly. The good news was easy to give, but what about the rest?

Chapter Seventeen

'We're going to stay at Craigallan?' said Callum, a huge smile on his face. 'Really?'

They had congregated, as ever, in the kitchen. Lucy was curled up on the floor with Monty, the boys sitting at the table with their grandmother. Ellen was leaning against the Rayburn. She felt in need of support.

'I'm glad you're pleased,' she said.

'When did you decide?' asked Angus. The next question was unspoken: *and why didn't you tell us straight away?*

'I don't know,' said Ellen cautiously. 'I've only been sure these last few days. And there's still a lot we need to talk about.'

'But we are staying *here?*' he asked quickly, looking about the room as though it might be about to disappear.

'That depends. If that is what you want – what we all want – then we can carry on living at Craigallan. I have, in any case, put my flat in Edinburgh on the market. There is no way all of us could live there, even if we moved to the city.'

'But we're not moving, are we?'

'Not unless you want to.' Ellen looked around at them all. Callum and Angus seemed happy, or as happy as Angus could manage. Lucy was stroking the dog's tufty ears. So far she had said nothing. 'Realistically, there is nothing to stop us living in this house. The mortgage is paid off, you like it here, and there are schools nearby which ... well, we can talk about schools later.'

'The Academy's OK,' said Angus quickly.

'But what we can't do long term is run Craigallan as a farm. Not while you are all so young.'

Now she had the full attention of all three children. 'But...' said Angus.

His grandmother had been looking from one to the other as the conversation progressed. Now she put a hand on her elder grandson's shoulder. 'Angus, darling, Ellen and I have talked about this. There is no way you can manage this place between you.'

'We can. We are doing.'

'We're not doing it properly,' said Ellen. 'We're just getting by. And we're relying hugely on Kit to help, which is unrealistic. What will happen when things start to get difficult, when fences need fixing, vets bills paying, silage cut? All of those things? I can't do those, Angus.'

'But I can. And Cal will help. Or we can get someone in to do them.'

'You boys are too young to take on the responsibility, even if you could do it. You've got school. It's not possible. I'm not saying that we need to sell absolutely all the animals, we could keep a few acres if that's what you want, and keep, say, a

197

dozen sheep?'

'You're going to sell the land?' Angus had shrugged his grandmother's hand away and was sitting tall and tense again.

'No, we'll look to rent it out. When you're older you can decide for yourselves what you want to do with it.'

'You're going to sell our animals?'

'We'll have to. I can't look after them. And nor can you, not properly.'

'Why not? I can! And you could learn, Mum and Dad did...'

'Angus, I'll need to find a job. I won't have the time.'

'You don't want to, that's what you mean, isn't it? You don't want to so we can't. It's always what *you* want.'

'Angus, that isn't fair,' said his grandmother.

Angus looked down at his clenched fists. Ellen had known this would be difficult, that it wouldn't be enough to stay at Craigallan if they couldn't farm it too.

'As I said, we'll be able to keep some of the animals. Angus, we have to be realistic.'

'Don't call me Angus!' he said fiercely. 'I could do it. If you'd let me try. I could...'

'No,' said Ellen.

His grandmother patted his hand. 'Ang ... Sam, we've all got to make compromises. Ellen is doing a lot, moving down here, giving up her job. You...'

Angus did what he did best, and got up and left the room.

'Well, I'm glad that went so well,' said Ellen.

When Ellen brought Lucy back from her swimming lesson a few days later, she found Kit in the yard talking to her eldest nephew. She sighed. They were probably discussing her wickedness in wanting to divest herself of the animals. Angus was refusing to speak to her about it, but she doubted he would have the same reservations with Kit. When she approached, however, she discovered they were discussing the best way to treat sheep's feet. She didn't even know that sheep's feet needed 'treating'. See, wasn't that proof she was making the right decision?

She said to Kit, 'I was hoping to have a chat with you. Do you want to come in for a coffee when you've finished out here?'

'No problem. Can you give me five minutes?'

Ellen started peeling potatoes for the evening meal and put some mince on to brown. She was getting so good at this mum thing it scared her. In Edinburgh she had lived off salad or ready-made meals, unless she was entertaining. Now it came as second nature to cook 'proper' food, and to take in to consideration all the children's likes and dislikes. This meant they had mince and tatties or bangers and mash far more often than she would have chosen, but she always made sure they had one or two healthy veg along with it.

'All right if I just wash my hands?' said Kit when he came in ten minutes later.

'Of course.' Ellen listened to see if Angus had accompanied him, and felt guilty when she was relieved that he hadn't. 'I've put the kettle on for coffee, or would you rather have a beer?'

'A beer'd be great. Chasing sheep can be thirsty work. They're gey stupid animals.'

'I noticed,' said Ellen, taking two beers from the fridge. She poured the boiling water on to the potatoes, pushed that pan and the mince to the cooler end of the Rayburn, then took a seat opposite Kit at the table. 'Has Angus said anything to you?'

'No, I don't think so.' He raised his eyebrows, interested. 'What about?' He had sluiced his face as well as washing his hands and he looked shiny and clean, if as dishevelled as ever. It was strange how someone who made so little effort could look so attractive. Ellen probably looked as scruffy herself, but she was sure it didn't suit her. She should make more effort. But what was the point of dressing up and putting on make-up if you were only going to meet animals and children? And Kit, of course, not that he noticed her appearance.

'About Craigallan.' She paused to take a drink from her bottle. 'I've decided not to sell. No, don't say anything, let me tell you the whole lot before you start approving.' So she told him quickly that she was selling her flat in Edinburgh and would be moving to live down here on a permanent basis, but that she had also decided that they couldn't run the farm any longer and the land and animals would have to go.

'I wanted to tell you for a number of reasons,' she continued, before he could comment. 'I wanted you to know that we'll be selling most of the animals, even if we are staying, so Angus is still dead against it. But you won't be called on to help us out for much longer, which is good, isn't it? I wanted to thank you again for all you've done for us.' He seemed about to speak, but she ploughed on. 'Also, do you have any idea who farms the land adjacent, and whether they might want to rent our fields? And finally, I've agreed with Angus that he can keep a small number of animals, and I mean small, only as many as he can reasonably take care of himself, but I've no idea what that might be, so I wanted your opinion.'

As she had been speaking Kit had listened carefully, a slow smile spreading across his broad features, brown eyes crinkling. Even when she mentioned letting out the land, he didn't throw up his hands in horror. She hadn't meant to seek his approval, because she hadn't expected it, but now she said, 'So you think I'm doing the right thing?' For the first time in a while, her heart felt lighter.

'I think you're doing great,' he said, swinging the chair back on two legs and shaking the sun-bleached hair from his eyes. 'I'm in no position to advise you on whether you're doing the right thing, maybe there isn't even *one* right thing, but I'm glad you're staying.'

She smiled back. Amazingly, she was glad too. All she said was, 'The kids are relieved. I was mad to think about uprooting them, when they have already had such a shock. But Angus wants to keep the farm going. I'm not sure how much is for himself and how much is for the memory of his parents, but he's pretty cut up about the thought of selling off the animals.'

Kit shrugged, as though this wasn't that important. 'He'll come round.' He grinned broadly.

201

'So you're staying?'

'It looks like it.'

The one beer turned to two. Ellen found a note pad amongst the clutter that had accumulated on the dresser and began to write down some of Kit's ideas. He knew two of the neighbouring farmers who might be interested in the land, and suggested which one she should call first.

Then they moved on to discussing animals, at which point Callum put his head round the door. 'When're we going to eat? Can I have a packet of crisps?'

'Heavens.' Ellen jumped up and stirred the mince. 'I'll put the peas and sweetcorn on now, it won't take five minutes. Will you stay, Kit? Plenty to go round.'

'I wouldn't say no.' He seemed happy. Ellen wondered what could have happened to make him so.

Kit made a point of seeking out Angus the following evening. They usually came across one another in the course of their animal husbandry, and often exchanged a few words but normally they spoke only about practical things. Kit hadn't had much success when he tried to broach the subject of school, and now he had to do something even more difficult. He wasn't sure how to start.

'I bet you're pleased to be staying here?' he said as they manoeuvred ewes and lambs from the lower to the upper fields. He could hear the falsely cheery note in his voice, and wasn't surprised at the scowl Angus threw his way.

'Hmm,' he grunted.

'Craigallan's a great place,' said Kit encouragingly.

'Craigallan's a farm. That's why Mum and Dad bought it.'

'Ye-es.' Kit didn't know what to say. 'But your mum and dad aren't here now' was far too cruel.

'Has she told you what she's going to do?' asked Angus abruptly.

'Ellen mentioned you're thinking about renting out some of the land.'

'*She's* thinking about it. And what she wants to do she does.' Angus kicked a mole hill which was more solid than he expected and made him stumble. He looked very like the child he claimed not to be, lost and vulnerable.

Kit cleared his throat. Giving the youngster a hug, which was what he most wanted to do, would not solve anything. 'Your aunt has agreed to stay here. That's not necessarily doing what she wants. And I know she thinks you should keep some of the animals.'

'It's not enough,' said Angus.

Kit wanted to say, 'well, it's all you're getting.' How did Ellen manage to stay cheerful in the face of this? He continued in the same bright tone. 'Do you think Lucy will want to keep the pony? We've got to be practical about this. And the hens are supposed to be Callum's, aren't they? Do you think he'll want to keep them?'

'Why don't you ask them?' said Angus. 'I'm keeping Melly. I don't care what anyone says, I'm keeping her and the calf. And my own ewes, the Suffolk crosses. They're mine, Dad bought them for me, she can't make me sell them.'

'Well, that doesn't sound impossible,' said Kit quickly, before the list could grow any longer. 'I don't think that sounds too unreasonable at all. Why don't we go and talk to Lucy and Cal now and see what we can sort out?'

'I don't see why you get landed with arranging all this,' said Angus. 'Why doesn't she do it?' But he followed Kit back down to the farm buildings and stayed to listen while he negotiated with the youngsters. Kit felt he had made some progress. Ellen would be pleased, and he had gone a little further towards making up for the awful wrong he had done Jess and Sam.

Chapter Eighteen

Kit parked his muddy estate car outside Clare's cottage and climbed slowly out. He and Clare were friendly enough, but he'd never previously visited her uninvited. It had never occurred to him to do so. He felt uncomfortable because he was only calling now because he wanted information.

He tried to think of some plausible excuse for his arrival, but couldn't.

Grace answered the door. 'Oh, it's you. Mum's in the workshop.' She stood and looked at him through tangled hair.

'Do you think I should go through?'

'If you want. I'll show you.' The child set off with a skip, leaving Kit to close the door and follow. The cottage was small, chaotic, and colourful, rather like Clare herself.

'I hope I'm not disturbing you,' he said as he peered in through the open doorway of the workshop. 'I...'

Fortunately Clare didn't seem to need any explanation for his arrival. 'Great to see you. Any excuse for a hot drink. You will have one?' She flicked her hair over one shoulder and stood up. Kit looked around the workshop with interest. There was a massive barrel of what was presumably wet clay, wrapped in multiple layers of plastic, a foot-powered turning wheel, and any number of partially completed artefacts, from the grey uncast to the fully painted. Clare had been in the process of removing items from the kiln.

'You make some lovely stuff,' he said appreciatively. Apart from the candle holder she had given to Ellen, he hadn't seen much of it before.

'Glad you like it. Perhaps you can commission some amazing and original pieces for your new house when it's finished? I'll give you a good price.' Clare grinned. 'Come on through to the kitchen. Tea or coffee? Something herbal?'

Compared to Craigallan, the kitchen here was tiny, but like the rest of the house it was full of colour. One wall was canary yellow, another sky blue, and the tiles behind the sink were a hand-painted rainbow. Clare pulled out a ladder-back chair beside the small table. 'Have a seat. How's the building work going?'

'Actually,' said Kit in a surprised tone, 'It's not going too badly. Building Control are being fairly reasonable and the foundations have been dug. If it doesn't rain tomorrow, I'm having the cement delivered to fill them in.'

'Wow. Amazing. You're doing really well.'

'Yes. It's only taken me, what, nine months to get this far.'

'Jess and Sam were in Craigallan for ten years and they didn't make much progress with that.'

'Mmm,' said Kit. Even Clare's bright smile dimmed as she recalled that mention of Jess and Sam was not a happy topic of conversation. 'And look how I'm getting on here. Not.' She waved a hand around. 'No skirting boards, no curtains.'

'You've got the place very nice. Those tiles are great.'

'Yes, they are, aren't they? They were an experiment and I think they worked out really well. But it's the finishing off I'm not so good at. Look, I was supposed to seal the edge here between them and the sink but somehow...' Clare laughed and brought two mugs to the table. It didn't seem to worry her that water dripped down behind the porcelain sink every time she turned on the tap.

'Have you heard that Ellen has decided to stay with the kids at Craigallan?' he asked, working around to the topic he really wanted to discuss.

'Yes. Good on her. I think it's the right thing to do, although I have to say I was surprised.'

'Yes, I think we all were.' Kit took a sip. 'The kids are relieved. Even Angus, I think, although you wouldn't necessarily know it.'

'He's a strange boy,' said Clare. 'Always was. It's good news for the village school, isn't it?'

'Is it?'

'It'll keep the numbers up, which is essential if

we're going to fight closure. Losing Cal and Lucy would have been a blow. And now Ellen'll have to join the Parent Council and I can rope her in to help with the campaign. We need all the support we can get.'

'Oh,' said Kit. He wanted to talk about Ellen, but not the school or the children. 'It must be quite a wrench for her, leaving the city life behind.'

'You should know. Weren't you enjoying the bright lights of Sydney before you came back here?'

'It wasn't Sydney, exactly. And I was coming back to something I knew, whereas Ellen...'

'It's good she's made up her mind,' said Clare firmly. 'It wasn't doing any of them any good, the not knowing. I wanted her to go and see an astrologer friend of mine, see if that would help her make her decision, but she wasn't keen.'

'No.' Kit had to smile. 'No, I don't suppose she would be.'

'It's a perfectly sensible place to seek advice,' said Clare, not taking offence.

Kit cleared his throat. 'I suppose this means things with that Edinburgh boyfriend of Ellen's aren't going so well, then.' He let the comment hang.

Clare grinned, dark eyes laughing from behind that mass of hair. Kit fidgeted. This was important. 'I suppose it does,' she said.

'Has she, er, said anything?'

'Anything about...?'

Kit sighed. Maybe it wasn't the done thing to go asking questions behind Ellen's back, but Ellen wasn't the communicative sort, and there were some things you just had to know. 'I would have thought he'd want her to move back to Edinburgh.'

'I got the impression that he'd love her to move back, but that he wasn't so keen on the kids.'

'Oh,' said Kit. 'Poor Ellen.'

'I don't think she's that bothered.' Clare watched him consideringly now, no longer laughing. 'She broke up with him a while back, didn't you know?'

'Did she?' Kit couldn't keep the smile off his face. Ellen was single? This changed everything!

He looked down at his coffee, wanting to finish it quickly now. He had masses to do at home, and if he just happened to wander down to Craigallan after that, well...

'I wondered if you were interested in her yourself,' said Clare, still watching him.

'Me? Ah, well, she's a lovely person and...' Kit could feel himself blushing.

He was, literally, saved by the bell: by the little Tibetan bell that Clare had hanging by her kitchen door. A man rang it with one hand as he opened the door with the other. 'Hiya, couldn't resist, I just love that sound. Sorry I'm late.' He looked vaguely familiar, but all the same Kit was surprised when Clare raised her head to kiss the newcomer on the lips.

'This is Kit,' she said, holding on to the stranger's hand. 'You might remember him from the ceilidh? Kit, this is Grant McConnell.'

'How do you do?' said Kit. He did remember him now. This was Angus's music teacher, the one whose things had got smashed up in the fight. 'Did you manage to get your van fixed up?'

'Aye, it's fine. It was just a door hinge. And amazingly the keyboard works as good as ever.'

Kit rose. This was a good time to make his departure. 'Nice to see you again. Clare, thanks for the coffee...'

'Any time.' Clare also stood up, leaning into the younger man, tucking an arm around his waist. Kit wondered if Ellen knew about this development. 'And don't forget what I said about any commissions for your new house.' She glanced up at Grant. 'Kit's building a house near Craigallan, you know, where Angus Moffat lives?'

'Aye, I remember. That reminds me, is young Angus OK? He's missed a couple of lessons since the ceilidh. I wondered if he was avoiding me 'cos of all the hassle, like.'

Clare looked at Kit. He said, 'I think he's fine. I'll mention it to him, if you want.'

'I'd appreciate it. I should have his phone number somewhere but I haven't got around to looking it out.'

Kit frowned. During all the recent troubles only Angus's guitar and his animals had been the constants. There could well be a good reason for missing the lessons that Kit didn't know about. But if Ellen did know about it, he was surprised she hadn't phoned Grant to cancel.

He wondered if he should say anything to Clare about not mentioning this visit to Ellen but decided, on balance, it was safer just to leave it.

There was something calming about the weather today. The mist from last night's rain lingered in the hollows of the hills and drifted like smoke here and there. The fields were a deep, rich green, and the sun rising over the eastern side of the valley flooded it slowly and completely with a golden light. It felt good to be here.

Ellen still didn't know if she had made the right decision in agreeing to stay, either for the children or for herself. But today it felt good, and she would have to go with that.

Angus was still being ... Angus. They had come to a tentative agreement over animals, negotiated by Kit, but he refused to talk to her about that or anything else. After his initial euphoria about staying at Craigallan, he seemed no happier than before. He must be missing his parents, she knew that, but she wished he would let her know if there was something else as well. The fight with those horrible boys was an unresolved issue in her mind. Were they still bullying him? She had no idea.

Today Ellen had something else to think about. She had a sort of interview at the higher education college in Dumfries. It was the first job interview she had had in years and although it was supposed to be very informal she couldn't help feeling nervous.

After walking Monty through the sunny fields, and trying not to think how she would feel when the animals there no longer belonged to Craigallan, she put on a smart suit, and set off into town.

This was a familiar journey now, down through the hills, past villages that were little more than clusters of cottages, and then the scattering of

newer bungalows as you drew nearer to civilis-
ation. The trees were fully in leaf and the birds
fluttered in the hedgerows. It was a pleasant thirty-
minute drive at this time of day and this time of
year. What would it be like in winter, when time
was short and roads treacherous? Ellen remembered Jess saying that was the worst part of living
out at Craigallan, the driving into town for her
nursing shifts. But there wasn't any work nearer at
hand, so it had to be done.

Ellen had obtained this interview through her
former head of department in Edinburgh. Shirley
had been at college with one of the lecturers in
Dumfries, and in the small world that was higher
education in Scotland still bumped in to him at
conferences and seminars. She had put in a good
word for Ellen, and although she had been told
there were 'no vacancies as such, just now' she
had been invited in for a chat.

It wasn't Shirley's friend who was to interview
Ellen, but one of the senior lecturers. He introduced himself as Mark Gillespie and shook
Ellen's hand at length before ushering her into a
small, institutional office. It could have been her
own room in Edinburgh, with the books along
the walls and piles of papers to be marked, except
that here the view was out across farmland to the
Southern Uplands.

'Now, Miss Taylor, or may I call you Ellen? I
hear that you are looking for employment? You
come very highly recommended from your previous employer, but as you know funding is tight
and I'm not sure we have anything we can offer
you right at this moment.'

'I understand,' said Ellen. 'It's good of you to see me. I just wanted to let you know that I'm here, so that if you have an opening in future, you know you can call on me.'

'Excellent, excellent.' The man was in his early forties, casually dressed as befitted a college lecturer. Now that he had got the awkward matter of telling Ellen there was no work out of the way, he settled down to the interview. He asked her a little about her CV, chatted about shared acquaintances in the academic world, queried her areas of special interest. His questions were pertinent, his comments amusing, and he made it clear he was impressed with her experience. Ellen wondered why it was she didn't like him. Perhaps it was the way he threw himself back in his seat, arms raised above his head, as though putting that long, athletic body on display for her. Or the fact that he made just a little too much eye contact.

'Of course, we close for the summer in a few weeks' time,' he said. 'We're still finalising the courses for next year, dependent on student numbers. I take it you wouldn't have a problem with part-time work? And evening courses are very popular, we have a lot of mature students who combine studying with work.'

'Part-time work would suit me best,' said Ellen. He knew enough of her situation to realise that, surely? 'But I'm afraid that evenings would be difficult. The children are still young.'

'Hmm, mm,' he said non-committally. 'Well, we'll have to see what comes up. How about I have a chat with Personnel about keeping your details on file and if anything suitable arises, I'll get back in touch?'

'That would be fine,' said Ellen. She didn't want him to think that she was desperate.

'Well, why don't we go and have a coffee in the canteen and you can tell me how you're settling in to life in rural Dumfriesshire?' He ushered her down the stairs, walking a little too close. 'Must be quite a change from the hustle and bustle of Edinburgh. Have you been out in Dumfries much? Perhaps I could show you around the town one evening?'

'That's kind of you,' said Ellen politely. 'But as I said, evenings are difficult.'

He smiled. 'I'm sure you could find a babysitter if you tried. You don't want to shut yourself away in the sticks, do you?'

It felt very odd to have someone asking her out. It was so long since anyone had done that she could hardly remember it. She and Richard had been a couple for years. Strange how she hardly missed him. Not nearly as much as she missed Jess. Poor, lovely Jess. In these last few months men and relationships had been the last thing on her mind. Now here was someone, reasonably good-looking, who looked at her not as the poor aunt left with those orphan children, but as a woman, herself.

And she had no interest in him at all. Eventually, after she turned down his invitations a couple more times, he seemed to get the message.

For some reason, as Ellen drove back out to Craigallan, she remembered how Devon had dragooned Kit into taking her as his partner to the ceilidh, angled after an invite to his house. She had seen no sign of the girl since, which made her smile.

'Right,' said Ellen as the children trailed in for their evening meal. 'Time we had another talk.' The interview at the college might not have produced a job, but it had perked her up in a way she hadn't expected.

Angus immediately looked as though he wanted to leave the room. His pale hair was now a soft halo around the narrow head. His head drooped, but at least he stayed.

Ellen placed a Lancashire hotpot in the middle of the table with a pan of broccoli beside it, and began to dish out.

'I don't want much,' said Angus. 'I'm not hungry.'

'It's good for you,' said Ellen, putting a reasonable portion before him. She knew he was saying that because he wanted to leave the room.

When they had all been served she took her own place and, with a fortifying sip from her glass of water, began. 'Right. We've agreed we're going to stay here, I mean in this area. But I want to be sure you definitely want to stay in this house. It's a fair way from town, there are no neighbours very nearby, do you really want to live here?'

'Of course we do,' said Angus quickly.

'Let everyone speak for themselves. An ... Sam, you want to stay at Craigallan, yes? Now, Callum, what about you?'

Ellen smiled encouragingly at her second nephew, who looked uncomfortable to be the centre of attention. ''S fine here.'

'OK, but what would you want, if you had the choice? Here, or Kinmuir village, or Dunmuir itself? I'm not suggesting we sell Craigallan, but we could rent it out, just as we are doing with the fields.'

Callum glanced nervously at his brother and Ellen wondered if having a 'family' discussion had been the right thing to do. The younger two were bound to be influenced by what Angus said. She said gently, 'Think about it, Cal. And now, Lucy, what about you?'

'I want to live with you,' said Lucy. 'Where are you going to live?'

Ellen didn't think she had a heart that could melt, but it seemed she did. She felt tears rise to her eyes. 'We'll all live together, where ever we are. Don't worry about that, sweetheart.'

'Oh. Good. I'd like to stay at Craigallan, then, but can we move it closer to Grace's house?'

'We can't leave Craigallan. You said I could keep Melanie and the sheep. You said...' Angus hadn't touched his food. He was breathing hard, building himself up to a full-blown argument.

'Yes, that's what I said, and I keep my word.' Ellen raised her voice too, which made him pause. 'But we don't have to have them right on our doorstep, do we? We could live in the village but keep a few acres out here. I'm just consider-ing the options, Angus. Remember, you said I should discuss things with you more.'

Angus's lip curled.

'Craigallan's our house,' said Callum slowly. 'I think I'd like to stay here.'

'Even with all the walking back and forth to the village?'

'Well. It would be easier if I had a better bike,' he said, eyeing her hopefully. It was the first sign of natural cunning that Ellen had seen in her easy-going nephew, and she had to smile.

'We'll see. So, it's unanimous for Craigallan, is it?'

'Yes,' said Angus fiercely. 'Of course.'

'What about you?' said Lucy. 'Don't you have a say?'

Ellen was amazed. Perhaps she should talk to the children more. 'I'm quite happy to stay here,' she said.

'So that's all right then,' said Angus, starting to fork food into his mouth at his normal breakneck speed.

'That's just the beginning,' said Ellen, and took another deep breath. 'If we're going to stay here, we should think about what we want to do with the house.'

Angus put his fork down again. 'The house is all right.'

'What would we do?' said Callum.

'Well, we could do some redecoration.'

'Can I paint my bedroom pink?' said Lucy.

'It's a possibility. But what we need to think about is,' another even deeper breath, 'is your parents' room. We can't leave it shut up like it is for ever.'

Lucy and Callum looked at her in surprise. 'You're not having it,' said Angus.

Ellen clamped down on her irritation. She said firmly, 'We'll talk about who will have the room later. What we need to do first is sort out what's in there. You might want to keep some of the things, some of them can go. I can sort out things on my own if you want, or we can all do it together. What do you think?'

Lucy swallowed and moved fractionally closer to Ellen. Callum looked blank.

'We'll do it together,' said Angus gruffly. Ellen had the feeling he would rather have excluded her, but didn't dare.

It was a relief to have got this far. 'Right, why don't we tackle it tomorrow morning? It's Saturday, no school. How about it?'

'I was going to go to Simon's,' said Angus.

'OK, well, we can do it in the afternoon.'

'I've got a school football match in the afternoon,' said Callum.

'We'll do it in the morning. I'll tell Simon I can't go.'

'Sunday would be soon enough,' said Ellen. She didn't want to scupper any plans he had to meet up with Simon Scott. 'And in the meantime, we need to talk about what we should do with your mum and dad's room once we've sorted things out. Would one of you want to move in there?'

She waited. Three pairs of eyes turned to her but no one spoke.

'We don't have to decide now,' she said. She was going too fast. 'You can think about it.'

'Angus is the oldest,' said Lucy.

Angus narrowed his eyes at Ellen. 'You want it, don't you? You want to move in there.'

Ellen sighed. She really, really did not want to move into her dead sister's room. But she couldn't say that to him and even if she did he probably wouldn't believe her.

'I think one of you children should have it. You two boys could even share, it's big enough. But we'll talk about it again after Sunday, OK?'

On Saturday evening, as bedtime approached, Lucy crept up to her aunt and tapped her arm. 'Auntie Ellen,' she whispered. 'Can I sleep in Mummy and Daddy's bed tonight? P-please? Just this one time. I know you said I shouldn't but – please?'

All the children had wanted their parents' bed in those first dark days after their loss. It had been a struggle to get them back to the normality of their own rooms.

'I don't know...'

'Let her, why not?' said Angus. 'It's the last chance she's going to have.'

That evening he went in and sat with Lucy after Ellen had read her story. She didn't hear the sound of voices. Eventually, when he came out, he went to the bathroom and spent a long time in there before retreating to his own room. She guessed they had both been crying.

Callum said nothing, but watched movies on television until he was so sleepy she had to guide him up the stairs.

Chapter Nineteen

Kit had done the sensible thing and arranged for extra carers to go in and help his mother. She wasn't as mobile as she used to be and everything was an effort, getting herself up and about, preparing meals, seeing to the house.

He was pretty sure the time had come for her to think about moving into a care home, but he had no idea how to broach the idea with her.

So he was completely flummoxed when she said, during one of their occasional Saturday runs out in the car, 'You know, I wouldn't mind going to call in on my friend Nora. She's in Westerwood House, I think that's what it's called. Do you know it?'

'Westerwood House?' This was one of the two local care homes he had found information on. And then done nothing about. 'Yes, I know where it is. Shall we head out in that direction, pop in and see if she's free to see us?' he remembered from the literature that visitors were welcome.

'Would you mind, dear?' His mum beamed at him, seeming delighted. Why hadn't he thought of this himself? How lonely she must be at home, with only the carers and him going in and out. She rarely got to see any of her friends, because both she and they were so immobile.

The visit was quite a success! Mum and Nora had a great chat, and Kit had the opportunity when he left them alone for a while to speak to the manager. She was a woman in her late fifties, smartly dressed but homely in her manner. She said they didn't have any vacancies. However, if Kit's mother wanted to come back for a proper visit and was interested in moving in, she could go on the waiting list.

He didn't have the nerve to sound Mum out about this straight away, but he felt more hopeful than he had in a while. She had seemed to enjoy her visit. And the whole place had a really pleasant atmosphere, not at all institutionalised. He'd give her the chance to bring it up, but if she didn't then he would suggest a visit himself. Definitely, he would.

He was glad to be distracted from these thoughts by the sight of Ellen coming up the track early Sunday afternoon. She had the dog with her, but she didn't normally walk him in this direction, so he could only assume she had come to visit.

His spirits rose, and he greeted her with a smile. 'Not a bad day, is it?'

'I've seen worse,' she agreed, but she hardly glanced at the view. She looked troubled, the hazel eyes narrowed and frowning, as they used to be so often. He offered her a drink, to break the ice, and she accepted gratefully. They sat on one of his own-design wooden benches (a plank of wood balanced on breeze blocks) and gazed out over the valley.

'How're things going?' he asked encouragingly.

'I think I've just messed them up,' said Ellen with a long sigh. 'Again.' She took a sip from the mug and looked out over the foundations of his house, which she didn't even seem to see, to the hills beyond.

'I'm sure you haven't.'

'I decided it was time we went through Jess and Sam's room,' she said, still not looking at him. 'So that's what we did this morning. Me and the kids.'

'Oh.' A small warning voice in Kit's head said, 'not good, you don't want to get in to this'. It had been bad enough going through his late father's possessions with his mother, and that was some-one at the natural end of their life. How much worse was this?

'I didn't want to do it without them,' continued Ellen flatly. 'My mother offered to help, but I thought the kids had the most right to say what happened to everything. And I thought it might be a way for them to say goodbye...'

'Yes, I suppose I can see that.'

'But I think it's just made it all worse. Lucy insisted on sleeping in her parents' bed last night, Angus wouldn't come out of his own room. And when we actually started going through things...' Ellen shuddered. 'It was too awful. The smell of the clothes, the little bits of Jess's jewellery, Sam's work overalls. God, it brought it all back. Lucy was wailing and Callum in tears. It was Angus who insisted we go on now we'd started. So we did. We divided everything up into what could go to charity shops, what could be sold, what we wanted to keep.'

'It sounds like you achieved something then.'

'Yes. And now it's not even their room any

more.' Ellen sniffed and swallowed. 'It's just a room with piles of stuff in it. It's as though we're wiping them out.'

'You have to move on.'

'I know, I know.' She rubbed fingers across her eyes. 'Oh god, I don't know if I can do this.'

Kit took her mug from her and put it with his own on the ground. Then he did what he would have done for anyone in distress; put his arms about her and drew her in. He had wanted to do this many times, but Ellen had a way of keeping you at a distance. Now she wept against his shoulder, and he held her close, rocking her like a child.

'It's not easy, what you're doing, but you are doing it,' he said. 'Everyone says how marvellous you're being.'

'Except Angus,' she said, her voice muffled by his T-shirt. 'Angus hates me.'

'He doesn't. He's just ... missing his mum and dad.'

'So am I. Oh God, so am I.' Ellen began to cry in earnest.

Kit stroked her hair, murmuring nothing much as encouragement. What could he do, what could anyone do? Ellen felt so slight in his arms it was heart-breaking. He wanted to surround her with his care.

He wiped the tears gently from her cheeks, feeling the smoothness of her skin and bent to touch his lips to her hair. Maybe she felt the change in the caress because she sat back and pulled out a tissue. She gave him a watery smile. 'Sorry.'

'No bother. Any time.' Even tear ravaged and

tired, she was very beautiful. 'They say a good cry can make you feel better.'

'Maybe.' She blew her nose loudly. 'God, it was so awful... But I'm not going to think about it any more. What's done is done. I'm sorry to be so feeble, crying all over you like that.'

'Not a problem,' said Kit. It was a struggle not to pull her back towards him, not to kiss away the tears this time and distract her with other thoughts entirely. That clearly wasn't what she wanted. He suppressed a sigh and passed back her coffee, now tepid. 'Where are the kids just now?'

'Angus got a bus in to town to see that friend of his, Simon. I offered him a lift but he wouldn't take it. Lucy and Callum are watching television. I know it's a waste on a nice dry day like this but I didn't have the heart to make them come out with me. I can hardly blame them for not wanting to. I think we all needed time on our own.'

'Television never did me any harm,' said Kit.

She smiled at him, almost properly this time. 'I'm glad to hear it.'

After a while she shook her head, and said in a determinedly cheerful tone, 'Now, tell me some more about your house. I see you've got the foundations laid. What happens next?'

This was a nice, unemotional subject and one on which Kit was usually happy to hold forth for hours. With an effort, he managed to force his thoughts away from Ellen. 'Ever heard of the autonomous house?' he asked. He had been re-reading the book last night.

'Er, no.'

'I suppose not everyone has,' he said understandingly. 'It's the idea that a house, or any building really, should have no impact on the environment. You know, things like zero CO_2 emissions, have its own water supply and sewage? It has to be carefully situated and constructed of certain materials. I'm compromising on some things, unfortunately, but that's the general idea I'm aiming for.'

'I see,' she said doubtfully. She looked more closely at the foundations, trying to make sense of them. 'So is this going to be the front?'

'That's right. South facing, which is important in a climate like ours. And I'll have a big conservatory along the full length of the house, for passive solar gain. Also it'll be a great room, with views down the valley. And there are porches around any outside door, see, to reduce draughts, and I'm really going overboard on the insulation...' He chattered on and saw to his relief that it was working, Ellen was really listening now, distracted from her own worries.

'So what do you think?' he said when he had spoken for perhaps a little too long.

'It sounds ... fascinating. I think it's going to be a far pleasanter building to live in than Craigallan. Now why wasn't that built south-facing? And with bigger windows? And even minimal insulation wouldn't go amiss.' She smiled wryly.

'That's the way they used to build. But Craigallan's essentially a good house. You don't mind it really, do you?'

'The kids want to stay there and I've agreed, so even if I did it's too bad now. I thought I'd start making some small changes, you know, maybe insulate the loft and repaint some of the rooms, but after this morning...'

'Leave it for a few days. Then you'll feel better. And if you want any help, give me a shout. I'm the person you want to speak to when it comes to insulation. It's a good idea to use the cellulose fibre stuff, it's low energy in production and just as efficient... Oops, there I go again. You'll be sorry you ever asked me.'

'Not at all.' She put her mug to one side and rose. 'Thanks for the coffee. And everything. I'd better get back.'

'Don't forget what I said about helping out.'

'Kit,' she said, and her tone was suddenly grim. 'You do far too much for us already. I'm trying to rely on other people less, not more.'

Which was a shame, as far as Kit was concerned, but he didn't know how to put that into words. It was only after she had gone that he remembered he still hadn't mentioned about Angus missing his guitar lessons. Maybe that would be a good excuse to pop down sometime soon.

Ellen was embarrassed by the interlude with Kit. What on earth had she been thinking, going to him when she was in such a fragile state? She hadn't needed to rush to anyone in the past and she certainly couldn't start now. It had felt ridiculously good to be in his arms, but that didn't mean he had liked it. He was just the sort of man who had to offer comfort. She cringed. She hoped she had handled it successfully, drawing back before he realised how much she wanted to stay there. Wanted to put her arms around him,

225

too, and...

Anyway, no point in thinking about that. He was four years younger than her, for goodness sake, and who would be interested in a woman sobbing with grief, with three children in tow? What an idiot she was.

She walked Monty around the top of the copse and back to the house where she rounded up a willing Lucy and reluctant Callum to help her in the kitchen.

'Come on, what shall we make?' she said brightly. You just had to get on with things, didn't you? 'Cakes? Biscuits? Pancakes? What would you like?'

'Dunno,' said Callum, in a worryingly Angus-like voice.

'Cupcakes,' said Lucy. 'Have you got those sprinkly things to put on them?'

'Not sure,' said Ellen. But it was good to see how Lucy could bounce back from her tears, she wasn't going to disappoint her. 'I'll check the pantry, shall I? I know your mum used to have lots of those food colours, we can make our own icing. And Cal, why don't you look through this book and see if there's anything you fancy?'

'Make that milkshake you used to do,' suggested Lucy. 'Go on, it was yummy.'

'If we've got enough ice cream,' said Callum, but his face brightened. Ellen listened with interest. So they had used to cook with their mum? Callum was a milkshake specialist? Why did she not know this?

The rest of the afternoon passed in messy but mostly cheerful chaos. Ellen tried not to question

226

the children directly but to listen to what they said, to learn more from them obliquely. This unforced chat was much more fun than the struggle around the table at meal times. It was good to do things together.

It was gone six o'clock when she realised that Angus still hadn't come home, and wondered if she should start to worry.

'Have you seen your elder brother?' she asked Lucy, who was decorating buns with her tongue sticking out the side of her mouth. Callum had retired to watch television with an enormous glass of banana milkshake. 'Is he back?'

'He might be outside,' said Lucy, not looking up. She was all too used to Angus being out with his animals.

'I thought he would have come in to change first,' said Ellen, doubtfully. 'I'll go and have a look.'

But there was no sign of Angus. The animals were grazing peacefully in their various fields. The horses hadn't yet been brought in for the night, which was apparently necessary when there was so much grass around. Angus might be hiding in one of the many dips and valleys, but she thought on the whole he probably wasn't. She tried his mobile but it was switched off. Now she had to decide whether to phone Simon's house and check up on him. Would that be unforgivably intrusive? After inviting Simon to the disastrous birthday party, she was trying not to meddle.

She decided to give him until seven, and went back indoors to begin preparations for the evening meal. An afternoon of baking had exhausted her, but the fact remained the children still needed to be fed. The process of child-rearing was endless.

Ellen had just gone to find the phone book to look up the Scott's number when Lucy called, 'Angus's here now,' She pushed the directory quickly back on the shelf and returned to the kitchen.

'We thought you'd got lost,' she said.

'I missed the bus.' Angus was looking at his feet so she had no way of telling if this was true.

'You missed ...? But why didn't you phone me? How did you get home?'

'I walked. 'S all right.'

'What can I have to eat now?' said Callum, appearing from the sitting room, without the empty glass he had been specifically reminded to bring through. 'Did you say you walked from Dunmuir? Coo, you must be mad.'

''S not that far.'

'I would have come and got you,' said Ellen. 'Didn't you have your mobile with you? Why didn't you phone?'

'It's, er, run out of credit.'

'Well, why didn't you tell me before?' Ellen tried to remember when she had last given him money to put on his phone. It didn't seem like long ago.

'It was fine. I got a lift a bit of the way with John Thompson's mum. Anyway, you're always saying exercise is good for us.'

'Mmm.' Ellen resisted the urge to shake him, to make him look at her. She felt that something was wrong, but how to find out? 'Did you have a good time with Simon?'

'It was OK. I'm going to get the horses in now.'

Ellen watched him withdraw with that familiar sinking feeling. Was it her fault he was in this mood, less communicative even than usual? Had it been a mistake forcing them to face their parents' room? Would she ever know?

She sighed and said, 'Callum, feed Monty please. You should have done it ages ago. And Lucy, if you wash something up it's supposed to be clean afterwards, not covered in pink icing. Do that bowl again.'

Sensing the change in atmosphere, both children obeyed without complaint.

Ellen wasn't like Sal.

This thought came to Kit in the middle of the night, as he tossed and turned on his thin mattress. Sal was happy go lucky, easy come easy go. Ellen was – the opposite. Therefore his only hope of progress was to take things slowly. He couldn't forget the slight shape of her in his arms, the powerful attraction that surely couldn't be just on his side.

She no longer had a boyfriend, but she did have an awful lot of worries. Well, he could help her with those. All he had to do was convince her she needed him in her life.

With this thought in mind he set off for Craigallan after work the following day, taking a quick detour through the fields and actually being disappointed that there were no problems evident for him to deal with.

He found Ellen in the back kitchen, emptying the washing machine. Her smile of welcome was

229

guarded. He wondered if she was remembering the embrace. He said brightly, 'Just thought I'd pop in and say hello. Children all right after – after yesterday?'

'Yes, they seem fine, thank goodness. They went to school as usual.'

'That's good.' He paused, suddenly uncomfortable. Things had always seemed so easy before, when he had been unaware of what he wanted.

Ellen shook out the last T-shirt and hung it on the drying wrack. 'Time for a coffee? Or were you wanting to use the shower?'

'A coffee would be good.'

By the time they were settled at the kitchen table, Kit was feeling at ease again. They chatted amicably, and Kit's only concern was that he shouldn't appear to be out-staying his welcome. Just as he was about to leave, he remembered the one thing he needed to mention. 'How's Angus's guitar playing going?' he asked carefully. He didn't like the idea of being the cause of further worries.

'Fine, I think. If anything, he's even keener now that he used to be, with this chance of being in Simon Scott's band.'

'That's good. It's just that I happened to bump into his guitar teacher the other day, and he mentioned Angus had missed a couple of lessons. I made me wonder...'

Ellen stared. 'Angus had done what?'

'He said he'd missed a couple of lessons, and he was surprised...'

Ellen pushed her mug away and tapped her fingers on the table, tense and concerned again in exactly the way he didn't want her to be. 'How can he have missed lessons? He's being going after school. I gave him the money to pay and he said it fitted in with band practice and he'd get the bus home, I didn't need to pick him up.'

'Well,' said Kit, cautiously. 'Apparently he hasn't been going to Grant's. I wonder what he has been doing.'

'He's lied to me. I've had my suspicions that he's not always exactly honest but this... He took the money, he never said. And he likes Grant McConnell, I know he does.'

'It does seem strange.'

'I don't like it.'

They both heard the back door swing open at the same time. Kit called, 'Angus? Sam? Is that you?'

Angus muttered something in response. Ellen rose and went to the intervening door. 'Could you come through, please?' she said. 'There's something I'd like to ask you.'

Angus entered the room slowly, looking nervously from one adult to the other.

'We were just wondering,' said Kit, trying to keep his tone friendly. 'If...'

Ellen interrupted. 'Angus, have you been going to your guitar lessons?'

The hunted look on the boy's face was definite now. He backed towards the door. 'I've been doing my practice.'

'That wasn't what I asked. I hear that you haven't been going to Grant's for your lessons, is it true?'

'I might have missed one or two.'

'But Angus, I thought you loved those lessons. And why didn't you say anything? What on earth must Grant think of me? Don't you realise he'll have been hanging around, waiting for you.'

Angus glanced up in surprise. 'I – didn't think.'

'And you took the money from me.' Ellen didn't raise her voice, but her tone was dangerous. 'That was dishonest.'

'I didn't spend it,' Angus flashed back at her. 'You can have it back if you want.'

'What we really want to know,' said Kit, 'is why you've been missing the lessons. Is there something wrong?'

'I told you, I've been busy.'

'Have you fallen out with Grant?' said Ellen.

'No! Grant's cool.'

'Then why? Is it something to do with those boys?'

Angus didn't meet her eyes. 'Look, I'll start going again, OK? I think I need to, some of the stuff Simon's writing is really hard.'

'That's good,' said Kit encouragingly.

'I'll have to phone Grant and apologise,' said Ellen, still looking very put out. 'And you had better apologise too.'

'OK,' said Angus, so quietly you could hardly hear him. 'Is that all?' He hurried back out before they could reply.

'Now why was he so cagey?' said Kit, turning back to Ellen.

'Perhaps you haven't realised, but he's always like that,' said Ellen grimly. 'And I still don't know why he missed those lessons.'

'No, we don't, do we?'

'It's not your problem,' said Ellen, with more emphasis than he would have liked. And it was a bit much, when she had asked him not so very long ago to try and speak to the boy. What had he done wrong now?

Ellen rose and took the coffee cups to the sink. Kit decided that perhaps now wasn't the time to do as he'd intended and invite her to a movie. He had even been going to include the kids in the outing, so he didn't scare her off with a 'date'. He'd have to wait for another opportunity.

Chapter Twenty

'Are you sure you don't want to come?' said Ellen, doubtfully, to Lucy and Callum. She was taking Angus, plus electric guitar and amplifier, to Simon Scott's house. Even Angus had had to admit that he couldn't manage that amount of equipment on the bus. The acoustic guitar was fine for lessons at Grant's, which appeared to have re-started, but it was electric or nothing when it came to the band.

Callum had complained about missing his *favourite* TV programme and insisting on being left at Craigallan, and Lucy had jumped on the bandwagon and said she wanted to stay too.

'I'm fed up of sitting in the car,' said Callum. 'What's the point? You'll just be dropping Ang ... Sam off and coming straight back. We'll be fine here.'

233

'Yes, we'll be fine,' echoed Lucy.

'I don't know

'You leave us when you're walking Monty and stuff,' said Callum. 'What's the difference?'

'I'm going to be late,' muttered Angus.

'OK, OK,' said Ellen. This was an important day for Angus, and she didn't have the time or energy to argue with the younger two just now. She told them to behave, promised not to be long, and set off. She turned onto the tarmac road at such speed she had to swerve to avoid Mrs Jack and her fat little terrier. Since the incident with the cows, she and Mrs Jack had only just got back onto nodding terms. This time all she received was a glare.

'What is it with that woman?' she said, half under her breath.

Angus didn't bother to reply. He was alternately looking at his watch and biting his nails. Today was the band's first gig – if you could call it a gig. They were performing at the fifteenth birthday party of an acquaintance, in Deer Bridge village hall. It wasn't exactly the big time, but it was an opportunity. Ellen had been delighted for Angus, happy to see him taking such an interest. It was only now that it occurred to her that he might be feeling nervous.

'You know, I've never heard you all play together,' she said. 'When do I get to come along and listen?'

'You won't like it,' said Angus immediately. 'It's not your kind of stuff.'

Ellen wondered what he thought 'her kind of stuff' was. The Beatles? Frank Sinatra? Or were those so old-fashioned he hadn't even heard of them?

'What kind of music is it?' she said.

'Kind of, like, Imagine Dragons, you know, and other stuff. Simon sort of writes it.'

Ellen hadn't even heard of Imagine Dragons, but she was impressed at the idea of Simon writing songs. Of course, she didn't know what the quality was, but it showed an application that she hoped Angus might copy. 'Do the rest of you contribute?'

'Not really. Simon likes to do it himself.' They turned the corner into the smart little housing estate where Simon lived and Angus let out a sigh of relief. 'They're still here.'

Simon and his two friends were standing in the driveway of the house, with instruments piled around them. As soon as Ellen and Angus climbed out, it was clear something was wrong.

'Try your dad again,' Simon was saying to one of the other boys. 'Or what about a taxi? Couldn't we get a taxi?'

'Who's going to pay?' said the other boy. 'And we'd have to get one to come from Dumfries, right? That'd take forever.'

'What's happened?' asked Ellen.

Simon straightened and tried to adopt a relaxed expression. 'Slight, er, hiccup. My dad's car was in for a service and it's not ready yet. Mum's away in Edinburgh. So we're just a bit, er, stuck for transport.'

'Your dad said he might be here in half an hour.'

'Yeah, *if* the garage get a move on. Even if he

makes it, we won't get to Deer Bridge till nearly seven.'

'The party only starts at seven.'

Simon shot his friend a pitiful look. 'What about setup time? Checking the sound system? We need to be there *now*.'

'Maybe I can help?' said Ellen. They seemed like nice boys, and she was infinitely grateful to them for involving Angus. 'Would all your things fit in my car?'

They examined the hatchback doubtfully. Ellen was reminded yet again that it would really have been more sensible to keep Sam and Jess's old estate car. 'We can try,' said Simon.

It was only when they had crammed in every last guitar-lead that Ellen remembered the two children she had left at home unsupervised.

She hesitated for a moment. But nothing was likely to happen to them, was it? And she couldn't let Angus down now. He was smiling at the older boys' jokes, agreeing that as he was the smallest he'd sit on someone's lap. He seemed almost happy. She would just drop them off and get home as quickly as she could.

The little car struggled under the extra weight, but they arrived at Deer Bridge in one piece, and without meeting any police who might have objected to the unconventional seating arrangements. 'Thanks a million,' said Simon. 'You can stay for a bit and listen if you want.'

Angus looked horrified at this offer, then relieved when Ellen had to turn it down. They unloaded the equipment quickly and Ellen wished them well. 'Are you going to need a lift home?'

'No, definitely not, my Dad'll be here by then. I've texted him.' Simon gave her a cheery wave and set to carrying the gear into the hall.

'I'll see you later,' said Ellen to Angus.

He nodded, and swallowed. 'Thanks for helping us.'

Those words, and the half smile that accompanied them, made the added worry more than worthwhile. And, of course, Callum and Lucy were perfectly all right when she arrived home. They hadn't even realised she had been away longer than expected.

As Kit walked with Angus amongst the cattle, he thought for the hundredth time what a shame it was that they had to be sold. He knew it was the sensible thing to do, even Angus had grudgingly come to admit that, but it was sad. Sam had intended these to be the core of a top-class herd of Galloways. He had selected and bred them himself, starting with only two heifers. On Friday, apart from Melanie and her calf Molly, they would all go to auction, and as likely as not be sold in different lots and end up all over the country – or in the abattoir. Absolutely no point in dwelling on that now.

'How's school?' he asked cheerily. He knew Ellen was still finding the boy difficult, and was determined to show an interest himself.

'OK. But I'm not going in on Friday.'

'Ah...?' Friday was definitely a school day. 'Is your aunt letting you go to the auction?'

'I told her I'd go whether she agreed or not, so she said yes. Anyway, it's the last day of term, no

237

one will care.'

Kit could see why Angus wanted to go, and why Ellen had given in, but he wasn't sure it was a wise decision. The boy would be more upset than ever to see the herd split up.

All he said was, 'When's the lorry arriving?' The least he could do was be there to help load the animals.

'Half seven.'

'I'll come down at seven, help you see everything is OK.'

'You don't need to. I can manage.'

It was strange to think that a thirteen-year-old boy *could* manage. Angus was brilliant with animals. A pity he wasn't so good at inter-personal skills.

'I know you can manage, but I'll still pop down. I've got quite familiar with the beasts over the last few months. I'd like to.'

'OK ... I mean, thanks.' Angus said gruffly, speaking to his feet, 'And thanks for helping us out so much. I know you didn't need to. It'll be easier for you when the animals are gone.'

Kit put a hand gently on the boy's shoulder. 'I haven't minded a bit. I've enjoyed it. If things had been different...'

'Ellen says you've got your work and the house and your mum to worry about, you don't need us to take up your time as well.'

'I've done it willingly, for you and your mum and dad.' He didn't mention Ellen. He gave the boy a playful push. 'And don't you try keeping me away, even when most of the animals are gone. I'll still expect to be able to come down and keep my hand in.'

Angus looked at him doubtfully. 'If you want.'

'I do want.'

The conversation left Kit feeling cheered. Angus was growing up, finally seeing things not only from his own point of view. If only he could start to be a little more understanding towards his aunt.

In the last week before the schools finished, Ellen had an unexpected visit.

It was a woman from the social work department.

It started off pleasantly enough. The woman, large and untidy in a motherly sort of way, asked politely if she could come in, if Ellen would answer a few questions. She commented on the lovely position, the character of the house. But all the time she was looking about, taking things in, so that Ellen began to feel uneasy. Eventually, the conversation moved on.

'It must be difficult, finding yourself suddenly responsible for three young children?'

'It's not been easy, but I think we're coping. And Angus isn't that young, he was thirteen last month.'

'I see. And you think that's quite a responsible age, do you?'

'Angus is very responsible, sometimes too much so.' Ellen shifted uneasily. What did the woman want?

'And what about the other two?'

'They're good enough children, but they don't worry about things like Angus does.'

'I meant, what are their ages?'

'Ten and, er, seven.' As she spoke, the woman nodded knowingly. Ellen's unease increased.

'I see. And do you feel that at that sort of age they're old enough to be left at home alone?'

'Angus, yes. The younger ones on their own? No, I wouldn't do that.'

Even as she said the words Ellen remembered that she had left them alone that afternoon last week. But it had been unavoidable. And Social Work couldn't possibly know about that, could they?

'So you haven't ever left the younger two alone?'

'Maybe occasionally, if I'm walking the dog, checking on the animals close by.'

'No other time?'

'Look, what is this about? Do you have the right to come into my house and start asking questions?' Suddenly, Ellen didn't feel so keen to co-operate.

'I hope you'll realise that we always have the children's best interests at heart.' The woman, who had introduced herself as Kathy, or was it Kathleen, waited a moment, and then said, 'It has come to our attention that the children may have been left alone in the house recently for quite a number of hours. Can you recall if that might have been the case?'

'I don't see...' Ellen felt blood rush to her face, as realisation struck. 'Somebody has reported me, haven't they? That's what this is about. Someone has reported me to the social services.' She couldn't believe this was happening. Anger bubbled up inside her. 'You're coming round

240

here to investigate me, because some busybody had the cheek to tell tales? They didn't come to see me, to see what the problem had been, if there had been a problem. They didn't look to help, oh no, they just ran straight to Big Brother...'

'So there was a problem last week?' said Kathy/Kathleen imperturbably.

'I left Cal and Lucy for twenty minutes, twenty minutes, while I went to drop their brother in Dunmuir. And then, well, something came up, and I was out a little longer. But they were perfectly all right.'

'I understand the children may have been alone for a number of hours before you were back.'

Ellen clenched her fists, holding on to her temper. 'It was an hour, an hour and a quarter at most. And who on earth... Ah, don't tell me, I think I can guess.' For an awful moment she had wondered if it was Kit who had told tales on her. And then she remembered Mrs Jack had seen her leave. She'd probably waited to see her come back, and then exaggerated it. Now it all made sense.

'I'm sure you'll understand when I say that we don't divulge the sources of our information.'

'Don't worry, I can put two and two together.' Ellen took a deep breath. She would concentrate on hating Mrs Jack later, just now she needed to mollify this woman, and get her out of the house before the children came home. 'Look, you're just doing your job, and I understand why you had to visit, but I can assure you this was a one-off. I wouldn't dream of leaving the children alone. I'm not saying I'm perfect but I do realise that they're far too young to be left in a remote place like this.'

'Too young to be left anywhere, without adult supervision.'

'Yes, of course, that's what I mean. I'm just so aware of how remote it is here, that's why I mentioned it. But as I said, I don't make a habit of leaving them here. And even though it is remote, we do have a very helpful neighbour just up the track there.'

'I suppose we're using the term neighbour rather loosely here, aren't we?' The woman looked out of the kitchen windows at the hills all around. 'And where are the children just now?'

'At school, of course. The younger two are at the school in the village. Angus goes to Dunmuir Academy.' Thank goodness the woman didn't know she was allowing Angus to take the day off school tomorrow. Best not even to get in to that conversation.

'What time do they finish?'

Ellen glanced at the clock. Too soon for her liking. She didn't want this woman cross-questioning her charges, she couldn't see that that would do them any good at all. 'Cal and Lucy usually get home about half past three.'

'Oh.' The woman formed her face in to an expression of great surprise. 'You don't go and collect them yourself? Perhaps they get a lift with someone else?'

'Actually, they walk. Isn't that what we're supposed to encourage them to do? The school walk not the school run? Sometimes I take the dog and go and meet them, or go in the car if it's raining. But more often than not they walk. It's less than a mile. My sister used to let them walk, you know.'

'I see.' The woman looked thoughtful. 'I assume you have checked that they have good road sense, have you? It's rather a narrow lane, no pavements.'

'I'm aware of that.'

'I see.' The woman folded her plump legs and sat back in the chair. Ellen felt she was inspecting the kitchen now, noting the unwashed coffee cups, the clutter on the table, dog hairs on the floor.

'Kinmuir Primary is a very good little school,' said Ellen, warming to the topic. 'Ideal, in fact. Small enough for the teachers to really know all the kids, near enough for most of them to walk there. They've been very supportive of the children during these ... difficult months.' Which is more than can be said of some people, she added silently. For the first time she realised how much the children did benefit from that school, what a tragedy it would be if it closed. She vowed to stop moaning about being drafted on to the Parent Council.

'I'm glad to hear it,' said the woman, in the same unemotional voice. 'If you don't mind, I'll just stay until they get home and have a wee chat with them myself.'

Ellen did mind, but she had no idea what her rights were. The last thing she wanted to do was antagonise the woman. 'Of course, if you want to wait.' She had her temper under control now and was able to say almost naturally, 'Can I offer you

243

a tea or coffee?'

'That would be nice. Tea please. Lots of milk, no sugar.'

Ellen rose to prepare it and found she felt better just to be moving. She cheered up even more when she remembered it was Thursday and Lucy's afternoon for swimming lessons. 'I'm afraid you won't see much of them,' she said, smiling sweetly. 'We have to dash out almost straight away, to take my niece to the swimming pool. Callum comes with us and usually plays in the park nearby. I suppose it is all right to let him go to the park alone, is it?'

She had meant the question to be ironic but the woman answered seriously. 'Naturally, you need to consider each situation on its merits. We have started to offer parenting classes, for people who have difficulty knowing what to do and what not to do. They wouldn't normally be aimed at someone like you, but I suppose that not having much experience of children you aren't aware of their limitations.' The woman smiled sympathetically. Ellen told herself that she was probably a very nice woman, and that she was *just doing her job*. It wasn't her fault she came across as nosy and self-satisfied. 'Would that be of interest?'

'I'll think about it.'

'Good, good. And how does your older nephew get home?' Nosy didn't come near to describing it.

'Usually he gets the bus to the village and then walks home from there.' Ellen didn't add that he then changed and went straight back outside. No doubt this would be interpreted as neglect as well.

244

'However, today I'm picking him up on our way through Dunmuir. He's coming into Dumfries with us as he needs some new trainers.' There, that sounded good, didn't it? It showed that she cared for her charges, bought them new clothes when required. Fortunately Kathy/Kathleen wouldn't see how bad a state the current trainers had got into before she noticed they needed replacing.

'I see. I'll probably pop out again in a week or two's time, see how you are all doing. Perhaps I'll meet with – Angus, is it? – at that point.'

'Perhaps you will.' Ellen smiled with a complete lack of sincerity.

These are my children, she wanted to say, *my* children. Don't you dare to interfere!

And then she caught herself, because it was the first time she had thought of them as her children. They were hers and she loved them, even Angus in all his thorny inapproachability. Lucy was easy to love, always had been, and was generous with her affection. Callum was less open, but had been willing to give his aunt a chance, willing to accept what she was doing for him, and as he turned more and more to her, in his easygoing way, she had found herself turning to him. Angus still didn't trust her, possibly didn't even like her, she knew that. But he was *hers*.

She had never had anything worth defending before, except her small place of silence, and no one had seriously threatened that. This fierce possessive anger she felt stunned her.

Chapter Twenty-one

Kit was pondering his next steps, with Ellen and with the house, as he prowled his plot of land.

It was easier by far to plan for the house, so he concentrated on that. He enjoyed having the place to himself, which was now only possible at this time of evening. Progress was welcome, of course, but three or four workmen on site, with the blare of their radios and sound of their tools, changed the feel of the place. He moved slowly between the timber-frame walls. It was good to see what had been achieved today. He was just thinking that perhaps it wasn't so surprising how quickly the money was going out if so much was being accomplished, when he heard the phone ringing in the caravan.

'Oh, Kit, I'm that glad I've reached you. It's your mother, she's been taken bad.' It was Mrs McIver, sounding desperate. 'I had to call the ambulance and they've rushed her off to hospital. I didn't know what to do. You weren't answering your phone. I hope I did right.'

'What's happened?' said Kit, feeling suddenly sick with fear. His mother had been so much brighter the last few weeks. With additional carers going in, he had been lulled into a false sense of security. He had taken her to visit her friend Nora a couple of times, but she hadn't mentioned the possibility of moving to Westerwood House herself, and nor had he. 'Did she fall? Is she OK?'

'I don't rightly know. I came to look in on her, as I do, like, in the evening. And there was no sound, and when I found her she was on the floor in the kitchen. It's a gey hard tiled floor, that one. There was blood coming from her head...'

'Was she conscious?' Kit swallowed. He pictured his lovely, heavy mother sprawled out, no one to help her.

'Not conscious, no, but she was breathing, like.'

Kit thanked her for her trouble, ascertained that the ambulance was heading for Dumfries Infirmary, and said he would go directly there himself.

Over the next few hours, time crawled by. He waited in Casualty for news, waited to be allowed to see his poor, unconscious mother, waited for the results of scans and tests, waited, waited.

He let his gaze dwell on his mother's broad face, now slack and silent. His mother had always been such a solid background to his life. She had always been there, a plump and cheery presence through his harum-scarum childhood, sticking plasters over cuts, providing food for picnics, giving all-engulfing hugs, a counterpoint to his more austere father. She had been so proud of him when he graduated. To have a vet for a son had meant something to her, given her something to boast about. He smiled and squeezed her limp hand as he remembered his embarrassment at her public delight.

He sat at his mother's side and the hours passed. It was like being in a twilight world, nothing to do but wait and think.

Ellen was disappointed that Kit didn't come down to Craigallan to help load the cattle on to the lorry taking them to market. He was under no obligation, of course, but somehow she had expected he would. Angus seemed to have expected it too, because when she mentioned Kit to him he said, 'He's probably got better things to do,' in a hurt tone.

At his own insistence, Angus was to travel to the auction in the cab of the lorry. The driver had been a friend of his father and seemed to take the arrangement for granted. Ellen was to meet them at the mart, once she had dropped the younger two off at school.

'It's not fair, why can't we go?' moaned Callum most of the way through breakfast. 'They're our animals too and...'

Eventually Ellen lost her patience. 'You weren't so interested in them being your animals when there was work to do! So you can keep quiet and finish your cereal. You're going to be late.'

As always when she raised her voice to the children, she was met with shocked stares. Their mother would never have shouted.

She sighed. It was getting easier to think of Jess these days, but she still preferred not to do so. Little things could so easily throw her all over again. Finding a Tupperware container of bolognese sauce at the bottom of the freezer, marked in Jess's distinctive writing; receiving mail addressed to Sam; seeing the raspberry bushes they had so proudly planted bearing their first fruit...

And now she was allowing – causing? – the dispersal of Sam's precious herd. It was no wonder she was tense. She couldn't help but feel she was letting her sister down.

The auction mart was a large, echoey place, filled with the sounds and smells of animals. Ellen stood beside Angus as the bidding got under way. She was completely out of her depth, glad to have at least one person she knew. Maybe he felt the same. At least he didn't edge away.

They watched as the various single animals and groups went under the hammer. It happened a lot faster than Ellen had expected, the animals moved in and out of the mart ring with surprising efficiency.

'It's us next,' said Angus, almost under his breath.

Ellen wished she could hold his hand, or pat his shoulder. Do something to make things better. Instead she clasped the cool metal barrier and told herself this would be over soon.

And then things, amazingly, took a turn for the better. There was something about one farmer, one bid, some more discussion, and then the hammer fell.

'What happened?' she hissed, confused.

Angus was almost smiling. 'They've all gone to one farmer. The whole herd. Someone who had heard of Dad – Dad's reputation. I think. He must want to keep them together, breed from them.'

'That's brilliant,' said Ellen. 'I'm so pleased.' And they'd gone for a good price, too, but the main thing was the compliment to her late brother-in-law, and how pleased Angus seemed to be.

She thought he might actually have been humming under his breath on the way home. And he answered all her questions, and didn't grunt or sigh once.

The following day was the first of the summer holidays. Angus was up and out early as usual. The younger two chose the more understandable option of watching television in their pyjamas. Ellen allowed herself a second mug of tea with her breakfast and was just wondering whether she could contemplate the luxury of reading her book when there was a knock on the door.

'Hi there, how's things?' It was Kit.

Ellen gave a silent sigh of relief. She couldn't help wondering what had happened to him. He hadn't been around at all the previous day.

She was about to give a light-hearted response, to show that she hadn't missed him at all, when she realised something was amiss. He looked pale and tired, the normally broad, smiling face tense. 'How are things with you?' she asked, concerned.

'Not so good.' He slumped down in a chair and in short factual sentences told her about his mother's collapse and admission to hospital. 'They say it's a stroke. A full-blown one, not like the possible TIAs she's been having. I was there with her all day yesterday. I'm sorry I couldn't help with the cattle.'

'You don't need to apologise.' Ellen was glad there had been a reason for his absence. If only it hadn't been such a horrible reason. 'And, anyway, Angus managed fine.'

'I'm glad. How did the sale go?'

Ellen told him. 'Isn't it great? Someone from

over by New Galloway, apparently. So no dealer, no abattoir, no splitting them all up. Angus was happier than I've seen him in a long while.'

Kit smiled too, his white face briefly taking on a more normal expression. Then he pushed himself to his feet. 'That's good. Look, I must dash. I'm working at the vet practice until lunchtime, then going back to the hospital. I'll probably stay there until the end of evening visiting. I just wanted to pop in and ask about the cows, and...' His words trailed off. He looked exhausted, which he probably was.

'Of course, I won't keep you. Give your mother my regards, if she's up to receiving them.' It occurred to Ellen that, for once, Kit was the one who needed some help. 'And why don't you come and eat here when you do get back? That'll save you having to worry about food, at least.'

'That's very kind, but it'll be late, after eight. I'll try and look in on the animals, of course...'

'No, forget the animals. It's mostly sheep now, Angus can manage them fine. But if you want to eat, eat here. I don't get round to cooking until late on weekends and as it's the holidays it'll no doubt be even later. Eight thirty or after would be fine.' And then she wondered if she was being too pushy. 'Or will you be wanting to stay with your mother?'

'Probably not. I'll stay for visiting but they don't really make you welcome after that, once the crisis is over.'

'We'll see you here then.' Ellen felt a glow of satisfaction that remained with her throughout the day. It must be that she so rarely did anything for others, voluntarily.

It was almost nine by the time Kit reappeared. Ellen was glad she had given in to the children and let them have fish fingers and chips while watching the DVD they had got from the library to celebrate the start of the holidays. It meant they were happy (even Angus) and not starting to whinge from hunger. The chicken casserole she had made for Kit and herself was in the warming drawer, ready to be heated when required.

She got him a beer.

'Tell me how things are going. You look pretty knackered.'

'I am.' Kit wiped a hand over his face that was still as pale as it had been in the morning, but now more tired than ever.

'Not good news?'

'No change really. It's hard to know how much she understands, but she's not able or not willing to speak. She is conscious some of the time. She opens her eyes, and she'll squeeze your hand, but... Oh, who knows?'

'It's hard for you.' She tried to remember how she had felt when her father had been diagnosed with Parkinson's. One thing was sure, she and Jess had been there to support each other. Ellen had taken that all for granted then, Jess rushing up to Stirling, being her normal caring self, and Ellen happy to talk things through but relieved she didn't have to take the strain. Ha! How things change.

'Here, have some crisps. Maybe what you need is sustenance.' Ellen tossed a couple of packets on the table and went to move the casserole to the main oven.

The happiness that had been with her all day was still there. Kit might be tired and worried, but he was still the person she felt most at ease with. She paused behind his chair, tempted to hug him, to cheer him up as he so often did her, and then wondered what on earth she was thinking of. She went quickly back to her own seat on the far side of the table.

They chatted some more about Kit's mother, and Ellen's father, laughing sadly at how they found themselves in the same boat now. 'Except you don't have the kids,' Ellen pointed out. She suppressed a sudden shiver as she remembered about the social worker. 'Poor you, only got one generation to worry about.'

'I don't know. What about worrying about myself? I'm sure I'm quite as much trouble as three well-behaved children.'

'Well-behaved? Pouf. And speak of the devil...' Lucy drifted in looking for food, or possibly attention. Of the three, she was the one most likely to seek Ellen out and it wasn't always clear why.

When she saw Kit, she gave a little skip and said, 'Kit! Did Auntie Ellen tell you about the cows? Angus did so well. We're going to go over to this man's farm to see them. And Melanie's not *very* lonely, she's still got her calf, and...'

Angus must have heard her because he came through to join them – of his own volition! He, too, wanted to talk about the auction, and basked in Kit's approval in a way he never did with Ellen. He talked happily of breeding lines and the best bull to put Melanie to in the autumn. Even when they discussed a date for taking the sheep to market, he didn't seem too downhearted.

Eventually the children went back to the sitting room, where Callum was summoning them to watch deleted scenes on the DVD, and Ellen brought the casserole to the table. It was strange how at home she felt in this kitchen now, how used she had become to its space and far from convenient arrangement. She scooped knives and forks from the drawer, plates from the dresser, with hardly a second thought. It was a pleasant room. With a lick of paint – maybe a dusky peach to pick out the tiles on the floor – it would be more than acceptable.

'You seem settled here,' said Kit, as though thinking along the same lines.

She smiled. 'I think I am. Amazing, really. There's still lots to do, of course, but I'm getting used to being here. In fact, it's hard to remember anything else. Kids and animals somehow take over your life.'

'You don't miss your flat?'

'No.' Ellen considered as she spooned food on to both their plates. 'No, it was convenient, but I realise I never loved it like Jess and Sam did this place, or you will with your house. I'm relieved it sold so quickly. My only worry is what I'm going to do with all my stuff when we get it down here. Now the kids are on holiday, we're going to go up and do some packing. I need to have it cleared by the middle of next month.'

'I could help,' said Kit immediately.

'No, we'll be fine, thanks. You've got more than

enough on your hands. I'm going to hire one of those big transit vans for a couple of days and see what we can fit in. I want to make a kind of expedition of it, make it fun for the kids.'

Kit grinned. 'Have you ever driven one of those vans?'

'No, but I'm sure I'm capable.' Ellen felt a flutter of irritation. She still didn't like people laughing at her, thinking her useless. it was all the more galling as she had given Kit plenty of reasons to think that over the last few months.

'I'm sure you are. I'm just saying, if you need a hand, give me a shout. Even if it's only to help you take stuff out at this end.'

'Thanks,' she said, determined not to take up the offer.

'How's the decorating here coming on?'

Ellen was glad of the change of subject. 'We've made one big step forward. Did I tell you, we've sorted out who'll have which room? Angus gets his parents' old room. Not surprising, really. He's the oldest, and although Lucy suggested I have it, I knew the boys wouldn't be happy. So I'm going into Angus's room, which is half as big again as the cubby where I am now, and Lucy and Cal stay where they are. And we're painting all the rooms.'

Kit nodded approval. He lounged back in his seat, shaggy hair falling over his brow, eyes lazily interested. 'You know, you could do some interesting things rearranging the rooms downstairs. You could knock the spare room and that never-used dining room into one, it would make a great space. But you probably don't want to get into that just now?'

'I thought of it,' admitted Ellen. 'I could have had that, with the downstairs toilet and shower as an en suite. It was a nice idea, but I couldn't face it just now. Plus I didn't want to upset the kids.'

'Upset Angus, you mean.'

'Yes, upset Angus.' Ellen couldn't help glancing towards the doorway, but the children seemed still to be ensconced in the sitting room. 'He seems a bit ... happier at the moment. I hope it lasts.'

'The holidays'll help. No more problems with those bastards at school?'

'Not that I know of. And now we don't need to have anything more to do with them for seven whole weeks.' Ellen beamed at the thought of it: no more chaotic early mornings, no more pressure of leaving one thing unfinished because you had to move on to the next. Yes, they were all looking forward to the holidays.

Kit insisted on doing his share of the evening chores. Unsurprisingly, Lucy, when given the choice, opted for the treat of a visitor reading to her. Ellen wondered if she should be jealous, but decided it wasn't worth worrying about. One less job. And surely soon the child would do as Angus and Cal did, and read for herself?

She put the kettle on for coffee and took the tray through to the sitting room. It was used more by the children than her. But today she had given the room a spring (or summer?) clean, and was determined to get some benefit of it before it deteriorated into a crumb and DVD-strewn pit.

'Milk and sugar?' she asked Kit when he eventually joined her, having been coerced by Lucy into a mammoth story-reading session.

'Yes, both. Tonight, I think I need them.'

He came and sat beside her on the settee and Ellen wondered if it was for this she had moved through here. Now there was no longer a table between them, what might happen? How lucky it was that Angus was in the habit of going to bed early, so that he could rise at some ungodly hour as befitted a farmer.

They sat in companionable silence.

When Kit had finished his coffee, he put his arm around her, as though it was the most natural thing to do. She let herself lean very slightly in to him, and he turned and touched her lips with his own, hardly a kiss at all, just a question. She felt that strange tautness in her stomach that she hadn't felt for years, the thrill along her skin where they touched. 'Mmm?' he said, but she didn't want to talk. She pulled his head down towards her and kissed him properly.

Kit was warm and solid, an untidy, gentle bear of a man, but as the kiss deepened she became aware of a new side to him. Passion, fiery and hot, as he pulled her closer, losing himself in the moment.

Ellen felt stunned, desperate for more, burying her fingers in the thick hair, pulling him closer and closer. And at the same time part of her was listening for sounds from overhead, steps on the stairs.

It was Kit who pulled back first. 'Wow,' he said, but the shake in his voice wasn't laughter. He leant his cheek against her hair and took a long slow breath.

After a moment Ellen gently disengaged herself and sat back.

'What is it? What's wrong?'

'Nothing's wrong.' She could feel colour rush to her cheeks as she met his eyes. Things were quite the opposite of wrong. 'It's just – I was surprised. And I'm worried if the kids come down...'

'They'll be asleep by now.'

'Probably, but...' Ellen couldn't bear the thought of the children finding them like this. It felt totally right and at the same time completely strange. She didn't know what to think herself, let alone how they might react.

'I should probably go,' he said with a slow smile. He kept her hand in his. 'I need some sleep, and you need some time to think. Perhaps?'

Ellen didn't want to think just then. 'I'll walk up the track with you,' she said. 'Monty needs to go out.'

It was a good plan! The kiss outside Kit's door was longer, uninhibited by the possibility of interruption by children, but they neither of them suggested taking it further. It was new and exciting and who knew where it would lead.

'Now I should walk you back to your door,' said Kit shakily.

'Don't be silly. You're dead on your feet.'

'I think you've just woken me up.'

She stood on tiptoe to kiss him again briefly. 'I hope not. Sleep well.'

As she strolled back down to Craigallan, she heard the rustle of leaves and the whistled hoot of an owl. She could still feel the warmth of Kit's arms around her, the glow of the excitement he had kindled. So *this* was why she had been so happy all day.

Ellen lay awake for a long time. Her body felt tingly with excitement, as though she were on the verge of something momentous. She had known for a while she found Kit Ballantyne attractive, but hadn't dared to hope the feeling was reciprocated. Still less had she thought anything might come of it. She didn't do intense relationships, did she?

And yet tonight she thought maybe she could.

She had only to close her eyes to see Kit's broad face before her. She loved the way his eyes crinkled at the corners, as though he had spent too long looking into the sun. His wasn't a conventionally attractive face. The features were too broad, the jaw too heavy, but as a whole, with those deep brown eyes and framed with the shaggy, dark blond hair, it made him into someone very special.

Chapter Twenty-two

Angus loved the school holidays. He always had. He'd never enjoyed school, and the last few months it had been the pits. Now he had seven weeks at home. And Craigallan *was* still his home. Selling the cows had been a wrench, but Kit was right, he had to be realistic and look on the bright side. He had Melanie and Molly, who were both doing well, and his Suffolk crosses would be staying. He hated to admit it, but that was probably as much as he could cope with for the next few years.

The kids seemed happier now, too. He couldn't help feeling a little bitter. He wondered how much Lucy would remember of their parents in years to come, and how much Callum really noticed of the changes, as long as he could play football. But if they were content he didn't need to worry about them, so he tried to swallow his resentment.

'Ang ... Sam, we've been waiting for you. Remember we were going to start moving furniture?'

Angus suppressed the irritation at his aunt yet again trying to boss him around. He was thirteen, he didn't need someone to nag him all the time. 'If you're never going to remember to call me Sam, you might as well stick to Angus,' he said. 'I'm getting a bit fed up of Angsam, you know.'

'Angus?' said his aunt doubtfully.

'Oh good,' said Lucy. 'I was never going to remember.'

'Are you sure?' said Ellen.

He didn't know why she was surprised. 'Yeah. What's in a name, anyhow?' Angus was what his parents called him in his dreams.

'If we're not moving the furniture now can I go down to the village?' said Callum.

'We are moving the furniture. Come on, upstairs everyone.'

Angus kicked off his Wellington boots and followed them through the house. He had been triumphant when it was agreed that he was to have his parents' room, but now he wasn't so sure. He had pretended to be too busy to help with the painting, so Ellen had given the walls a covering of white emulsion herself. Personally, Angus thought that if his parents had been happy with the room the way it was he would have been happy too.

Ellen seemed a little strange this morning. Some of the time she was joking, in high spirits, and then she would go quiet and thoughtful. He hoped she wasn't having doubts about Craigallan. Maybe she just didn't like having them all around so much in the holidays? If that was the case, why did she constantly drag him back inside?

It took longer to re-arrange the rooms than Angus would have imagined. The furniture was awkward to lift and the stairs were a nightmare. But by lunchtime, the room that was to be Angus's was almost complete, and he had to admit it looked pretty good. It was bigger and, with the new paint, brighter than his old room. There was plenty of room for his desk and his guitar and music stand.

'Do you like it?' said Ellen. She always had to ask questions.

He shrugged. 'It's fine.' After a moment's thought he added, 'Thanks.'

Callum was just beginning his refrain of, 'I still don't see why you should get the best bedroom,' when the phone rang.

'I'll get that,' said their aunt. 'Will you lot wash your hands and then start getting things out for lunch?'

Angus grinned at his brother. 'I get the room

'cos I'm the oldest. So hard luck.'

'It's not fair...'

Angus smiled smugly. He made his way down to the kitchen, leaving the whine of Callum's complaints behind him.

Lucy went with him. She began to lay the table, collecting butter and cold meats from the fridge and bread from the breadbin.

'I can't find the bread knife,' she said after opening two or three drawers. 'Why is it you can never find anything in this place?'

'Dunno.' Angus watched her. How was he supposed to know where the bread knife was?

'Auntie Ellen's going to bring all her kitchen stuff down from Edinburgh,' said Lucy happily. 'That'll make things better. She's got lots and lots of really smart things. Did you see her knife block? Mum always wanted one like that.'

Angus frowned. As far as he was concerned, the knives they had were perfectly satisfactory. They might be a bit battered, but they still functioned, didn't they? Ellen would probably throw them in the bin once her own things arrived. He had noticed this tendency she had to chuck things away that weren't even slightly old.

He picked up the small knife Lucy had put beside the cheese on the table. Its wooden handle was smooth with age. As he turned it over in his hands, he thought of a use he might have for it. His jacket was hanging on the back of the door and when Lucy wasn't looking he slipped it into a pocket and got another, newer knife from the drawer.

He might no longer need to go to school every

day, but he would still be going into Dunmuir to see Simon, and to have lessons with Grant. And Jason bloody Armstrong lived just round the corner from Grant. He would feel a lot happier if he knew he had that in his pocket.

Kit slept late, which was a blessed relief, and then spent the afternoon at the hospital. He managed to be bored and anxious at the same time, an awful state of mind. His mother was unchanged, occasionally restless, but mostly she lay still and silent in the high, white bed. When he tried to ask questions, the staff brushed him off with reminders that it would be a while before they knew the full effects of the stroke. He sat beside the bed, holding her hand.

There was so much to worry about, yet he couldn't stop his thoughts turning to Ellen.

He was amazed at what had happened the night before. The attraction he felt had been growing for some time, but he hadn't known how she felt in return. And it wasn't in Kit's nature to hurry things. It must have been the tiredness and the wine had made him less cautious. Ellen was lovely, beautiful in fact, and kissing her had been – well, pretty mind-blowing. Perhaps she wasn't as reserved as he had thought!

But now wasn't the time to get into a new relationship. He should be thinking about his mother, not himself.

He groaned and turned back to the pale, motionless figure beside him. How he wished he had spoken to his mother properly about Westerwood House. He had no idea what state she would

263

be in if when she recovered, but he doubted it would be a good idea for her to go back home.

He found his thoughts straying back to Ellen. Was she wondering why he hadn't contacted her? Regretting what had happened between them? Expecting him for a meal once again that evening? Or hoping never to see him again?

Eventually Kit decided to call in at Craigallan on his way home. He couldn't not go and see Ellen, whether it was right or wrong.

He had stayed longer at the hospital this evening. It was only when he reached the house that he thought he should perhaps have made some effort at communication during the day, even if it had just been a text.

Ellen didn't kiss him on arrival. She seemed reserved again, cautions. 'The kids have already gone up to bed. They were keen to go up. Angus is in his new room and we've done some reorganising in the others. Lucy was definitely over-excited.'

'That's good,' said Kit, although he wasn't sure that it was. She seemed ill at ease and he didn't know if it was because of the children, or to do with him.

'Would you like something to eat?' she asked politely.

'No, thanks. I had something in the hospital canteen. I wanted to stay later tonight as the staff said Mum roused a bit in the evening yesterday, but there was no sign of that today.'

'She's no better?'

'No better,' confirmed Kit grimly. He accepted a beer from the fridge and automatically took a seat at the kitchen table, and then wondered if that was the right thing to do. Wouldn't it be friendlier if they sat in the sitting room? Before he could rise again Ellen sat down opposite him.

'It must be hard for you,' she said warily.

'I'm not the only one in this boat.'

'Presumably she's over the worst now?'

'I suppose so. Nobody seems prepared to say.' Kit took a drink and sat back, enjoying the cosy chaos of the room after the sparseness of the hospital ward. 'Let's not talk about that now. How are you? Have you got anything planned for this first week of the holidays?'

'Actually,' said Ellen, frowning, 'I've got a not-very-welcome visitor coming on Thursday.'

'Oh?' Kit wondered who it could be, to make Ellen seem suddenly tense. He had just been thinking how pretty she looked, in old jeans and a pale mauve T-shirt, relaxed and at ease in these surroundings in a way he would never have expected four or five months ago.

Now she grimaced. 'I didn't tell you about the social worker, did I?'

'Social worker?' The very word made Kit feel depressed. Weren't these the people he was going to have to deal with over his mother's future?

'Yes. One popped in unexpectedly last week.' Ellen's colour rose as she described the encounter to him. He could understand why she was annoyed. It was *unbelievable* what some people would take on themselves. He wished she had told him before.

'She was questioning your ability to look after the children, after all you've done?'

Ellen smiled. 'I know, ridiculous isn't it?' she said with faint irony.

'But you've done so well, given up so much. The kids are really happy now, well as happy as they can be, what on earth are *they* going to do?'

'Hopefully nothing. But apparently leaving the two little ones alone is a terrible sin. I'm afraid they're going to keep an eye on me now. I suppose as long as I don't put another foot wrong I'll be OK.'

'Interfering busybodies. And how on earth did they know you had left them alone?'

'Ah, now that's an interesting question.' Ellen pressed her lips together. 'I've no proof, but my suspicion is that the lovely Mrs Jack reported me.'

'No!' Kit put his beer down with a bang. It was a relief to have somewhere to direct his anger. 'That woman! Why am I not surprised? Someone has got to tell her to keep her nose out of other people's affairs. I can't believe she reported you to Social Services.'

'I've no actual proof. It's probably best if we just ignore her.' Ellen was coolly sensible, trying to bank down his anger, which annoyed him all the more.

'I don't know how you can be so calm.'

'I'm fine,' she said emphatically.

A short while later he got up to go, and she smiled politely. 'You look tired. I hope you get some sleep.'

He hesitated in the doorway, determined not to go without saying something. 'About last night...'

'You want to say it was a mistake?' A faint pink

266

came to Ellen's face, otherwise he would have thought her as calm and collected as ever. 'That's fine...'

He put a hand out immediately, wanting to touch her. 'No, not a mistake. Not a mistake at all.'

She smiled. 'I'm pleased.' Yet still neither of them made a move.

After a moment she said, 'Let's just take things slowly, shall we? I've got the kids to think of, and you've got your mother.'

'I suppose...'

She kissed his lips, but only briefly. 'It's for the best. Believe me.'

He had no idea what that meant.

Ellen watched Kit kicking the ball around with the two boys, all of them laughing, loving the rough and tumble.

She wished she could go out and join them, but that wasn't her way. And things were a little odd between her and Kit, not awkward exactly, but as though they were both unsure how to take things forward.

She was pleased to be interrupted from these thoughts by the ringing of the phone.

'Hi, Mum,' she said as she picked up it. This was the normal time for motherly phone calls. 'How's things?' Unfortunately, it wasn't her mother.

'Ah ... Could I speak to Ellen Taylor, please? Is that Ellen?'

Ellen groaned silently. 'Yes. Sorry. I was expecting someone else.'

'Mark Gillespie here, Senior Lecturer at the College. You will remember, I'm sure, that we met when you came in for a chat a while ago?'

'Yes, of course.' Ellen grimaced. What a fool he must think her. 'How can I help you?' she said, her tone now ultra-professional.

'I was wondering how you were situated for work at present?'

'I don't have anything definite yet,' she said cautiously.

'Perhaps you could help us out then. We're running a two-week summer school starting next week and one of the lecturers has had to back out at very short notice. It's not exactly your subject area, but as you're local and were looking for work, I thought I'd sound you out.'

'Can you tell me a bit more?' Ellen felt her spirits rise. The idea of work – the money and the stimulation – was quite exciting!

He described the course, which was intended to support weaker students in the transition from school to college. She hadn't done much of this kind of thing previously, but was willing to give it a try.

'So you would be interested? I'm afraid I'll have to press you for a quick decision, time's running short.'

'I'm very interested,' said Ellen. And then common sense reasserted itself. 'Oh. But I'll have to think about it.' She sighed softly, coming down to earth. 'I'll need to see if I can arrange childcare.'

'Excellent,' he said. Clearly he had no idea of the difficulties of childcare. 'Once you've sorted that out you can get back to me. Tomorrow morning at the latest, OK?'

As Ellen put down the phone her thoughts were

in turmoil. She wanted to do this more than she would have imagined, but she didn't see how. The children seemed finally to be accepting their new life, was now a good time to throw another change their way?

Normally she would have invited Kit in for a coffee and discussed the options with him. But he popped in briefly to say he had an appointment with the consultant in charge of his mother and had to dash. Which was fine. Absolutely fine.

She couldn't ask her mother for help. Her father hadn't been well this last week and her mother didn't need more worries.

Then she thought of Clare. She hadn't seen a great deal of her neighbour since the holidays began. A wander down the road to pop in for a coffee seemed like a very good idea.

'I shouldn't disturb your work,' said Ellen, when Clare jumped up from the sitting room floor where she was packing pottery into boxes.

'Rubbish. I deserve a break. Come and sit out the back and watch the girls.' Ellen had brought Lucy with her, and she and Grace had fallen on each other as though they had been apart for months. Callum had walked on to the village to look for someone to play football with and Angus had, inevitably, stayed at home.

Ellen hoped that was all right. The social worker's visit might have passed off fairly well, but the thought of it still made Ellen nervous. Angus had surprised her by being pleasant and co-operative, which must have made a good impression. The other children were merely themselves, and the only hiccup was when Lucy asked why the house was so tidy.

'How's life?' asked Clare cheerfully as they carried glasses of homemade lemonade outside.

'Fine.' Ellen perched tentatively on a rickety bench and looked around at the wilderness that was Clare's garden. 'You've cut the grass,' she said, surprised.

'Not me,' said Clare happily. 'Grant decided it needed doing. I didn't even know I had a lawn-mower, but he unearthed one at the back of the garage. Makes quite a difference, doesn't it? Rather nice.'

Ellen wished she could be as easy-going as Clare. True, her standards had slipped since taking on three children, but even now she wouldn't have said the weed-infested borders and over-grown shrubs comprised a 'nice' garden. 'It's a good place to sit,' she said equably. 'So I take it you're still seeing Grant?'

Clare tossed back the long hair and smiled, embarking on a long discussion of the good and bad points of her boyfriend. She was funny and indiscreet and made Ellen laugh out loud.

'And what about you and Kit?' continued Clare blithely. 'Any progress there?'

'What do you mean, me and Kit?'

'Come on, anyone can see he's interested in you. And you can't tell me he hasn't got a certain earthy attraction.'

'Kit's very caught up with his mother at the moment,' said Ellen primly. She told herself she wasn't disappointed he'd accepted 'taking things slowly' so easily. She definitely didn't want to discuss him with Clare. 'You know she's in hospital in Dumfries?'

'I'd heard. Is she bad?' Clare, as ever, was keen to know the details of other people's lives, but she hadn't yet finished with the topic of Kit. Once they had dealt with Mrs Ballantyne, she was back on the scent. 'You're avoiding the issue. Are you saying that if Kit wasn't so busy with his mum something might be happening?'

'No.'

'So what has happened?'

'Nothing,' said Ellen firmly. 'Absolutely nothing. I came to talk to you about something else entirely.' She was relieved to have other news with which to divert her friend.

She told Clare about the offer of work, and Clare was suitably impressed.

'Are you going to take it? You've got to take it, it could lead on to other things.'

'I'd really like to,' admitted Ellen. 'But I have the kids to think about. I wondered if you knew of any day care centres they could go to? I remember Cal or Lucy bringing leaflets home in their school bags, but I seem to have binned them.'

'There are always lots of things on in school holidays,' said Clare. 'Sports courses, arts and crafts. And most of it's not too pricey. But if you're just looking for somewhere for the kids to stay while you're at work, why not leave them here? I'm at home most days, as you know...'

'That wasn't what I meant,' said Ellen quickly. She was still amazed at how helpful her neighbours were (except Mrs Jack). And she was aware how hard she found it to reciprocate. She had

271

had Grace for one sleep-over at Craigallan and the hours of high-pitched excitement had totally exhausted her.

'I know it wasn't what you meant, but I still think it'd be a good idea. Grace is far easier when she has a friend to play.'

'Even if that's true for Lucy, I couldn't dump the boys on you.'

'The boys'll do their own thing, but they can have lunch here, use me as a base. No problem... Ah, you're worried about that social worker, aren't you? They'll be fine, I'm a very responsible person.'

'I know you are, it's not that. I don't want to take advantage.'

'Hey, I'm not saying I'd do it for the whole of the holidays, or every day after school, but a couple of weeks is nothing. As long as I'm here, of course. I've arranged to take Grace to her dad's at some point, let's check the calendar...'

Ellen found herself, as so often with Clare, carried along on a wave of good-humoured optimism. She put up more objections and Clare laughed them off. She went to fetch her calendar, artwork clearly done by Grace. 'Mmm, slight problem. On the Thursday of the second week I'm taking Grace down to her dad in York. But if you can make other arrangements for that Thursday and Friday I'll do the rest.'

'I don't know...'

'Think about it. I'm sure Kit would help if he could.'

'I'm not asking Kit.'

'Oh-oh? Well, I know someone who would like

to be involved for a couple of days at least. Your mum. She's desperate to see more of the kids. She said when she was down for Angus's birthday that she could come down for the occasional few days, but she didn't know if you'd think that was interfering.'

Ellen was astonished. She'd been trying to save her mother from worry. Had she been unintentionally excluding her? Something else to worry about. 'I'll think about it,' she said.

Chapter Twenty-three

Ellen's first two days working at the college in Dumfries had gone very well. She loved how interesting it was, how at home she felt in that environment. Best of all, the childcare arrangements with Clare were working out a treat. Although the boys moaned they were old enough to be left on their own, they dutifully appeared at Clare's cottage for lunch, so Ellen had at least the illusion they were being supervised. Lucy was finally losing that lost waif look that she had had since her parents' death. She was less clingy, her face was pinker, her laughter more willing.

Ellen's mother had arranged carers for her father and was looking forward to coming to collect the children and having them to stay at the end of the second week. She insisted she could cope and seemed to be looking forward to it.

Ellen hummed to herself as she prepared the

273

evening meal and didn't realise she had a visitor until there was a fierce rap on the door. Monty began to bark vociferously. Why couldn't he be more useful and bark *before* someone knocked?

She was surprised, when she pulled the door open, to find Kit on the doorstep. Normally he let himself in after a perfunctory knock.

'Hello,' she said doubtfully, standing back to let him in.

'Clare's just told me you're working and she's looking after the kids,' he said without preamble.

'That's right.' Ellen wasn't often aware of how big Kit was, tall and solidly built. Now he seemed to tower over her.

Kit came one step into the kitchen. 'Why didn't you tell me?'

'It was all arranged in a bit of a rush. You've been busy with your mum. How is she, by the way?'

'The same. So you didn't think it would be useful for me to know that you were all going to be away from the house all day. Who is keeping an eye on the animals?'

Ellen met his gaze coolly. 'Kit, that's my problem, not yours. And anyway Angus isn't away all day. He goes to Clare for his lunch. The rest of the time he's here, if he doesn't have band practice with Simon.'

Kit harrumphed.

'You've been a fantastic help to us all, but with the cattle gone and the sheep going next week life is getting easier. We *can* manage.'

'So now I'm not needed, it's thank very much and goodbye?' He glared down at her, the brown eyes that usually seemed so sleepy dark and angry. 'Or maybe you didn't think you even needed to bother with the thanks and goodbye?'

'Kit, it's not like that. You've been busy. We both have...'

'You should have asked me to help.'

'Kit, you're working, you've got your mum to worry about. The kids are my problem.'

'You didn't even think to discuss it?'

'I wasn't hiding it from you. It just never came up.'

'Well, fine. If you're not willing to discuss things with me there's no point, is there?' And he swung around and left without another word.

Ellen felt as though she'd been punched. Kit's good humour had been the one constant in the last difficult months. The growing attraction between them had surprised her, and she still wished they didn't have to be sensible, take things carefully. But she had been willing to be patient, and she thought he had too. What on earth had happened to make him behave like that?

Kit cursed himself for losing his temper with Ellen. All those months they had jogged along so well together, helpful neighbours, almost friends. It was he who had breached the invisible barrier between them, as he had wanted to for weeks. None of it was Ellen's fault. But he had been more furious than he could remember, when he had heard she had turned to Clare and not to him for help.

She had needed help, and she hadn't turned to him. It was so unfair, after all he had done for them. He'd assumed he would always be the first person Ellen would turn to. Clearly he was wrong.

But even if he still thought she should have told him what was happening, he had behaved like an idiot, totally over-reacted.

'Do you think I should say I'm sorry, Mum?' he said to the silent figure in the bed beside him. Her eyes met his, but she said nothing. It was hard to know how much was an inability to speak, how much a lack of understanding, and how much simple lethargy.

Of course he should apologise. He sighed and ran his fingers through the heavy hair. 'Do you think I should get it cut, Mum?' Still no response.

Sometimes she scanned the room as though looking for something, sometimes her lips moved but no sounds came out. What was it she wanted? He took the soft, lined hand and squeezed it. Even the hand felt frailer. This person was a mere shadow of his large and cheerful mother.

'I'll make arrangements,' he said, more gently this time. 'I'll look after you. Properly, this time.'

That was what he needed to concentrate on. He'd do that first, and then he'd think about Ellen.

'Why do you never talk about my mummy?' said Lucy, out of the blue.

'Your mum?'

'Yeah. And my dad. I was thinking...'

Ellen had just collected Lucy from Clare's. Now she needed to start preparing tea. Getting back to teaching might be interesting, but by the end of the first week she realised it was also exhausting. She suppressed a sigh. 'What were you thinking?'

'We want to know, I want to know, what happened. You know, when...'

Ellen stared at her. Lucy was so much the baby of the family she hadn't expected this from her.

If Lucy felt strongly enough to voice the words, what must the boys be thinking? Did Ellen really avoid the subject of their parents? In the weeks immediately after the accident it had been physically impossible to talk about them. She had developed a knack for avoiding the subject. That could be one reason they so liked to see their grandmother, she at least would talk endlessly about how wonderful their parents had been.

'What do you want to talk about?' she said, cautiously.

Lucy's lips, still so young and soft, did quiver then, but she stuck out the lower one and said, 'We want to know what happened, in Ch, Chec – that place where they were. Angus said the police had spoken to you, but he didn't know what they said.'

'They didn't have anything new to say. I would have told you, if they did.' Ellen shook her head, trying to get her thoughts straight. Why had she not seen this coming?

Just then Angus and Callum came in from the yard and she said, without pausing to think, 'Lucy says we never talk about your parents, and she'd like to. I didn't realise ... I hadn't thought... What is it you want to know?'

Angus halted in the doorway between the scullery and the kitchen and glared at Lucy. 'We don't need to talk about them to *you*.'

'But we want to know – things,' said Lucy, helplessly.

'I'll tell you one thing I can do,' said Ellen. Why hadn't she thought of this before? 'I can get back in touch with the British Embassy in Prague and get as much detail as possible about the accident and what has been found out since. If they can't tell me, they'll know who can. I suppose I hadn't really wanted ... I didn't really see the point... Would you like me to do that?'

'Yes,' said Lucy. Callum gave a slight nod. Angus's face was impassive.

Angus was wondering if he could get together enough money to buy the new Ed Sheeran album. He really wanted it. Simon had it and if Angus had an iPod he could have downloaded his friend's copy. But of course he didn't have an iPod. His aunt would never let him spend money on something like that. To be fair, his parents wouldn't have either. Apparently he was too young. As if everyone else in his class didn't have one. And probably half of Callum's class, too.

He was thinking these thoughts as he made his way by a back route to Grant McConnell's house. Grant had offered to call off lessons during the holidays, but Angus felt he really needed them now, to keep up with the rest of the Dudes. And he had decided he wasn't going to let Jason Armstrong and his gang keep him away.

At that moment an unwelcome voice said, 'So *this* is the way you come. Hey, Annie, how ye doing? Look, guys, it's little orphan Annie.'

It was Jason Armstrong, who else?

Angus swore under his breath. How could he be so stupid? He'd let his guard down, and look what happened. He kept his head down and walked more quickly. He was glad he had taken to playing one of Grant's guitars during lessons and didn't have his own with him. At least they couldn't wreck that.

Jason sauntered out onto the pavement in front of Angus, murmuring something over his shoulder as he did so. Angus's heart fell when he recognised his companion, a spotty youth with glazed eyes. He was the one who had taken Angus's bus fare, weeks ago, so that Angus had had to walk home. He was older and had an even worse reputation than Jason Armstrong.

There was a smell of smoke and alcohol hanging around the boys. Angus kept his head down and mouth shut and tried to push past.

'Not going to speak to us, Angus?' said Jason.

'That's no' polite,' said his friend, nudging Angus in the chest.

'Get lost. You're making me late.'

'Get lost. You're making me late,' mimicked Jason.

'You think you're so clever,' said Angus, taking a step back from the beery breath. His heart was beating wildly but he didn't actually feel afraid this time. He slipped his hand into his coat pocket. His aunt had said it was far too warm for a coat but Angus liked to have something to hide within. Thank goodness. The knife was still there, and felt comforting in his hand.

'Bin crying the day?' asked one of the Dawson

boys, and sniggered. 'Crying for yer mum-mee?'

Angus's anger rose a notch. 'You shut up, OK? Just shut up.'

'Oooh, isn't he the tough guy.' Someone nudged him on the shoulder, someone else raised the empty bottle they were holding and gestured with it at his face.

Did they think Angus was scared of a bottle? He drew the knife from his pocket with a vicious sweep, and was gratified to see pimple-face waver at the sight of it. 'Let me past or I'll use this.'

'Oo-ooh,' said someone, but doubtfully. No one came any nearer, but they didn't retreat either.

He brandished his weapon. 'Get out of my way.'

He heard someone smash a bottle on the pavement. As he glanced over the pimply boy took the chance to lunge forward.

Angus reacted instinctively. The knife made contact with a sickening thunk.

Chapter Twenty-four

Ellen's heart was thudding as she drove the short distance into Dunmuir. Lucy and Callum sat silently in the back of the car, too stunned to speak.

Angus had been arrested!

Angus was being held at Dunmuir police station because he had been involved in a knife fight. This latter fact she had kept from the children, but the words reverberated in her head. Presumably her nephew wasn't hurt, or she would be on her way to the hospital and not the police station, but what on earth had happened? She felt cold even thinking over the possibilities.

She swung the car too fast around the last corner and parked with a skid by the station door. 'Stay there, OK?' she said to the other two as she leapt out.

She introduced herself at the reception desk. 'What happened?' she demanded of the officer who came out to meet her.

'That is what we are trying to ascertain.'

'Where's my nephew?'

'He's along here.'

'And the other boys? The ones he was fighting with?'

The officer was an older man, and he turned to her now with a look that might have been sympathetic. He said quietly, 'I believe one or two people have been taken to hospital.'

'Oh.' Ellen was having difficulty taking this in. 'But Angus is all right? Are the others badly hurt?'

'I'm afraid I can't say. I'll take you to your nephew now.'

'I want my mum! No, I want Ellen. I want Ellen!' Angus was sobbing out the words as she was led into the interview room. His head rested on the table and the efforts of the plain-clothed woman at his side were not so much brushed off as totally unnoticed. 'I want *Ellen*.'

When Ellen saw that Angus was, truly, uninjured, she felt her legs quake beneath her. Then he turned a pale, desperate face towards her.

'Auntie Ellen.'

She fell onto the chair beside him and pulled him clumsily close. 'Angus. Oh, God, Angus. Are you all right?'

Angus collapsed against her, crying in earnest now. 'I'm sorry, tell them I'm sorry. Auntie Ellen, I'm so sooorreee...' And then the words became indecipherable and he was a shaking, sobbing bundle of bones and skin.

'It's all right.' She held him tight, arms completely around him, keeping him safe.

The plain clothed woman had moved to a seat by the door but she kept her eyes on them. Ellen recognised her now. It was Kathleen, the social worker.

Ellen met the woman's eyes. 'Can't my nephew and I have a few moments on our own?'

To Ellen's surprise, the woman rose and left the room. She kept the door ajar, but Ellen could cope with that.

She held the slight figure of her nephew and let him cry himself out. She felt swamped with love. She stroked the short, light brown hair and whispered words of comfort. It didn't matter what she said so much as that she was there and he knew she was there and he trusted her.

After ten minutes or more she pushed him gently away and reached in her pocket for a tissue. 'Here, have this.'

He sniffed and took it and began to dab at his eyes.

Ellen took a deep breath. 'Thank goodness you're all right,' she said slowly.

Angus sniffed again and looked down. He must

know he couldn't avoid the questions for ever. She put a hand to his thin cheek and said, 'Angus, look at me.'

He looked up, then away, then back.

'Whatever happened, Angus, you're not on your own. OK? I know there have been problems with these boys for – ages. I should have done some-thing about it sooner. And I don't even know exactly what happened, but whatever it was we'll get through it, OK? No one was killed ... were they?'

He shook his head and gave the first glimmer of a smile. 'Naw, it was just a scratch. But you should have heard him scream.'

'Right, so it's not the end of the world. We can sort it out. But first, suppose you tell me exactly what did happen?'

Angus blew his nose on the disintegrating tis-sue. 'I – I suppose so. You could tell those other people to come back in, too. I might as well tell you all at the same time.'

She dropped a kiss on his forehead, something she had never dared do before, and went to the door to summon officialdom.

Ellen couldn't believe the amount of bureaucracy involved in one little fight. It hadn't been like this when the boys had beaten up Angus and Simon, had it?

There was the charging and being released on bail, the allocation of a solicitor and going through the whole story again with her, then dealing with Social Work. She kept calm because she had to, and the strength that Angus's new trust gave her

283

was amazing. But she still needed to talk the whole thing through with an adult, and as she couldn't worry her mother, and Kit was clearly out of bounds, she turned to Clare once again. This time she insisted that Clare and Grace come and eat at Craigallan, as a thank you for looking after Callum and Lucy while she and Angus were otherwise occupied. She bought ready-cooked chicken, pre-prepared salad, baguettes, and lots of wine.

'Well, this is very nice,' said Clare, surveying the victuals with pleasure and managing in her usual wonderful way to ignore the tip that was the rest of the kitchen (and, indeed, the house). She tossed her hair back and regarded Ellen closely. 'So, time to draw breath?'

'Yes, thank God. Everything seems to have gone quiet for a bit.'

'Have you found out yet what happened?'

'Not entirely.' Ellen had to smile as she remembered the garbled versions of events she had heard from Angus. 'I don't think he's quite sure himself.'

'No, I gathered as much from Grant.' It was Grant who had been the first adult on the scene, having heard the screams from his house. It was he who had called the ambulance and the police, deciding sensibly that there was no way he could keep the latter out of things. He had also notified Clare of events and she had rescued Callum and Lucy from the car outside the police station when Ellen had totally forgotten them.

'Should I have invited Grant tonight?' said Ellen. Someone else she had to be grateful to.

'He couldn't have come. He's at a gig. There's

a lot to be said for going out with a musician, you know? No way they can hang around and get under your feet every evening.'

'I suppose.'

'So, tell me what you do know, at least.'

Ellen took a sip of her wine and considered. The last few days had been so hectic it was a relief to catch her breath and try to get things clear in her mind. 'Jason Armstrong and those other boys were hassling Angus again. Whether they were waiting for him on purpose or it was pure chance, I don't know, but they stopped him on his way to Grant's. Angus says they wouldn't let him past and when he tried to get by they began to push him about. He took the knife out of his pocket but he swears he never meant to use it.'

'But why was he carrying a knife?'

'You might well ask. This bullying has obviously been carrying on all summer, despite his denials. Why he couldn't talk to me about it... However, he knows now that carrying a knife was definitely not the right way to deal with things.'

'Can he claim it as self-defence?'

'Whatever happens, he'll be done for having the knife. As I said, he shouldn't have had it. Carrying an offensive weapon, or something like that. But he says hurting the other boy was an accident, there was a scuffle and he must have lashed out. He doesn't remember clearly.'

'Grant said there were broken bottles at the scene as well. I know he's told the police that two of the youths were threatening Angus with them. It's lucky he came along, God knows what they would have done.'

'What I can't understand is that only the boy Sean seems to have been hurt, despite all the blood and screaming. And he was cut on the face, but Angus says the knife went through his sleeve and got stuck there, so I really don't know what to think.' Ellen shook her head. Maybe talking things over wasn't going to make them any clearer.

'Does anyone know how badly Sean was hurt?'

'The police won't say, but from the solicitor I understand it wasn't a bad wound, didn't even need stitches.'

'And what does Kit think about it all?'

Ellen frowned. Why did they need to bring Kit into this? 'I haven't seen him,' she said shortly. It wasn't strictly true. Every time he went in or out he had to drive past Craigallan, so she had seen him – or his car – often enough. It was just that they no longer seemed to be speaking.

'Don't you think it's time you and he made things up?'

'We haven't had an argument, how can we make up?'

'I realise that Kit has a number of issues he needs to work through,' said Clare earnestly, helping herself to another glass of wine. 'He's got this great need to care for people, and when he feels he isn't achieving that, he doesn't cope well.'

Ellen grunted. So Kit had only hung around all that time because he could care for them?

'Someone needs to get him to loosen up a bit, you know?' continued Clare. 'It's a shame his mother is ill but it doesn't mean he should put his own life on hold.'

The words rang uncomfortably true with Ellen.

286

Hadn't she put her own life on hold during those first awful months following Jess and Sam's death? She wondered what the situation with Kit would be like now if she had behaved differently then.

'It's Kit's life,' she said shortly.

'Does he know about Angus's latest?'

'I haven't told him. I don't know if Angus has.'

'He'll be hurt if he finds out and none of you have told him.'

'For goodness sake,' said Ellen. 'I've got enough to worry about without whether Kit Ballantyne is hurt or not.'

When Kit knocked on Ellen's door on the Monday morning, she met him with a guarded smile. He couldn't blame her. She must be wondering what had happened to make him appear now.

He should have apologised days ago, although he couldn't now quite remember what it was he thought he had done wrong. But his mum had needed him, and he'd promised himself he'd put her first. Now the hospital were confident they had her medication right and were even talking about a moving her to the local cottage hospital. So he had time to think of other things.

Ellen must have washed her hair that morning and it was still damp, combed tidily back to reveal more of her face than usual. She looked calm and collected and very pretty, even in jeans and a loose cotton jersey. It made him feel nervous, at how she could always be so calm, so immaculate.

'Er, hi,' he said, bending to pat Monty, who was perfectly welcoming.

'Hello.' She went back to the sink where she had been washing up. When he said nothing she sighed and made a move to dry her hands again. 'Do you want to come in? Coffee?'

It made him smile. She couldn't not be polite. She frowned suspiciously at the smile and he said hurriedly, 'That'd be great, thanks.' At least it got him in to the house and seated at the kitchen table. 'Lovely day,' he said, as the silence lengthened.

Ellen glanced out of the window at the fields where the sun slanted through an early morning mist, picking out the golds and browns of the grass. 'Mmm.' She put a mug down on the table in front of him and then returned to the sink. He stared at her back. It wasn't encouraging.

'Er, Ellen?'

'Mmm?'

'How's Angus getting on?' It wasn't what he meant to say, but he had to start somewhere.

Her expression darkened. 'I presume you've heard what happened?'

'No. Why? What?'

Ellen sucked in her lip. 'I thought that was why you were here. Angus got into another fight.'

'With those same kids?' Ellen nodded and he felt the anger rise in him as he remembered the smug nastiness of the youngsters on the evening of the ceilidh. 'I hope he sorted them out properly this time.'

'Maybe you could say he did.' Ellen gave a faint smile. 'He knifed one of them.'

'He *what?*' Kit leant forward, horrified. How could she smile about something like that? Angus in a knife fight! He couldn't believe it.

'He didn't do much damage. In fact, it's debatable whether he did any at all. The other kids were using broken bottles. A boy called Sean got cut on his face and another boy on his hand, but no one is clear how.'

'Is Angus OK?'

'Physically, he's fine. He was a bit – shaken.' Ellen looked shaken herself as she described briefly what had happened. 'There have obviously been ongoing problems the whole time, but I didn't realise. I can't understand why I didn't know.'

'Where is Angus now?' asked Kit, but what he was really thinking was, *why didn't you tell me?* Angus had been involved is something as serious as this and nobody had thought to let him know? Did he count for nothing in the lives of Ellen and the children?

'He's at Simon's. He's fine – well, fine-ish. He's on police bail while we find out what is going to happen.'

'You've let him go into Dunmuir where those other kids are?'

Ellen glared, the green-brown eyes cold. 'I took him in. I'll pick him up. Simon's mum knows what happened. She'll keep an eye on him. I think I'm doing the best I can, don't you?'

'Yes, of course. I only thought...'

'You think I should keep him locked up at home? What good would that do?'

Kit took a deep breath. 'I'm only concerned about Angus.'

'You think I'm not?'

'No, I didn't mean that. Shit. What's going to happen now? Will he have a criminal record? This could be really serious, don't you see?'

'Yes, of course I see. You think I'm not worried sick? But I can't let Angus know that. He's upset enough as it is. We're just waiting to see what will happen. Apparently there'll be a Children's Panel hearing, whatever that is.'

'Is there anything I can do to help? Do you want me to talk to Angus?'

'No *thank you*. I can talk to Angus perfectly well myself.'

Everything he said was wrong, but Kit couldn't seem to stop himself. Didn't she know how much Angus meant to him, how desperate he was to help? He admired and liked the kid, and he owed it to Jess and Sam to do everything he could. 'Maybe I could take him out somewhere for the day? Take them all out. Give you a break.' Why hadn't he thought of that before?

'I don't need a break, thank you. Despite the opinion of the social workers and others, I'm perfectly able to cope.'

'I didn't mean that. Perhaps I can put in a good word for him, you know, as a character witness or something? And surely they'll take into account all he's gone through this year, losing his parents, he's had a difficult time. They won't be too hard on him, will they?'

'I'm sure they'll take all that into account.' Ellen's eyes flashed with anger now. What had he said? 'And the fact that he's now being looked after by his feckless aunt who has no idea of the rules of child care, but I'm sure a character reference from a pillar of the community like you will make all the difference.'

'Ellen, I'm only trying to help...'

'Just leave it, OK? Look, I've got things I need to get on with, and I presume you have too.' She rose and took the mugs to the sink.

Kit rose too and moved a step towards her, and then hesitated. 'Ellen, I'm sorry.'

'Why are you sorry? It's not your fault.'

'I know. I mean, I don't mean to interfere...'

'Then don't.' She turned to face him, her eyes steely and implacable. 'That's what everyone says they want to do, isn't it, they only want to help. Give their opinion. Criticise. Well, the children are my problem and I'm going to look after them, all on my own. OK?'

He could feel the cold waves of fury, driving him away from her. 'If that's what you want.'

Chapter Twenty-five

Ellen shuffled the papers nervously in her hands as she waited for the children to take their seats at the table. As she looked around she wished she had suggested the sitting room. This felt far too businesslike, and already Lucy's eyes were red and tearful. She had brought out the beautiful candle-holder that Clare had made for them.

'What's that for?' asked Angus.

'I thought ... maybe we could light it,' his sister whispered.

Angus shrugged.

'We'll light it this evening,' said Ellen. It wasn't the first time the candle had been brought out. It appeared in times of stress and lighting it appeared to calm the children, as Clare had surely intended.

Then she took a deep breath, and began. 'You remember I said I would try to find out everything I could about what happened to your parents?' They nodded. 'I want to tell you what I know.'

Ellen spread the papers before her with nervous hands.

This was the hardest thing she had done, harder than the funeral, harder than taking on the children. She'd had to force herself every step of the way, asking questions, insisting on answers she didn't even want to know. Forcing herself to face up to the facts of her sister's pointless death. Because the children needed to know.

She took a deep breath and began.

As you know, the taxi your parents were in was in a collision with another car. The Czech police have now finished their investigation and it seems that the taxi driver was not at fault. The driver of the other car had been drinking and he went through a red light. It was all very fast. His car hit the one your parents were in hard. They – they wouldn't have known anything about it.'

She swallowed hard. She had seen the photographs of the wreckage, but she wasn't going to show those to the children. 'The report says that death was instantaneous. That means it happened straight away, so neither of them would have suffered. The driver of the other car died later in hospital and the taxi driver was injured. The other

driver wasn't insured. He would have been pro-
secuted for dangerous driving and for having no
insurance but obviously if he's dead that can't
happen.'

'I'm glad he's dead,' said Angus.

Ellen raised her hands in a gesture of help-
lessness. She didn't feel able to make any excuses
for this man who had caused such misery.

She squeezed her eyes shut to force back the
tears that were threatening to fall.

The children asked a few questions, and she answered them as best she could. Really, despite all
her efforts, she didn't have much to tell them. But
they seemed relieved, as though this had helped.

After a while she said, 'One thing I found when
I was going through everything last week was the
camera your mum had with her during the
holiday. The film wasn't quite finished but I've
had it developed. I thought you might like to see.'
Jess had had an old-fashioned camera, no new-
fangled digital stuff for her.

Ellen slid the shiny pictures from the paper
packet and there was Jess's pretty face, flushed
and happy, laughing out at her. 'If you gather
round a bit we can look at them together, see if
we can work out where they are.'

The children did as she asked. She thought for
a moment that Angus would refuse, but after a
moment he moved to look over her shoulder. It
meant she couldn't see his face, which might
have been his intention.

There were fourteen pictures, some of the
beautiful buildings of Prague, one of Jess's feet,
and the remainder shots of Jess or Sam as they

posed against the unfamiliar backdrops. They looked so happy. Ellen reminded herself that this was the first break they had had in years, a chance to spend time alone together again. And it looked as though they enjoyed it. In every picture they were smiling or laughing, pulling faces, throwing snowballs – having a good time, with no idea what lay ahead. There was only one picture of the two of them together, taken presumably by some waiter or willing passer-by. They had their arms around each other and looked like a couple very much in love. They had been married nearly fifteen years and were still very much in love. It could happen.

'They look very happy,' she said gently. 'It's nice that they had a good time, isn't it?'

Lucy put her finger on one picture and said nothing.

Callum said, 'They shouldn't have gone.'

'We can't change it now,' said Angus, and his tone was bitter again, the way it had been in those long resentful months.

'No, we can't change it.' Ellen turned to put an arm around him, trying to enfold them all in an embrace. 'It's awful and unfair, but there's nothing we can do except try and get on with our lives. I miss Jess too. Not as much as you do, of course, but she was my only sister. We've all lost something. But we've got each other. I'm really, really glad I've got you and I hope I can be as good an aunt as it is possible to be.'

Angus stayed close longer than she expected, even putting his arm tentatively around Lucy.

'Is there anything else?'

'No, I don't think so.' There was no point in telling them that as the drunk driver had not been insured there was no money forthcoming from him. The officials had made a big thing of this, but, really, what was money? They had enough to live off, that was all that mattered. Although it would definitely help if she could find some more paying work soon.

'I thought of getting some bigger prints made from these photos,' she said cautiously. 'It might be nice to frame them and put them up some-where.'

'We don't need pictures to remember,' said Angus. Lucy had been about to nod, but now she fell silent, hiding her face against Ellen's shoulder.

'Of course you don't,' said Ellen. 'It's up to you. But I thought it might be nice, somehow...'

'I think we should have that one,' said Callum pointing to the one of his parents together. It might be slightly blurred and off-centre, but it caught the moment well. Callum's voice wavered, but he spoke loudly. 'I think it would be good to put that up in here.'

'Yes,' said Lucy.

Angus shrugged.

'I'll get some enlargements made and we'll see,' said Ellen.

She shuffled the pictures together and sat up-right. That was enough emotion. 'Now, I hate to nag but there are still some chores to be done. No one's collected eggs today and Monty needs feeding and...'

The children seemed as thankful as she was to have tasks to distract them. They drifted out.

Ellen left the photographs on the table in case they wanted to look at them in private later.

Then she went to pick up the post which she had heard arriving a short while before. And there was the letter she had been awaiting and dreading, the one summoning her and Angus to the Children's Hearing. There was a similar letter addressed directly to Angus. She put it to one side until tomorrow. He didn't have to cope with everything all at once, even if it sometimes felt like she did.

Kit had to do something. Ellen was point-blank refusing his help, but that didn't mean he should just give up.

His mum was in the cottage hospital and plans were in hand for her to move to Westerwood House. She was making good progress. With the input of the physios and the speech therapist she was now able to sit up and feed herself, even hold short conversations. And she actually seemed happy! She explained, slowly, that it would be nice not to have to worry about the house, about being on her own. He should have realised that living on her own was too difficult for her.

'I should have moved back home...'

'No, why would you do that? You're a good boy, Kit, but...' A pause. 'But it'll be nice to be with people my own age. Westerwood House is nice. You did like it, didn't you?'

'Yes, Mum, I've said already.'

He shook his head in bewilderment. His mum's speech might be slow, and she might be a little confused at times, but one thing was clear. She

296

was looking forward to this move.

And now he had to do something for Ellen. He decided to get in touch with Social Services. They obviously had no idea what a brilliant job she was doing under incredibly difficult circumstances. Ellen might not like it, but if he didn't tell them, who would?

His months of dealing with the bureaucracy of the planning department stood him in good stead now. He phoned ahead and after numerous diversions eventually secured the name of the social worker allotted to Angus's case (Kathleen Mitchell) and obtained an appointment to see her. He put on his best pair of corduroy trousers and a clean shirt and set off in plenty of time.

Kathleen Mitchell was a plump, untidy woman who ushered him into a tiny meeting room amidst chatter about the weather and apologies for keeping him waiting. She seemed rather pleasant, which was off-putting. Kit had been all ready to face down an ogre.

'What was it you wanted to see me about?' She sat at right-angles to him, with a small round table at her elbow, pad and pen laid at the ready.

'Angus Moffat.'

'Ah, yes.'

'I'm a neighbour of the Moffats. The nearest neighbour, as it happens.'

'I see. Mr Ballantyne, isn't it?'

'That's right. Christopher Ballantyne. I work at the veterinary practice in Dunmuir. I bought a plot of land off the Moffats just over a year ago now, and I had got to know them quite well before the – the accident.'

Still the woman waited, smiling pleasantly. Kit urged himself to get to the point.

'I have also got to know Ellen Taylor very well in the months since she moved down to Craigallan.'

'Ah, yes. Are you the neighbour she asks to help out with the children?'

'Ellen rarely asks anyone to help out with anything. She is very hard-working and takes far too much on herself. Before most of the farm animals were sold I helped a little with them but I don't think she has needed assistance with her nephews and niece. You know that she gave up a good job and her own life in Edinburgh to come down and look after them, which she currently does full-time?'

'Yes, I know she hadn't had much to do with children before this happened.'

'I don't think most parents have had much to do with children until they become parents, have they? This was just a bit more extreme a situation. And Ellen, Miss Taylor, has coped with it admirably.'

Kit was getting into the swing of things now. 'I don't think you realise how hard a time she has had, how much she has done. Those kids were absolutely devastated to lose their parents, you can imagine, and she has stuck by them through thick and thin. Angus isn't the easiest of people but Ellen has tried and tried to get through to him, to make things right.'

'Angus has been a bit of a problem, has he?'

'Angus is a thirteen-year-old boy who has recently lost both his parents and has had one or

298

two difficulties at school. You wouldn't expect things to be easy there, would you? But he's basically a good kid.'

'I see. Do you think that getting into a series of fights, as this youngster seems to have done, is the behaviour of a good kid?'

'It wasn't his fault, for goodness sake.'

'I realise that the adults with responsibility for him have a role to play...'

Kit could feel his voice rising. 'So you really are trying to blame Ellen? I knew you'd try to twist things like that. Don't you realise that sometimes it's just the circumstances that make things happen in a certain way? Ellen has done everything she possibly can for that boy, why don't you look at the school and see if you can say the same for them?'

'And would you say Miss Taylor takes the same amount of interest in the younger children?'

'Yes!' This woman seemed determined to twist his words. 'Yes I bloody would. She's been an absolute marvel. You've only got to see Lucy with her to see how good their relationship is.'

'And there's another boy, isn't there? Callum?'

'Callum's fine too. It's not that Ellen doesn't worry about him, she does, she worries because basically he is so much easier than Angus. She does her best for all of them. They're always going to football and swimming and all that stuff, and she makes sure they have a good diet, and everything. For goodness sake, aren't there any kids with serious problems you should be worrying about?'

'Just because children come from a middle-class background doesn't mean to say there can't be problems at home.'

Suddenly the cool tone struck Kit as ominous. 'You're not going to take the kids away from her, are you? You couldn't do that?'

'I'm not at liberty to discuss the situation with you. I'm grateful to you for taking the time to come in and talk to me. I appreciate the effort you have clearly made to help the family.'

'They don't need my help. That's what I'm saying. They're managing absolutely fine.'

'As I said, I do appreciate your taking the time to come in.'

Kit stared at her. Had he made things worse?

'Do call me Kathleen,' said the Social Worker to Angus for the third time. Why should he call her Kathleen? He didn't want to call her anything. He didn't even want to talk to her.

'Why d'you have to see me at school?' he asked. It was the first week back and he'd been embarrassed to be called out of Geography like that.

She smiled kindly. 'This was the time I happened to have free, and your headmaster was good enough to allow me to see you here.'

'Does Ellen know?'

Kathleen cleared her throat, a good sign that she was trying for time to think. 'Your aunt knows that I was planning to have a follow-up chat with you sometime soon. We didn't discuss any details.'

'She's my guardian, isn't she? Shouldn't she be here?'

'Your guardian doesn't need to be present at every interview. Sometimes it can help you to relax if there are fewer people around.'

'I won't tell you anything I haven't told Ellen.'

'No, no, of course I'm not asking you to do that.' The woman sighed and pushed strands of hair back from a face that was beginning to look red and uncomfortable. Good. Angus didn't think it was his job to put her at ease.

'Are you going to tell the rector everything I say? And the police?' It felt good to be bolshie again. He had spent the last few weeks feeling so remorseful he hadn't been able to get things in perspective. Now he'd had time to think, and Simon Scott had told him that git Sean was just putting it on. That made him feel a whole lot better. He wasn't angry with his aunt any more, he didn't know why, but he still had plenty of resentment for the school and the whole stupid system he was caught up in.

'Whatever you tell me will be entirely confidential,' said Kathleen, looking hopeful.

'I didn't do anything,' said Angus. 'Much.'

'I'm sure you didn't, but if we could just go over the series of events again...?'

'I didn't start it. They started it. They surrounded me and started pushing me about. I'm the victim here, you know.' Even as he said the words Angus felt an insane desire to laugh. He could just imagine Jason Armstrong coming out with those exact words. I'm the victim, life's not fair, it's not *my* fault... This thought made him change tack. 'Actually, I was being a bit ... stupid. I shouldn't have been carrying the knife. I knew it at the time but it made me feel safer, you know?' He paused. 'Will I go to prison?'

'Of course not. You're far too young to go to prison.'

Angus sighed. Grown-ups were so stupid sometimes. 'You know what I mean. To a Young Offenders place or whatever they call it. I want to know if that's possible. It'll be hard on my aunt if I do. And the kids.' He was sorry they had been dragged in to all of this. Lucy was really upset. Angus wondered if he should have listened to his aunt and moved to a school in Dumfries.

'That will depend on what happens at the Children's Hearing. I wanted to fill you in a little more about the hearings.'

Angus shrugged.

'This is a unique system of care and justice for Scotland's children,' said Kathleen. She looked more relaxed now, spouting jargon. Angus let the words go over his head. Why should he want to know about the stupid child-centred justice system? He just wanted it to be over.

'Why does it take so long?' he interrupted. 'It's really upsetting my brother and sister.'

Kathleen had opened her mouth to continue with her boring explanation. Now she closed it and frowned.

'The system in Scotland prides itself on dealing with these kind of matters quickly.'

'Yeah, well, it's still been weeks.' Angus hoped she couldn't hear the catch in his voice. 'Look, I know I'm in the wrong. Can't I just admit it and they can decide what to do?'

'I'm very glad that you see the error of your ways,' she said.

'But I'm not the only one in the wrong, you

know.' His aunt had been very keen to make sure he knew she knew that, and he was grateful. 'And I bet Jason and the rest aren't sorry. Not *really* sorry. Not so as it would stop them doing the same thing again.'

'Are you worried they might try to find you and cause trouble?' Kathleen picked up her pencil.

'No way. They'll leave me alone now. But I'm not the only one they bully, you know. If they get away with this then they'll be even worse the next time. Have you thought of that?'

'I'm sure that is being looked in to. I'm not the social worker allocated to their case, and even if I was I couldn't divulge to you anything that had been discussed.'

'Huh,' said Angus. 'That's a lot of help.' The woman coloured with annoyance, but he knew she wouldn't do anything to him. She was too keen for him to think she was on 'his' side. As if.

'Sean Mackay's dad's in prison at the moment, you know, for assault. And his brother's just come out after doing time for drugs.' Angus had learnt this from Simon, who was an excellent source of information. 'Doesn't that give you some idea of what he's like?'

'We shouldn't judge a child by their parents.'

'No.' Angus glared at her. 'Well, you can't judge me by mine, 'cos I haven't got any any more.' He knew that would make her feel uncomfortable and it did. She brought the interview to a close soon after.

He felt rather pleased with himself. He'd got her measure all right. He'd tell Ellen about it when he got home, and maybe help her start painting some of the downstairs rooms. Now they didn't have so many animals he had more free time, and it wasn't fair to expect Ellen to do everything in the house. He'd have to make sure the kids pulled their weight as well.

Chapter Twenty-six

Ellen was worried sick about the Children's Panel hearing. The solicitor had tried to be comforting, the social worker had dripped sympathy while being noncommittal, and Angus, surprisingly, seemed to be taking it in his stride. But she felt an immense weight of guilt that she had let him get in to this situation. It was she who had insisted he go back for those lessons with Grant, when he had clearly been intimidated away. She had been cross with him, had made him go into town on his own. Why hadn't she seen his side? She could feel panic rising. What if this ruined the rest of his life?

Her mother had offered to come down and accompany them to the hearing, but she had declined. That would just give her one more person to worry about.

Callum and Lucy went off (unwillingly) to school as normal and she made arrangements for them to go to Clare's afterwards, as she had no idea how long the hearing might take. No one could say she wasn't being responsible. She put on one of her dark work suits, which felt oddly uncomfortable after so long in casual clothes.

Angus, she discovered at the last moment, had no trousers other than his school ones or jeans. She didn't know what would look worse, the unnatural smartness of school clothes, or the I-don't-care attitude that might be portrayed by jeans. Why hadn't she thought of this before?

'Look, these jeans will have to do, I've ironed them,' she said, waving the offending garment at her nephew who looked horrified to see his favourite trousers now sporting a neatly ironed crease. 'Wear them with that shirt Grandma got for your birthday, that'll have to do.'

He looked ready to argue, but a knock on the door sent him retreating upstairs. Who could it be now?

Kit was standing on the doorstep, looking ill at ease.

'Yes?' said Ellen. She didn't have time to be polite.

'I, er, heard you were off to the Children's Panel this morning.'

'Yes. We'll be leaving in a few minutes.' Pointedly, she didn't invite him in. She didn't know what had gone wrong between them. He might have his own problems but she didn't have the energy for them just now.

'I wanted to wish Angus all the best.'

'That's kind. I'll tell him. He's upstairs getting changed.'

'Ah.' Kit looked relieved. 'Could I come in for a minute?'

Ellen sighed. He knew she was in a hurry. Hopefully whatever he had to say wouldn't take long. She let him in, but didn't take a seat, just in case he hadn't got the message that time was short.

'How do you think it'll go?' asked Kit.

'I've no idea.' When that sounded a little too abrupt she added, 'The solicitor sounded fairly positive, but really, I don't know what to expect.'

'I'm sure you'll be fine. There was one thing I wanted to mention. I've explained to the social worker how well you're doing.'

Ellen frowned. 'What social worker?'

Now Kit looked decidedly shifty. 'Er. Well. I got in touch with Social Services myself. I, er, wanted to do my best, to let them know that none of this is Angus's fault.'

'You what?' Ellen could feel her stomach tense, her throat tighten. She had been so near the edge of panic it only took one more thing to push her over. 'This is none of your business!'

'No, of course it's not. But I thought it would be a good idea for someone to put your side of the story...'

'And you think we haven't?'

'As an outsider, you know. I thought it couldn't do any harm and it might help. So I made an appointment to see someone in Social Services...'

Ellen could hear a strange buzzing in her ears. 'Thank you so much. I'm sure that counted for a lot.'

'I was trying to help. I just wanted you to know, that they have heard this from someone, from me. Don't let them pretend they've only heard bad things. If they have heard bad things. Look, I'm saying this all wrong...'

Ellen couldn't believe he had done that. Really, was there no limit to his interference? 'I haven't time for this. We have to go.'

'Yes, of course. I'm so sorry you have to go through this.'

'You think I'm not? Now...'

They were interrupted by the sound of Angus coming down the stairs two at a time. 'I don't see why I have to wear...' He paused when he saw Kit. 'Hi.'

'Hi yourself. I just popped by to wish you all the best.'

'Thanks.' Angus tugged at his collar and then shot them both an unexpected smile. 'It'll be all right, you know. They won't send me to prison, and nothing else is too bad, is it?'

Ellen tried to smile back. She didn't think there was any point in informing Angus of all the other measures that could be taken against him (and her). She had looked into it. They ranged from sending him to secure accommodation, through foster care, parenting orders, something called 'restorative justice', and simple, old-fashioned fines. And the worst of it was, she had absolutely no idea which was the most likely outcome.

'Time we were off,' she said, picking up her bag and keys. 'Thanks for calling by, Kit.'

'I could come with you, if you want me to?'

'No I definitely do not.' She just wanted him to leave, which reluctantly he did.

They drove to Dumfries in silence. Ellen thought Angus must be worried about the ordeal ahead, and tried and failed to think of words to comfort him. But as they drew into the car park behind the council buildings he said, 'Why are you so horrible to Kit these days?'

His words certainly distracted her from her other worries. She stared at him in amazement. 'What do you mean? I'm not horrible to Kit.'

'You are. Even Lucy has noticed. He used to be around a lot, helping and that, you know. Now he hardly ever is.'

'We haven't got so many animals now. And he's got his mum to worry about.'

Angus shrugged his disbelief. 'I don't think he means to annoy you,' he said.

They entered the red sandstone building in silence, but this time it was because Ellen was too stunned to speak. How could it possibly be her fault that she and Kit were estranged? It was far better for the children if she wasn't distracted by him. Determinedly, she put the whole topic out of her mind.

Three hours later she and Angus came out of the building by the same door, both equally shell-shocked.

'Let's go and get something to eat,' said Ellen.

Angus followed on behind her, saying nothing. The nearest café was down the Friar's Vennel, and they took the first table they came to. Ellen ordered a large black coffee and it was only when she had taken her first sip that she felt able to think.

'It could have been worse,' she said cautiously.

'Wonder what they said to the other kids,' said Angus.

The discussions had been firmly focussed on

Angus and his 'behaviour problems'. No mention had been allowed of the responsibility the other boys might have had in the matter. Ellen devoutly hoped that this was a matter of policy and not because it was felt the others were not at fault.

'Simon says they've got hearings too,' Angus continued. 'But he didn't know when. Can I have a burger and chips?'

Ellen nodded. She would have agreed to anything just then. 'Are you all right?' she said, examining his face, to which a faint colour had now returned.

Angus gave his characteristic shrug, but he didn't seem too downhearted. 'I thought when they said about compulsory supervision, you know, I thought they meant I'd have to go away...'

'So did I.' Ellen suppressed a shudder and gave him a quick hug, as much for her benefit as his. But she wasn't going to lose him. They'd had to agree to twelve months' 'supervision' by a social worker, and a few other things. But they could cope with that. 'It'll only be a few visits, really, and then those workshops she talked about.' *How to cope when we've been hurt. How to cope when we make mistakes. How to cope with resentment.*

She still resented that Angus was being punished when he really wasn't the perpetrator. 'Maybe I shouldn't say this, but I still don't think it's fair,' she said.

'I'm sorry you've got to go on one too,' said Angus, flushing with embarrassment. 'I don't get it, why they think you need to learn that stuff.'

Ellen thought there was a lot of stuff she

309

needed to learn. She just wasn't sure she'd learn it at a workshop. 'As I said, it could be worse. Hopefully this'll be the end of it.'

'As long as I don't re-offend within twelve months, in which case it might be more appropriate to resort to a criminal process.'

Ellen didn't like to hear the formal words on his lips, but she made herself smile and say, 'You better bloody not. You'll have me to deal with if you do.'

Angus made an effort and responded with a half-smile of his own.

When they had finished their late lunch Ellen said, 'What do you want to do now?' It was amazing how at ease she felt with the boy. One thing, at least, had come out of these troubles. She could speak to him without worrying how he would respond, could have a proper conversation with him. 'Home or what?'

'What time is it? If we hurry we can pick up the kids from school. Let's do that. They'll want to know what's happened.'

'Indeed they will.' As would Clare, and her parents, and the school... And Kit, but he needn't think she was going to seek him out to tell him. Just to think of him interfering, again made her flush with anger.

Kit didn't see what else he could do. He had offered the hand of friendship – twice, if you counted this morning – and Ellen had rejected it. Call it pride or simple common sense, he wasn't going to try again.

He decided to forget about neighbours and

310

went out for a drink after evening clinic with Alistair and Deb. He didn't even object when the vet nurse, Devon, brought a bunch of youngsters to join their table, seating herself triumphantly at his side. He bought a couple of rounds and laughed and joked, but he couldn't have said he actually enjoyed himself.

He had thought of a way to discover the news. He would call on Clare.

'I thought it was Grant,' was Clare's comment as she opened the door. Not an auspicious welcome, but she held the door wide which he took as an invitation to go in. 'Working late?' she asked, seeing the direction from which his car had come. 'Or were you at the hospital?'

'No, I had a drink at the Duke's.'

'Excellent,' she said encouragingly. 'Time for another one now?'

Kit declined. He just needed information. 'Have you heard how Angus got on today?'

'Yes! Brilliant news, isn't it?'

'It is?' He exhaled with a great gust of relief. 'He got off?'

'I don't know if you'd call it getting off. But despite Ellen's grumbles I think they were pretty lenient with him. They couldn't do nothing, could they, not after he'd been caught with a knife.'

Nothing was exactly what Kit thought they should have done, but all he said was, 'So what is his punishment?'

Clare examined him critically from behind the dark curtain of hair. 'Why are you asking me and not Ellen?'

Kit sighed and hunched down in his seat. 'Ellen

311

and I aren't getting on too well just now,' he said briefly. 'So are you going to tell me or not?'

Clare narrowed her eyes thoughtfully. 'You and Ellen, I don't know what your problem is.'

'Could you just tell me about Angus please?'

'OK.' She frowned, marshalling her thoughts. 'Angus has been given something called a Supervision Order...' She told him what she understood this to mean, and Kit felt his temper rising all over again at the unfairness of the system. OK, so the boy wouldn't have a criminal record and he wasn't being separated from his family, but it didn't sound like this was going to be any fun for Angus, or Ellen.

He thanked her as soon as he could and headed off. So that was that. No serious harm done.

Chapter Twenty-seven

Autumn had arrived with a vengeance, although it was only the end of September. Winds raged around Craigallan, making Ellen glad it wasn't situated in a more exposed spot. She examined the roof anxiously, but so far could see no problem slates, and the patching job done in the early summer seemed to be holding. The wild weather had blown the last of the leaves off the trees in the copse and if she had wanted to she could have had a good view of progress on Kit's house whenever she took Monty out. Mostly she avoided going in a direction that might tempt her to look. Since

312

their argument over his visit to social services they hadn't spoken. She couldn't remember, in retrospect, why she had been quite so annoyed.

Even without seeing the house, Ellen couldn't stop herself thinking of Kit. It wasn't just that she missed the practical help he used to give, she missed *him*. And that wasn't good. Kit had been the one who withdrew from her, who'd marched off, she should learn from that.

A Saturday evening a couple of weeks after the Children's Hearing Ellen invited Clare and Grace for a meal to celebrate the (relatively) positive outcome. She would prove to Kit, and herself, that she had the beginnings of a social life.

'Have you heard about Mrs Jack?' asked Clare as she mixed up a salad dressing.

'Heard what?'

'About Mr Jack, actually. He died a couple of weeks ago. None of us even knew.'

'That's a shame, now I feel bad. I never believed the husband was really ill.'

'Nor did I. Maybe he died just to escape from her! Anyway, she's moving back to England. Thank goodness. She can be someone else's nightmare neighbour.'

'And she won't be spying on us.' Ellen's spirits lifted at the thought. She knew, well she was fairly sure, she was doing a good job with the children. Every time she passed the Jacks' house she had the sensation of being watched, and judged. It would be such a relief not to feel that.

She found herself really enjoying the evening. Socialising, which had seemed so easy, just a natural part of life in Edinburgh, took some organising down here. There were the distances involved, the fact she was only starting to get to know people, and then the children. Everything had to be fitted in around them. But she was starting to make progress, wasn't she?

'Thanks for inviting us. It's good to get out.'

Clare said, 'It can't be easy for you. There must be all sorts of things you used to do in your old life that you can't do now.'

'It's fine,' said Ellen quickly.

'I know you don't complain, but you must miss things. What about your Edinburgh friends? And your climbing? Didn't you used to do lots of that? I'm sure I remember Jess talking about it, she was impressed and appalled at the same time.'

Ellen laughed. 'Yes, it wasn't quite Jess's kind of thing.' It was funny to think about climbing after all this time. Jess had thought it frivolous and dangerous, but perhaps there had also been a sneaking respect as well. 'I do miss it,' she said, with a soft sigh. 'But then I miss so much about my old life.' Not so much the friends, who she realised now had been little more than acquaintances, but the peace, the order, the... Well, no point in thinking about it. The change had brought other advantages. She loved the children, she really did.

'It's only normal to miss it. And Richard.'

'Oh, I don't miss him at all.' It was true, she didn't.

'Men do have their uses,' said Clare, with that distant look she got in her eyes when she thought of Grant.

'Things going well?' said Ellen with a smile.

'Mmm. He's thinking of moving in with me.

314

He's at my place so much it probably wouldn't be much different. But it seems like a big thing, you know, if he gives up his house. I'm not sure we're ready for it.'

Ellen admired the calm way Clare could discuss her relationship. That's how she liked to be herself, cool and in control. 'Grant seems a nice guy.'

'He is. Grace is very fond of him. Yes, you know, I think it might work out.' Clare pondered for a while, twirling her wine glass in her hands. The debris of the evening meal still cluttered the table but Ellen was enjoying relaxing with a friend. It could wait. 'Even if you don't miss Richard, don't you miss having a man around the place?'

'I've always lived on my own,' Ellen said quickly. She didn't want the conversation to become yet another of Clare's attempts to bring her and Kit together. 'And now it's alone with the kids.'

Kit's mum moved into Westerwood House in late September. It was amazing to see her there, settled in her own room with the few pieces of furniture she had wanted to take with her. She seemed proud of it, and desperate to get downstairs so she could have a coffee and a chat with Nora.

'You don't mind me moving here?' she said to Kit as he walked with her to the lift. There was only a very slight hitch in her speech now.

'Of course not! Why should I mind?'

'I liked to keep the house on for you, so you could visit. I didn't want you to know how difficult it had got.'

'I should have realised.'

'No, dear. You take too much on yourself, don't you know that? Now you'll know I'm being well looked after here, and in a while, if we decide, we can put the house on the market. You'd rather live in your new place than there, wouldn't you?'

'Yes, of course. But we don't need to put it on the market. Wouldn't you rather know it was there, that you could go back if you wanted?'

'I won't be going back,' she said. And she really didn't seem upset by the idea. It was Kit who was having more difficulty adjusting than she was.

'Now your mum is settled, when are you going to sort yourself out?' This was Debbie, of course. Always happy to ask the difficult questions. Kit had been invited for a meal with her and Alistair. He might not have been so keen to go if he'd known it would lead to this.

'I am settling down. If building your own house isn't settling down, I don't know what is.' Kit threw Alistair a pleading expression, but before his friend could speak Deb was in there again.

'That's not what I mean. You're not naturally a loner, Kit. What you need is a girlfriend.'

Kit cringed. He really liked Debbie, but sometimes she was a bit much.

'Leave him alone,' said Alistair. 'Kit has never had a problem getting himself a woman. If he wants a girlfriend, he'll find one.'

'But it has to be the right one,' said Debbie earnestly. They had just finished their first course and she didn't seem in any hurry to get up and clear the table.

'And there was I thinking just anyone would

316

do,' said Alistair ironically.

'He's had his fair share of short-term relationships. Someone like Devon would be OK for that, but she isn't what he needs now.'

'I don't think Devon would agree.'

'Excuse me, but do you mind not talking about me as if I wasn't here?'

'Well, say something if you want to,' said Debbie, smiling engagingly.

'Aren't the nights drawing in,' said Kit. 'It fairly feels like winter is on its way, doesn't it? Now, shall I clear the table? I can even do the washing up, if you want. That'll keep me nice and safe in the kitchen.'

At such a determined snub, even Debbie had the sense to let the topic fall. Instead she asked how Kit's mum was settling in at Westerwood House.

'Really well.' Kit grinned. OK, it might have been a surprise that his mother was so happy with the move, but it was a pleasant one. 'She seems so comfortable there, so relaxed. And the staff are really nice.'

'That must be such a relief. And do you think she'd enjoy visitors? I wondered about calling in on my afternoon off.'

'I think she'd love that. Thanks, Deb.'

Then Deborah blotted her copybook again by saying, as he was leaving, 'Don't forget you're coming for another meal with us on Tuesday. As it's Al's birthday it'll be curry. I'm going to do the whole caboodle: sambals, naan bread, the lot.'

'Of course I haven't forgotten, I'm looking forward to it.'

'And you could always bring someone with you, if you wanted? How about that neighbour or yours, what's her name? Ellen?'

'De-eb,' said her husband.

'Thanks but no thanks,' said Kit firmly.

Chapter Twenty-eight

It was Lucy who finally brought things to a head, one tea-time in early October.

'I want to invite Kit to my birthday party,' she said. 'He came to Angus's. He'll want to come.'

'Will he?' said Callum.

'Kit's busy at the moment,' said Angus quickly, giving Ellen a worried glance. She had never discouraged the children from visiting their favourite neighbour, but they must have known something had happened between her and Kit.

'Invite Kit, by all means,' she said brightly to Lucy. 'But don't be too disappointed if he isn't able to come. He has to work some evenings.'

The next day they awoke to a beautiful autumn morning. Ellen walked with the children down to the village for the sheer pleasure of being out in it. And as she climbed back up the hill she took a deep breath, and made a decision that had been hanging over her all night. She walked on past Craigallan and up the track. She hadn't seen Kit's car go out this morning so with any luck she would be able to beard him there and then, before her courage failed.

Monty scampered ahead of her, as though delighted once again to be allowed on this territory. When he saw Kit, warmly wrapped up and doing something to the window frames on the house, he gave a yip of delight. The house had progressed so much since Ellen was last here, the roof finished, the beautiful wide sheets of glass installed. She really liked the clean lines of the place.

Kit turned around slowly and watched her make her way over the rough ground. It was deeply rutted, which made walking awkward. Ellen was glad of the excuse to look down. The sight of him so close, his face stern and watchful, made her heart thud with nerves.

'Hi there. Beautiful day,' she said.

'Yes. Cold though. And there's heavy rain coming.'

'Hmm.' Ellen didn't want to talk about the weather. Kit remained beside the unfinished house, neither welcoming nor discouraging. She knew she had behaved the same way towards him a number of times recently, but that didn't make it any easier. She tugged her hat down further over her ears. The wind really was chilly up here. 'How've you been?' she asked.

'Fine. Busy.'

'That's good.' Didn't he realise how difficult it was for her to take the first step, how out of character? She seized her courage in both hands and said, 'I wanted to talk to you.'

'Yes. Well.' He put down the tools he had been using and brushed his hands together. 'Do you want to go inside?'

She wasn't sure if he meant inside the caravan

319

or the house, but neither appealed. 'Perhaps we could just walk a bit?' And that way she wouldn't need to meet his eyes, such lovely deep brown eyes, that were watching her suspiciously even now.

'Yeah, OK. Up and round the hill?' He stuck his hands in his pockets and set off, Monty bouncing delightedly around him.

'How's your mum?' she asked.

'She's moved into a care home. And she's really happy, amazingly. She likes the company, and I have to admit it's less of a worry for me.'

'That's good,' said Ellen.

They walked in silence for a while. Ellen could feel the stretch of her muscles as she pushed to keep up with him. He said, 'How did your climbing day go?'

He had clearly heard she'd taken the children to the Ratho climbing centre.

'It went well. Very well. Even Lucy gave it a go. I've high hopes for some outside climbing in the spring.'

They walked on in silence once again while she gathered her thoughts. So far so good. He hadn't rejected her company out of hand. Now she just needed to get the message across that she knew he didn't want to be more than friends, and she wanted that too, now. If it was for the good of the children, surely he would agree?

'Lucy wants to invite you to her birthday party. It's at that soft-play area in Dunmuir, in a fortnight's time. I thought I should come and warn you first.'

'Oh. Right.' Kit's broad shoulders sagged, as

though he had been expecting more than that.

'She's really keen for you to come.'

'That's fine. I'll be there.' He shot her the very briefest of glances but she couldn't read his expression.

'I don't want you to feel obliged or anything. It's just that she really wants her own people there, and I suppose she feels that's what you are.'

Kit didn't answer immediately. She wondered if she had said the wrong thing, when he finally nodded. 'It's good, if she feels that.'

'Yes. The kids really like you, you know. I think it's been hard for them when you and I haven't been – getting on so well. I know they walk up to see you sometimes but it would be better if things went back to how they used to be, wouldn't it? If you popped in to Craigallan and so on?'

Kit carried on walking. When she stole a glance at him he was frowning. 'So you want to see me around a bit more, for the sake of the children?'

'Yes. I mean...' Ellen knew she was no good at this sort of thing. She felt a strange lump rising in her throat. Somehow she had thought once she made the first gesture of friendship, his good nature would take over and he would do the rest. She had been so sure he wouldn't let her down. 'I just want us to be friends again, like we were.'

'For the children?' Kit stopped on the brow of the hill, so that they could look over into the next valley, a misty view of greens, golds, and rusts. He seemed to be examining it with great concentration.

'Well, for them and us. I mean, it's not great, is it, the way things have been recently...'

321

'I thought that's what you wanted. No more interfering?'

Ellen waved her hands vaguely in the cold air. 'It wasn't what I wanted. It was just ... oh, I don't know. Can't we start again?'

'And be friends?'

'Yes.' She looked at him hopefully now. He had dragged his gaze away from the valley and was studying her as though she was a complicated puzzle.

'Ellen Taylor, I do not want and never have wanted to be friends with you.'

'Oh!' It was as though he had slapped her face. She could feel her colour rising. All along he hadn't even liked her? 'I'm sorry, obviously I should have realised...'

'Ellen.' He put a hand on her arm, to stop her turning and fleeing, which is exactly what she wanted to do. 'Ellen, I don't want to be friends. I want to be *more* than friends. Surely you knew that?'

'But... You were so furious with me... Nothing was right...'

'Look, I've messed things up, I know that. I annoyed you, even though I was trying to help.' He moved a step closer and Ellen felt unable to move back, although surely that was what she should do, if they were just going to be friends? Isn't that what she had settled on? 'If we start again, can we start again as something else?'

'Something else?'

He put a hand up to her cheek. 'Girlfriend and boyfriend? Lovers?'

'I...' She had been determined to say no, take

things slowly. Wasn't that her motto? But it hadn't worked last time. She looked into those sleepy brown eyes, which were sleepy no longer, and she was lost. She had never seen eyes burn with longing like that. 'I...' He didn't bother to let her finish. He must have seen enough to know the answer, and when he bent and kissed her he would have felt it for sure. His lips were warm and hungry and she moved into his arms as easily as if she had always been there, putting her gloved hands up to his head, pulling him closer and closer.

This was what she wanted. She had told herself it was impossible, that Kit would never feel like this for her...

It was a very long time before he took a small step back and looked down at her, dropping a kiss on her nose. 'You're crying.' He was smiling, his arms still loosely around her.

'I am not. It's the cold.'

'It is cold, but you are crying.' He touched her cheek again, wiping a tear away. 'Far too cold to be doing something like this out here.' He grinned. 'Shit, and look at those dark clouds coming up. It's definitely time to head for home.' He took her hand and gave her a little tug to bring her back to her senses. Before she knew it, they were hurrying back downhill through the lightly falling rain.

It was all happening so fast Ellen didn't know what to think. They had been here once before, the passionate kiss, the heady exhilaration. And then they had parted and it had all gone wrong. She couldn't bear for that to happen again. By the time they arrived at the caravan the rain was falling harder and Kit pulled her towards the door. 'Better get some shelter.'

'No.'

He looked at her in surprise, doubt surfacing all too quickly in those brown eyes.

'Why don't you come down to Craigallan. Please? It'll be warmer, and I need to put fuel on the stove.' She wanted to add, and there'll be nobody there to disturb us, but dared not. She was inviting him to come home with her, not to leave her now.

He frowned for a moment, eyes narrowed as he surveyed the building site. She had no idea what he was thinking. 'I suppose it is a bit of a mess here.'

'I don't care about the mess. Please come with me.' She kept hold of his hand. She wasn't going to let him go. 'Unless you've got to get back to work?'

'No, no more work today.' Suddenly he was smiling again. 'Come on, let's run.'

Once inside Craigallan they stripped off their coats and Ellen piled anthracite into the Rayburn. She felt shy all over again, but Kit was having no second thoughts. He took her back into his arms and began to kiss her gently, then ferociously. 'I've wanted to do this for so long.'

Thank goodness she'd decided to approach him with that offer of friendship. And thank goodness he had said no!

'Do we stay here or go upstairs?'

'Upstairs.'

He hesitated. 'Are you sure?'

'Yes! Upstairs, please.'

She was trembling with yearning and nerves as they tumbled on to her bed. It was amazing that Kit could be like this, that he wanted her so much. She couldn't believe she had once thought him so patient. Considerate, yes, but not patient. But then, nor was she, now. She had waited so long to see him without all those layers of clothes, to touch the warm skin, now she couldn't get enough of him. She lost herself in the wonder of it. She had never known what making love really meant before.

Afterwards they lay in each other's arms, the covers pulled roughly over them, drifting off in sleepy euphoria. Part of Ellen couldn't believe what they had just done, in the middle of the day, with the curtains open (but at least they were on the upper floor). And the other part wondered why she had waited so long for this.

'I love you,' said Kit, planting a kiss in her hair. She thought he might have said it before, in the heat of the moment, but this was different. As she struggled to turn and read his expression, the phone rang.

'Oh, God, no,' she said. 'I don't want to get up, ever.'

He smiled sleepily and kissed her again. 'I'll go.'

'No.' That woke her up. She didn't want him answering her phone, whatever would people think? She was doubly glad when she picked up the receiver and found the head teacher of the village school on the other end.

'Ellen? So glad you're there, I was beginning to wonder. We're having to close the school. The river's far too high, it's already burst its banks.

Will you be able to come and collect Callum and Lucy?'

'Yes,' said Ellen faintly, trying to suppress a giggle. 'Yes, of course. I'll be down as quickly as I can.' Had she really expected that she and Kit would be left in peace?

Kit refused to go home. It wasn't that she didn't want him there, or wished him skulking in that draughty caravan in this weather, but what would the children think? Ellen was sure they would read guilt written all over her face.

'Boyfriend and girlfriend, remember?' he said, taking her hand for a moment before she went out to the car.

'Not lovers?' she flashed back with a smile and dared to lean in and kiss him. Everything seemed suddenly so easy.

When she returned with Callum and Lucy, however, she was relieved to see that Kit was almost back to his old self, didn't encroach on her space in a way that would have made them suspicious. He could make her heart race with a mere glance, but the children weren't aware of that. At least Angus, the truly observant, wasn't home yet.

Angus caught the bus from Dunmuir as usual. Ellen succeeded in reaching him on his mobile and offered to come and collect him, but he said it was only a bit of rain. 'Mrs Morton always panics,' he said knowledgeably.

He did agree to come inside for a hot drink before venturing out to check his beloved animals.

'Why's Kit here?' he said bluntly, holding the

warm mug in both hands.

Ellen looked at Kit. She hadn't expected such a question quite so soon.

'I was worried about the weather up there...' she said, gesturing vaguely towards the copse.

Angus examined the two of them, perhaps seeing the heightened colour, and who knew what else? 'I'm glad you're friends again,' he said.

Kit put out his hand and took Ellen's. 'Yes. Good friends.'

Ellen wanted to snatch her hand back, embarrassed and worried all at once. But Angus didn't seem put out. He merely shrugged in an off-hand way and said, 'That's all right, then.'

The birthday party was a surprising success. Ellen was worried she would do something wrong, as she had for Angus, but apparently a party at a soft-play area more or less took care of itself.

Afterwards Kit came back to Craigallan with them, as he did so often these days. It was wonderfully natural to have him around. Just being with him made Ellen happy, and if they couldn't be alone as much as they might have liked, well, who better than she knew you couldn't have everything?

'I still haven't got you a present,' he said to Lucy. 'Have you decided yet?' He had gone to put his mug by the sink and paused behind Ellen, letting a hand rest naturally on her shoulder. Ellen put her own hand up to cover his. It felt so good.

'A new dress,' said Lucy. 'A sparkly one. I've seen one in that new shop in Dumfries.'

Callum snorted and Ellen said, 'I don't think

Kit meant something quite so expensive. And anyway, why do you want another dress? You hardly ever have the chance to wear them.'

'But I want one,' said Lucy obstinately. 'And I've thought what I want from you, too. For my big present.'

'Oh?' Ellen smiled. This confident little girl was so different from the pale, quiet creature of the spring time. It was such a relief. She must be doing something right.

'Yes. I want a kitten.'

'A kitten?' Ellen was horrified. 'Don't we have enough animals around here?'

Angus and Callum began to snigger. They had clearly been in on this secret.

'One more won't make any difference,' said Lucy glibly. 'And I'll look after it. I'll feed it and everything.'

Ellen could feel herself weakening, but put up one last protest. 'What will Monty think?'

'He'll get used to it.' Lucy dropped her voice to almost a whisper. 'Dad said I could have a kitten when I was eight. He said then I'd be old enough to look after it myself. I can have one, can't I?'

Ellen gave her niece a quick hug, aware that the boys were watching her anxiously. 'We'll start looking tomorrow,' she said. How could she refuse?

The mention of 'when I turn eight' reminded her of something else. 'And do you still want to start learning the clarinet? That's something else we could look in to.' God, she must be a sucker for punishment!

Lucy jumped up and down. 'Yes! Yes! Now I'm

eight I can do lots of things. You won't need to make me practice like you have to do with Angus, I'll practice all the time.'

'I hope it sounds better than your recorder,' muttered Callum.

'I do practice,' said Angus, scowling.

You still not keen to learn anything yourself?' Ellen asked Callum, intervening before an argument could start.

'Naw. Wouldn't want to waste your money.'

'You don't have to buy the instrument,' said Lucy. 'I 'member Mum saying. You can borrow one to begin with.'

'That sounds like a good idea,' said Ellen, relieved. She would have found a way if they had to buy a clarinet, but she'd far rather they didn't. To begin with, at least.

She had been watching Angus out of the corner of her eye, and something in his expression made her ask, 'And what about you, Angus? Is there another instrument you'd like to learn?'

'Well.' He hesitated. 'If we really can borrow instruments from the school...'

'Yes?'

'I'd kind of like to have a go at the fiddle. Grant has been suggesting it. And I would practice. I do practice.' He scowled again at Lucy.

'That sounds like a brilliant idea,' said Ellen. Even more things to organise, but here was Angus actually asking for something, saying what he wanted. That was definitely a step forward.

Chapter Twenty-nine

Time passed quickly now, but not in a terrifying blur of never quite knowing what you were doing or whether you were doing it right. Life was busy, that was for sure, but Ellen was no longer overwhelmed. When the college offered her a couple of days' work in the run up to Christmas, she was even able to accept it without panicking about how she would cope.

Kit was happy to help out, and finally she was happy to let him.

He was still living in his caravan, though. Progress on his house seemed to have slowed down yet again. Ellen felt bad about him sleeping up there, but she didn't want to rock the boat with the children.

'Time I was heading up the track,' said Kit, after the evening meal one Saturday in December.

'I wouldn't like to sleep in a caravan in winter,' said Callum. The temperature was hovering around freezing. 'Isn't it really cold?'

'I'll survive.'

Angus cleared his throat. 'Why don't you stay here?'

Ellen looked at Kit in horror. It was true that the children were aware the relationship between the two of them had changed, but she had been careful. As far as she knew, the children had never even seen them kiss, so where had this come from?

330

'Grant stays at Grace's house. He sleeps in Clare's bed.' Lucy giggled.

'Ah...'

'You slept with Richard,' said Callum.

Ellen wanted to bury her head in her hands.

'Don't not stay here 'cos of us,' said Angus. 'We don't mind.'

'We think you should get married,' said Lucy.

Ellen was speechless. Where had this come from? Just when she thought she had the measure of the children, they would surprise her all over again.

'Lucy just wants to be a bridesmaid,' said Callum. 'It was her idea.' Then, noticing his sister's expression, he added, 'But I don't mind. We don't, do we, Angus?'

Ellen didn't even dare look at Kit. 'Phew,' she said shakily. 'You've quite taken my breath away. And I think you're *somewhat* jumping the gun. Now, where were we, wasn't it someone's bed time?'

After that startling exchange Kit didn't take himself off up the track. He offered to read Lucy's story and then busied himself tidying in the kitchen until the two boys were also in bed.

'I'm sorry about that,' said Ellen, coming back in and firmly closing the door between kitchen and hallway. Privacy was obviously something hard to come by in this house. 'I don't know where they got the idea...'

'They're not stupid,' said Kit. 'And I think it's quite a good idea, don't you?'

'You sleeping here? Well, yes, of course, but I still feel...'

Kit silenced her by taking her in his arms and

331

kissing her. After a while he pressed his cheek against hers and breathed in deeply. 'I love you.'

'I love you too. But the kids...'

'Ssh, this is about us, not the kids.' He stood back and looked down at her, the deep brown eyes seeming to seek the answer to some question he hadn't asked.

Ellen met his gaze. He was so beautiful she could have looked at him for ever. He was about to speak but she put a finger on his lips and said, 'It has to be about the kids, too. The kids are part of me now, you know that, and I can't expect you to want to take them on too. If you start sleeping here they're going to expect more and more of you and that isn't fair.'

'Marry me.'

Her heart gave a leap of pure emotion. She would love him for ever for asking her. 'Kit, you're not listening. I can't marry you. I'm four years older than you...'

'Three.'

'Three and a half. And I've got three children in tow. It's not fair on you. You need someone younger, who you can have your own kids with.' She made herself keep her eyes on his face, still so close to his own. 'Don't think I can't see that.'

'You might think that, but it isn't true.' Kit was smiling now. He leant in and kissed her gently. 'I love you. I love the kids. So what's the problem?'

'But they're my responsibility.'

'Hasn't anyone ever told you that you can share responsibilities?'

Ellen could feel hope burgeoning within her,

and pushed it down. 'Kit, you deserve your own children.'

'They will be my children. And if we should decide to have another of our own, well, all to the good. I've never quite been able to decide whether I wanted three kids or four.'

Ellen began to laugh. Another child to complete the family? Who would have thought she'd actually want that? She pulled him close and buried her face in his neck, kissing the warm skin. 'Do you never give up?'

'I'll take that as a yes, then,' said Kit, and returned to the serious business of kissing her.

Ellen paused at the top of Craigallan land. There might not be many Craigallan animals grazing it, but it was still their land, and she had a special feeling for it. A feeling that was nothing at all like the brisk, brief appreciation she had felt in the years of walking in other people's hills. Then she hadn't known what it all meant, how much work it took to keep the land looking and being as it was.

As she turned to gaze down the valley, through the steady drizzle, the sun came out behind her and for a moment it caught Craigallan in the last rays of evening. It made the long, low house look picturesque, pristine even, although she knew it wouldn't be long before it needed another coat of paint, not to mention new windows upstairs and some attention to that roof... Enjoy the moment, she told herself.

Recognise the sunshine through the rain, and be grateful for it.

This Large Print Book for the partially
sighted, who cannot read normal print, is
published under the auspices of

THE ULVERSCROFT FOUNDATION